THE
PRICE OF
TREACHERY

TED TAYLER

Vinci Books

vinci-books.com

Published by Vinci Books Ltd in 2026

1

Copyright © Ted Tayler 2016

The author has asserted their moral right to be identified as the author of this work in accordance with the Copyright, Designs and Patents Act 1988. This work is a work of fiction. Names, characters, places and incidents are the product of the author's imagination or are used fictitiously. Any resemblance to actual persons, living or dead, places and incidents is entirely coincidental.

All rights reserved. No part of this publication may be copied, reproduced, distributed, stored in any retrieval system, or transmitted in any form or by any means, including photocopying, recording, or other electronic or mechanical methods, nor used as a source for any form of machine learning including AI datasets, without the prior written permission of the publisher.

The publisher and the author have made every effort to obtain permissions for any third party material used in this book and to comply with copyright law. Any queries in this respect should be brought to the attention of the publisher and any omissions will be corrected in future editions.

A CIP catalogue record for this book is available from the British Library.

Paperback ISBN: 9781036700539

The EU GPSR authorised representative is Logos Europe, 9 rue Nicolas Poussion, 17000 La Rochelle, France
contact@logoseurope.eu

By Ted Tayler

The Phoenix

The Olympus Project
Gold, Silver and Bombs
Nothing Is Ever Forever
In the Lap of the Gods
The Price of Treachery
A New Dawn
Something Wicked Draws Near
Evil Always Finds A Way
Revenge Comes in Many Colours
Three Weeks in September
A Frequent Peal of Bells
Larcombe Manor

The Freeman Files

Fatal Decision
Last Orders
Pressure Point
Deadly Formula
Final Deal
Barking Mad
Creature Discomforts

Silent Terror

Night Train

All Things Bright

Buried Secrets

A Genuine Mistake

Strange Beginnings

Dead Reckoning

A Normal November

Into the Sunlight

Tame the Storm

One True Friend

Whispered Truths

A Morning Murder

Quick to Anger

Red Herring Season

Gathering Clouds

Still Standing

Chapter One

Good luck in your new venture, the card read.

It was one of a handful of cards from well-wishers that had arrived at the Hounsell house in the past few days. Phil Hounsell was making a fresh start.

The Divisional Commander had been a man of his word. Phil had walked out of his job with his head held high and a full pension. He had cleared his desk on Friday afternoon, then spent the best part of August in the garden at home or on holiday with Erica and the children.

The ACC saved his career by the skin of his teeth. A gullible public swallowed his story that 'heads had rolled' at Portishead after the debacle of the hunt for the Bulgarian killers; in truth, the shrinking numbers were more to do with austerity cuts or fellow officers giving up the pointless struggle and quitting the service.

The identities of the murdered men emerged as the new month progressed. Dimitar Marinov and his cronies were a collection of career criminals and ruthless enforcers. The media questioned how these murderers just waltzed through immigration control without anyone wondering whether they were the calibre of person the UK needed.

As for the gang's killers, there had been little progress on that front. A few residents had contacted the police to ask if they knew about the film crew in the area that weekend. However, confusion reigned over the name of the company involved.

Memories were hazy; it seemed so innocent at the time. A trifle inconvenient to have gunfire in the background while serving breakfast or when fetching the Sunday papers. Not significant enough to remember every detail on what looked to be an official sign. The local police passed the Met police the information, and when added to the sum of everything they gathered at Eton Wick, it amounted to very little.

The media's attention switched to new matters; the killings had stopped, and the Met was following up on dozens of leads gained from the Bulgarian's homes. Dimitar Marinov was proven to have been a trafficker of drugs and young women. They raided dozens of properties, and the smiles on the Met senior officers were getting broader by the day.

The possible existence of a second ruthless gang of killers slipped to one side for the time being. There were five hundred gangs from which to choose. They could only tackle one thing at a time. As for the involvement of third parties, such as the one stationed at Larcombe Manor, for instance, it never crossed anyone's mind. Giles, Artemis and the team could keep their misinformation tactics in reserve for another occasion.

At the end of the third week in August, as Phil Hounsell and family were stepping off the plane from Marbella, news broke the Met had discovered the bodies of the ram-raid gang. At long last, their families learnt what had happened to them.

The press portrayed them as 'victims', which their criminal shenanigans suggested they indeed were not. But they were British rogues, slaughtered by foreign killers that should never have been allowed to enter the UK. Nevertheless, the headlines caught the mood of the country.

Phil had read the newspapers the following day and wondered at the mentality of people these days. His leaving-do and the finalising of his exit from Portishead took place on Friday, August 30th. The DC was there both in the office and in the pub later. The ACC and others were otherwise engaged. Phil arrived home in a taxi at about two in the morning, three sheets in the wind; Erica saw that he was tucked up in bed safely but also made sure he got up by eight o'clock so he could get used to going shopping with her.

Phil had thought about what he might do now that his police career had ended. What were his strengths? Detecting was his expertise, but he didn't fancy starting as a private investigator. So instead, he thought he would try his hand as a security consultant. Erica came up with the name; she suggested Hounsell Security Services, or HSS for short.

"What nature of security work do you think you might get offered?" she asked.

"I'll circulate my details around the regional companies and offer my services to help them avoid being robbed or defrauded for a start. We'll see what that generates."

It's odd how the supermarket run sometimes finds one bumping into old faces. Erica had Phil on trolley duty and piled stuff into the basket while he coped with his hangover. He knew better than to expect sympathy from his wife, so he looked at the other poor souls passing him.

"Morning, Sir," said a voice, "I don't see you in here very often."

It was Wayne Sangster, his companion from the Glastonbury weekend.

"It's not 'Sir' any longer, Wayne. I'm retired," he replied.

"Got out at last, then? Good for you. What are you doing with yourself?"

"I'm starting a security consultancy, offering advice to firms, that sort of thing," said Phil.

"You don't want to be pissing around with that caper, mate," laughed Wayne, "big money is in personal security. Looking after celebrities and Russian and Arab oligarchs."

"How do you know so much about it, Wayne," asked Phil. Erica looked eager to move into the next aisle. Wayne manoeuvred his small trolley around to follow the couple.

"I did a bit of security before I joined; I told you I'd done quite a few jobs, didn't I?"

"You did, Wayne. Are you still enjoying life?"

"There haven't been many laughs since the weekend we worked together, it has to be said. So I thought of looking around for something else. I've got a couple of mates in the security business that I might give a call."

Phil decided to make an executive decision; Erica was shelf-surfing a few yards in front, hunting for a specific brand of whatever they had probably withdrawn from production. That might take a while.

"How do you fancy coming to work for me, Wayne?" he asked.

"Do you have a uniform?"

Phil thought quickly.

"Of course, it will be a navy-blue shirt with epaulettes

and the HSS logo on the sleeve, black trousers, and boots. That sound okay?"

"You can count me in," said Wayne.

Erica returned from a fruitless conversation with a spotty staff member to find her husband and a strange man shaking hands vigorously.

"Good to have you on board, Wayne," said Phil, "would these mates of yours be interested in joining us? What do you reckon?"

Wayne agreed to check and start the ball rolling on getting himself out of the police service. Phil breathed a sigh of relief; the shopping run had ended. Erica still seemed miffed about the item she could no longer find. For his part, Phil was staggered that two adults and two children could demolish the loaded trolley he struggled to push towards the car in one week.

Monday, September 9th, 2013

Phil had rented office space above a dry-cleaning firm, far enough away from Bath city centre that the amount didn't make his eyes water. Wayne arrived at two o'clock on the dot, as he had agreed when he rang Phil earlier in the day. Wayne was off-duty until Wednesday and counting the days. With holiday entitlement, he would change uniform for the umpteenth time after Friday. His two mates, Dusty and Leggo, had been interested. The newcomers just wanted to know when Phil secured a decent-paying contract that made it worthwhile packing in their current jobs.

"Do we have the uniforms yet, boss?" asked Wayne, always eager to start dressing up.

"All in good time. Let's find work first," said Phil.

"I might have an idea, boss," said Wayne, "while we worked together at Glastonbury, I picked up loads of contacts. Dozens of people handed out cards and fliers. You never know when one of them might come in handy, so whenever someone stuck a hand out with an offer, I grabbed it. You've heard of that Honey B, the singer?"

Phil shook his head.

"She's older than you, boss; she's been around ages and upset many people too. A bit of a diva, I've heard. She's starting a UK tour next Monday. I've just read in the Sun that she's fired her security people. A car never turned up where and when it should have. Honey B was left standing on the pavement in Chelsea for ten minutes with the grubby public. She got recognised, and people started grabbing hold of her and wanting photographs with her and all that stuff. Now advising *her* on security would be a nice little earner."

"We don't have the experience for that, Wayne," said Phil, "she'd hardly employ a brand new outfit like us."

"Her first concert is in Bristol, boss. She doesn't have much time to get something in place, does she? I'll get hold of her management people and tell her we'll sort Monday night out, and if she's happy, we'll take it from there. What have we got to lose?"

"What, just the two of us?" said Phil.

"I'll get Dusty and Leggo to phone in sick if they're working. We'll be fine. It's personal security boss, and it's only her we have to look after; the venue will have its own guys. We need to liaise with them, collect her from the hotel, get her to the gig and return afterwards. All without the lady breaking a nail."

Wayne's confidence started to grow on Phil. Finally, he

asked him for the number of Honey B's management company and made the call himself.

"Good afternoon, I am ex-Detective Superintendent Hounsell; we have staff available with decades of experience in personal security. I understand you have a pressing problem regarding your client's security at next Monday night's concert in Bristol. We are based in Bath and are prepared to step into the breach. We will waive our fee for the night. If your client is happy with our work, we can negotiate a figure for the other dates on her UK tour. What do you say?"

Wayne looked impressed. Not with the waiving the fee bit. He enjoyed how Phil covered all the bases and didn't give the bloke on the other end a chance to breathe. Let alone pass comment.

Phil was listening to a voice on the other end of the line and making notes. Wayne watched intently. Phil ended the conversation.

"Well, boss?" asked Wayne.

"HSS have their first client; Honey B's people will be in touch later in the week with the arrangements we need to make on Monday," said Phil with a smile.

"What's next then, boss?" asked Wayne.

"What size collar are you? What waist and leg measurements? What logo should we have? Big boots at a guess?"

"Seventeen. Forty-two, thirty-three. A white horse. Size twelve, boss."

"Forty-two?" asked Phil.

"At a push, boss, honest," replied Wayne, "shall I ring Dusty and Leggo to get their measurements too?"

Phil sorted uniforms for the three lads and agreed to a logo that looked remarkably like the Ferrari prancing horse but white with HSS below. However, he decided to stick to a suit and tie.

The Bristol concert instructions arrived from the management company's London office. Miss Honey B wanted plenty for her money, which in this case was something for nothing. Phil sat in the office and went through the items, and set out a timetabled procedure. If Wayne and the others followed this to the minute, they should be fine.

It was like planning a raid and getting the resources to arrive on cue precisely at the right time. Again, Phil found he enjoyed the exercise; this time, they had a result. Even if raids he organised went off without a hitch, someone screwed up further along the line, and the criminals only received a caution or got off altogether.

He sent the schedule he'd prepared off to London and received a reply within minutes, saying his plan was acceptable. Honey B had given HSS the task of keeping her safe on Monday night.

Phil asked Wayne on Thursday evening to track down a reliable limousine firm. Naturally, Wayne had half a dozen cards in his possession. A car was secured. The flowers and champagne were ordered. The exact blend of aromas was on standby to be introduced via the air-conditioning to the interior while Honey B was on board.

Wayne was the designated driver for the evening. Dusty Miller and Jake Legg stationed themselves outside the venue's stage door on the pavement.

The limousine arrived on the dot, and Honey B swept from her Clifton hotel and into the back of her sweet-smelling stretch limousine. The door closed quietly behind her. The drive to the venue was smooth. It left not a smidgen to complain over, even for a diva. Wayne eased to a halt beside Dusty and Leggo. Phil tapped on the stage door.

The Price of Treachery

Honey B waited until Dusty opened the door, and then she emerged to screams and flashing cameras and phones. Dusty and Leggo closed the gap to surround their charge, and she was inside the sanctuary of the theatre in seconds. The stage door slammed shut behind her. Honey B gave Phil Hounsell a head-to-toe appraisal.

"Mr Hounsell?" she asked.

"Yes, ma'am, Chief executive of HSS at your service. Your dressing room is this way."

"I've been here a dozen times before," she hissed. "I know the way."

The room also received the diva treatment. Phil was glad he wasn't paying for that lot, too; he thought this venue must be charging a fortune for tickets.

The concert got underway within ten minutes; a warm-up act played a short set, and then it was time for Honey B to take to the stage. The manager was praying nothing would go wrong.

"The audience will expect a two-hour show, but she can be fickle. If she gets it into her head that she's not feeling the love, she'll walk off after an hour. Another night she'll do an extra fifteen minutes."

"What will she do at the end, assuming she does the straight two hours?" asked Phil.

"Your guess is as good as mine. Honey B might run off the stage and collect her things from the dressing room. She'll expect you to be ready to whisk her straight back to Clifton. The last time she played here, she hung around in the room, cooling down and finishing her champagne, chatting to staff. She'll often have one glass before she takes to the stage, and the rest goes to waste."

Phil raised an eyebrow.

"Well, it would if the staff didn't look after it," the manager replied.

It was time for Honey B to sing to her adoring public. Phil stood in the wings and watched. He had to admit she sounded good. Phil recognised one or two tunes; his mother had several of Honey B's earliest hits on vinyl. However, he decided against mentioning it if she deigned to talk to him later.

Almost two hours had passed; Phil texted Wayne and told him to bring the car to the stage door. Dusty and Leggo lingered backstage, primed for action. Truth be told, they were having a coffee and nipping outside for a cigarette. Finally, honey B finished her set with one of her greatest hits. She left the stage to rapturous applause. She smiled.

Phil noticed that the smile didn't reach her eyes. As she made her way to the dressing room, her beady eyes appeared to be darting left and right. As if she was searching to find something to justify a tantrum. A strange woman and no mistake. He needed to tread carefully.

Honey B entered the room and went to close the door. She paused and turned back towards him.

"Will you drink a glass of champagne with me before we leave, Mr Hounsell? I hate to drink alone."

"I'll keep you company, ma'am," he said and took the proffered glass.

Honey B threw a wrap around her shoulders and sat in a comfortable chair. She studied Phil over the top of her glass as she sipped her drink. Phil didn't enjoy how she looked at him; not a pleasant inspection, more like a surgical dissection. He looked at the photos and cards adorning the table in front of them. The room was full of roses, dozens of them, all splashes of red and yellow.

Near her handbag lay a photo that didn't fit. The rest

looked like signed pictures of Honey B alone or unsigned shots with a fan at an exotic location worldwide. This one was a hastily framed shot of a man and a woman, snapped, leaving a building. Phil's heart almost jumped out of his chest. It looked like the two people he had met at Glastonbury at the end of June. He was sure of it. So why on earth did Honey B have a photograph of them?

Behind the public mask of Honey B, Demeter spotted the security consultant's sudden reaction; her mind raced. How could this ex-policeman know Athena and Phoenix? Her colleague had taken these pictures in Curzon Street as they left the Olympus meeting. Shortly before he travelled to Ibiza to carry out a small task for her and her friends, she hoped to unmask the true identity of her male opponent. Could this man hold the key?

Honey B soon switched back to her day-to-day persona. She drained her glass and told Phil she was ready to leave. Honey B caught hold of his sleeve as he moved to the door to summon Dusty and Leggo.

"Thank you for tonight. Call my office tomorrow; name your price, and you can be my security people for the rest of the tour."

Phil Hounsell thanked Honey B, trying not to sound too grateful. He didn't want to overdo it. She could be fickle, and the chill that ran through his arm as she touched his wrist unsettled him.

As she swept away from the stage door in Wayne's stretch limousine, he thought they must be doing something right. HSS was up and running.

Demeter was purring gently in the back of the car; what a stroke of luck to stumble across someone who recognised Phoenix.

"I believe we are hunting the same man, Mr Hounsell,"

she muttered. "I shall have to keep you close by my side. What fun we might have."

Monday, August 5th, 2013

While Phil Hounsell wrapped up his police career on one side of the county, matters in August had started on a more sombre note at Larcombe Manor.

Athena and a handful of mourners attended the funeral of William Horatio Hunt. Erebus was laid to rest between the graves of his beloved wife, Elizabeth and their daughter Helen. They could now seal the family vault. The generations of the Hunt family that had occupied Larcombe for five hundred years would see no other coffins arriving to join them.

Athena shed tears for Erebus, her mentor, as she stood in the vault beside Minos. Her cheeks were dampened by the showers that had greeted the small congregation as they followed the coffin onto the hillside cemetery that overlooked the Hunt family estate.

The gods expressed their displeasure at the manner of Erebus's death; as the mourners left the dark recesses of the vault, they emerged to violent claps of thunder. Seconds later, sheet lightning illuminated the hillside on the opposite side of the valley.

"I understand," said Athena quietly, "but you can rely on me. I will discover who was responsible for his death and take our revenge."

Minos placed a hand on her shoulder to comfort her.

"We owe Erebus a tremendous debt of gratitude. Olympus could never have existed without his vision and drive. This nation has no idea how many lives the missions our agents have carried out saved over the past six years. A simple ceremony such as that was a scant reward for his true significance."

Athena nodded. "We will each of us remember him in our way, Minos. But, the integrity of the Project had to be maintained. As much as we might wish to proclaim his name from the rooftops and demand the headlines he deserves, that would never be possible."

The party of mourners from the Olympus Project HQ gathered in the car park at the entrance to the cemetery. Athena stood for a moment and gazed across the hillside to the mausoleum. No one spoke.

Athena turned and walked to the cars from the transport section. Time to return to Larcombe. There was to be no wake nor no maudlin recollections of a life well-lived. It had to be back to business, battles fought, and debts paid.

In the orangery, Phoenix sifted through the reports Rusty prepared following his recce into the 'beds in sheds' situation in Outer London. Phoenix had missed the opportunity to attend his saviour's funeral, like many others who worked here at headquarters.

His true identity had been closely guarded since his arrival at the beginning of July three years ago. The day Colin Bailey ceased to exist and the Phoenix was born. The struggle to keep that knowledge hidden was doubly tricky now that Artemis worked in the ice-house. Zara Wheeler and Colin Bailey had a history.

The young ex-policewoman lived at Larcombe with Rusty Scott, his closest friend. Disillusioned with the current role of policing, she joined forces with Olympus. Phoenix had no idea what she might do with the knowledge of his past life should it ever be uncovered. Until Artemis could be trusted one hundred per cent, Phoenix had to resort to creeping around the estate. He moved between the rooms he shared with Athena and the orangery, which became his sanctuary. Trips to the ice-house and the other facilities needed strict control. Phoenix felt like a caged animal. Not a feeling he relished.

"Concentrate, man," he scolded himself as he leafed through the reams of intelligence that Rusty had gathered.

The background of the rent crisis in London was plain for anyone to see. The city had built new homes at around half the pace needed to satisfy the intensifying demand. Moreover, its population surged past nine million before the decade's end. As a result, average rents rose by over fifteen per cent in the past two years. As a result, the poor devils forced to rent the roof over their heads to live in the vast, sprawling metropolis parted with an average of over twelve hundred pounds per month.

Phoenix looked at his surroundings. He and Erebus used the elegant, refined orangery for their private meetings for over two years. He knew just how much he owed the old gentleman. How different his life might have been if Erebus hadn't marked him out as a potential recruit for Olympus.

After Sue Owens died, Phoenix became a wealthy man, but money was no substitute for family. Larcombe was now his family home. Erebus had been the father figure he never knew as a child. Athena was his partner for life, and she carried their child. Phoenix felt at one with his surroundings for the first time in his life.

Phoenix knew the direct actions he planned were challenging. The capital held thousands of families and individuals who wanted nothing more than to experience the sense of calm and 'belonging' he experienced. But, unfortunately, whenever an opportunity arose to profit out of ambitions such as those, unscrupulous people always stood waiting to take advantage.

Rusty identified two targets as meriting special attention.

Hounslow, a West London Borough, had its share of rogue landlords. Oscar Friedman, a grocery shop owner, started to expand his property portfolio twenty years ago. Oscar was a quiet, attentive grocer in his mid-sixties who charged over the odds for his fresh produce to the customers that visited his shop every day.

As far as anyone knew, Friedman merely rented out the rooms above the shop. Oscar and his wife lived in the more sophisticated climes just over the borders of the Borough in Richmond. Retirement beckoned, and they were sure to have put enough by to see them live out their days in moderate comfort.

The truth behind the public face of Oscar Friedman proved to be far more sinister. He employed an agent to look after the properties that provided his primary income. Sylvester Read, a former estate agent, was single and in his late thirties. He spent his leisure time watching or participating in his favourite sport. Sylvester was a cage fighter. Violence is his answer to most problems. If the problem needed extra muscle, he called Frank DeAngelo.

DeAngelo was a thug for hire. He had spent more than half his adult life in prison. Frank wasn't the brightest senior citizen on the planet, but he came from an Italian family that came to London in the 1920s. Since then, there had been a DeAngelo family member filling the role of 'enforcer' in nearly every organised crime gang in the capital.

Rusty had gathered evidence on the Borough and the impact of uncontrolled immigration. He identified the long list of properties Friedman owned and the methods Read employed to continually improve the returns on his employer's investments.

Hounslow had been a rural area in the not-too-distant past. Now, many areas resemble shantytowns. Twenty thousand gardens held ramshackle sheds or outbuildings of different sizes. Many of them rented out illegally. The census showed the official population at a quarter million two years ago. Only two years later, that number stood closer to three hundred thousand.

Shed renting had reached a crisis point. So the council set up a squad to tackle the problem. The squad now carries out dawn raids; properties that break planning rules face severe sanctions. Too often, though, the landlord only receives a warning.

The knock-on effects of the housing crisis are easy to see. Local schools have to accommodate hundreds of extra pupils. Many are the children of newly-arrived migrants, while others are from families who moved out of Central London to cut housing benefit costs. Doctors' surgeries, dental practices, rubbish collection and the sanitation system, are stretched beyond capacity.

Criminal landlords, such as Oscar Friedman, made huge profits from the most vulnerable people in society. Families trapped into living in filth in little more than shacks, yet paying hundreds of pounds a month in rent.

Sylvester Read's response to questions from inspectors from the council squad was as flimsy as the fabrications that Friedman's tenants occupied. Yet, it was tough to prove that many buildings were places people lived. The council squad needed to give the landlord notice of an inspection visit.

Oscar merely phoned Read, and when the inspectors arrived the next day, the families were at work; the children attended school. If a wife stayed home with an infant, she moved up the street to another house. The grocer owned more than a dozen properties on one street alone. The council might have suspicions, but obtaining the proof was as elusive as a winning lottery ticket.

Phoenix read page after page of escalating harassment and intimidation. Sylvester Read and Frank DeAngelo dished out racist and homophobic abuse regularly. The pair made frequent late-night visits to properties with no prior warning. Tenants complained locks changed while they worked. Services such as hot water and heating often got disconnected.

Repairs and maintenance on properties withdrew to the level where they became uninhabitable. That happened most often with single-occupancy apartments. Once the tenant had to move out, Friedman had a ready supply of families prepared to pay more rent. Overcrowding wasn't a word in his dictionary.

Rusty talked to a disabled lady in her fifties, who had lived in one of Friedman's flats for eight years. She kept herself to herself and always paid her rent on time. Despite her physical limitations, she kept the place clean and tidy. Read visited her.

He forced her to sign an agreement that reduced her rights. Then, two Somali men moved into the attic space above her flat. They tried to break into her flat to rob her on several occasions. The poor woman was terrified they might do far worse than rob her. So she quit the flat, and within a week, a family of seven migrants occupied the place she had called home.

Phoenix spotted another familiar story in the file. A young bank worker in her twenties moved into Hounslow from Brighton. Read told her initially; he had nothing available for someone wishing to live alone. He suggested she shared accommodation with a group of professionals, as the young girl was away from home for the first time. He persuaded her to at least meet her potential housemates.

Read picked her up after work and drove her to the property, a five-bedroomed Victorian house converted into flats. When they pulled up outside, he explained that each apartment already contained three tenants. As they climbed the stairs to the top floor, Sylvester Read pointed to a newly installed set of stairs leading to the loft.

"We're installing an apartment up there. Will you feel more comfortable being on your own? If so, this could be just what you need. You can still enjoy the company of the others in the communal areas."

The young girl was ecstatic; even though the rent was high, she grabbed the chance and arranged to move in soon as the flat became ready. Within six weeks, Oscar Friedman had decided rents needed to increase across his property portfolio. The young bank worker was distraught. The actual costs of living away from home had started to hit home. She called Sylvester Read to ask if he knew of anywhere cheaper on his employer's books. Was it possible for her to move into one of the other flats in the house to help her new friends with the extra burden they had to stand?

Read called around in person. Well, of course, he did, thought Phoenix. The slimy agent turned up at the loft apartment late at night. The young girl told Rusty 'his breath reeked of alcohol. He apologised; of course, he said he appreciated the financial impact of a rent rise was unfortunate. However, it wasn't easy to see a way forward. The landlord insisted on three occupants as a maximum and a minimum. He believed it resulted in less unwanted interference between the sexes with that arrangement.'

Read then suggested a solution to her problem; he could waive the rent increase in exchange for sex. The young girl had been horrified and ordered the agent out of her flat. Read merely shrugged his shoulders.

"I'll pop round tomorrow night, sweetheart, to see if you've come to your senses. If not, the extra money will be due in full for this month and next. If you can't pay, then you'll be in breach of our agreement. I will tell my boss you're a flight risk and might disappear without paying what you owe. He'll want you out of here in days. After that, it's up to you."

Rusty had detailed the sorry tale. The girl had opened the door to Read the following night. Sylvester Read visited her regularly for the next eight months while she hunted high and low for a flat outside the Borough. The violence that typified his lifestyle continued in the bedroom. She was depressed and withdrawn. Her haunted look when being interviewed shocked even Rusty, a hardened soldier. She was still battling to mend her broken life in a woman's shelter in Chiswick.

"This direct action is going to be a pleasure," said Phoenix as he moved deeper into the file. Friedman bought property after property in the same style as the semi-detached Victorian house he had just studied. Most were for multi-occupancy letting, and the tenants were white, middle-aged to elderly business people. Read and DeAngelo carried out Friedman's orders as the years passed. First, they moved these people out so that large migrant families could replace them.

Not everyone wanted to leave. DeAngelo called around late at night and used his fists to mete out a mild beating. Read and DeAngelo returned together if the message hadn't been received loud and clear by one visit. Then, the beatings became more severe.

The violence continued to escalate as the number of immigrants flowing into the country increased. Many of these new arrivals arrived here illegally; others had outstayed student visas and evaded deportation orders. It's not difficult to find a hiding place in a city of over eight million souls. As soon as there was any sign of trouble from one of these tenant families, Friedman reacted. Complaints about the state of the dilapidated properties they occupied resulted in Friedman getting his lackeys to pay a visit.

They warned that their illegal status could become known by the authorities if they didn't pay up and keep quiet. If they didn't heed the message, then Read forced himself on the wives while DeAngelo subdued the husbands and made them watch.

Fewer and fewer of Friedman's properties remained in the hands of the tenants living there at the outset. Indeed, the turnover was rapid. There was evidence in Rusty's file of dozens of tenants living in fear, too frightened to seek protection from the police. So instead, the thugs targeted anyone that didn't fit their twisted idea of normality.

Read and DeAngelo terrorised two men in a civil partnership. They suffered verbal abuse for months. Then, when the thugs wanted to persuade them to leave the flat they shared, they arrived on a Sunday afternoon and tried to force the pair to agree to go. The older man tried to argue with Read. He insisted they had rights. He had arranged to see a lawyer in the morning to end this harassment.

DeAngelo grabbed the younger man's wrist. He forced the palm of his right hand flat on the tabletop in front of his partner.

The Price of Treachery

"Rights?" he bellowed. "You ain't got no rights."

With that, he pulled out a knife and stabbed it into the man's hand, pinning it to the table. The screams echoed around their apartment and the other flats in the house for days. There was no visit to the lawyer, and the whole property became available for new tenants within days.

Phoenix looked at his watch. Athena should have returned from the funeral. He was sick to his stomach with what he had read so far. He identified the first targets and confirmed the punishment. There would be time to read stories of the Irish mafia in Ealing later. He needed a breath of fresh air.

Phoenix checked there was nobody in the vicinity of the orangery, and the pathways were empty. Then, he headed to the main house with a glance towards the stable block and ice-house for signs of Rusty or Artemis.

He found Athena sitting by the window, looking over the manicured lawns. She held the silver-framed photograph of Erebus and his wife Elizabeth against her bosom. Phoenix could see her tear-stained cheeks. He wrapped her in his arms and kissed the top of her head.

"Hard saying goodbye to those you love, isn't it?" he said.

"Even harder when you know they died before their time," said Athena.

"We'll find out who was responsible and avenge him soon enough, Athena."

"Have you kept busy while I was gone?" she asked.

"I feel dirty," he growled. "After reading Rusty's reports on the vermin living in the big city, I need a shower."

"I think I might join you," Athena smiled and took his hand. "I have a favour I need to ask."

"Lead on," said Phoenix, trying not to appear too eager.

"Mummy and Daddy are home soon from the south of France; we need to visit them. I want a united front when we tell them they will be grandparents in the New Year."

"Ah," said a deflated Phoenix.

"You're going to be there, so that's final," said Athena.

The thought of interrogation by her father inside the Fox family home in Vincent Gardens, Belgravia, was terrifying to a simple West Country lad.

"How do you think they'll react to having a vigilante killer as a prospective son-in-law?"

"One step at a time," replied Athena, "we'll tell them our news of the baby first. Then we can let them get used to the idea we're a permanent item before we mention the 'M' word."

"Oh, they know we're a permanent item then?" asked Phoenix, surprised.

Athena blushed. "They know we work closely together for the charity; I always catch them looking at one another whenever I mention your name. With them being abroad most of the year and Mummy's heart problem always having to be taken into account, I haven't confirmed their suspicions in so many words."

"Awkward," said Phoenix as they reached the shower in their en-suite bathroom.

"Maybe we should discuss what we're going to say to them?" said Athena, slipping out of her clothes.

"Later," said Phoenix.

Chapter Two

I never imagined myself as a sailor. My parents enjoyed the sea-going life while they lived together as long as it came with a crew and plenty of bottles of champagne. We could be found on the Isle of Wight in August for Cowes Week with monotonous regularity when I was a teenager. My mother left on a cruise ship for the Mediterranean or the Caribbean not long after we returned home in those days.

My stepfather didn't want me hanging around while they wined and dined with the yachting fraternity. So I got packed off with an old local fisherman every afternoon of our three or four-week stay. He took his boat out to the lobster pots and pootled around the coastal waters, teaching me how to steer his tiny craft. When we were lucky, and I wasn't bored out of my skull, we even caught a few fish with a rod and line. I still recall the occasional flounder or bass I managed to land unaided.

My guardian didn't worry about success with his fishing expeditions; my stepfather paid him well. As the summers ticked past and I grew older, Michael Woodford passed on more valuable information than I realised at the time. He was a man of few words, for which I was grateful.

The silences were heaven. Life at home had become one screaming match after another. It was only a matter of time before my parents parted ways. Michael explained the vagaries of the tides, vectors, and races in the currents around the island. I thought it went in one ear and out the other, but by the time we made our ferry trip from Yarmouth to Lymington, I had subconsciously absorbed enough information to help me through what lay ahead.

Michael Woodford had retired. My stepfather was adrift. Not literally, of course, but he no longer travelled the ferry crossing in August after I turned seventeen. I accompanied my mother to social functions during Cowes Week for the first time.

Although she was at pains to point out I was her companion, not her toy boy, I spotted a knowing look on several faces we met. Those faces belonged to upper-class clientele in the clubs and harbourside restaurants we visited that summer. They thought after her last husband went that, my mother had hunted down his son as her new partner.

Mother had her reasons for denying my existence. Of course, I didn't fully understand them as a child, but I appreciated the logic behind her misdirection at seventeen.

The links between a mother and son and vice-versa are more robust than in marriage. We stayed in close contact no matter where she went or who she lived with. I owed her everything. I could refuse her nothing.

When I moved to London at eighteen to seek my fortune, I did so with a generous allowance. However, she promised that capital was available should I identify a market opportunity that helped me make my fortune.

The Price of Treachery

When that opportunity arose, I grabbed it with both hands. A decade later, I still reaped the benefits. From time to time, my mother needed a favour in return. How could I refuse? She had made other similar requests to the one she made in January. So I flew out to Ibiza for a weekend visit.

I watched from inside a café on the marina as Gavin helped William Hunt carry his small suitcase on board the yacht 'Elizabeth.' I followed Erebus as he walked along the tree-lined promenade after breakfast. I stood twenty feet to his left, leaning on the black-painted iron railings as we both admired the sandy beach.

I strolled up the Calle San Jaime around lunchtime as he whiled away an hour with this blessed newspaper under his arm. I thought of ways to dispose of him on his river walk up to the Roman bridge, but the waters were too shallow to conceal the body. So, in the end, I decided to stick with what I knew best. I have taken risks throughout my business life, doing things my competitors never dream of doing. So I decided to do the deed in plain sight. Risk everything on the roll of the dice.

I flew home on Monday morning and called my mother. She was in Australia with her latest husband. Even younger and less appropriate than the last. She was in no immediate rush. William Hunt wasn't going anywhere, and she had other things on her mind. I didn't ask what they might be; I knew better than to question her motives.

We met for only the second occasion that year in mid-July in London. A few words passed between us, enough to get me on a flight out to the Balearics early the following week. I visited the marina café once more and watched the comings and goings on 'Elizabeth'. Gavin, the crewman, fetched supplies, started the regular clean-up and looked to be kept busy for the next couple of hours.

William Hunt sat on the verandah of the Ring O' Bells with a cup of coffee. His copy of The Times was neatly folded in front of him on the circular table. He was too preoccupied with his preparations for his crossword to notice my approach.

I bounced up the steps, eager to fulfil my mother's wishes. I stabbed Erebus in the neck and hurried past the pool table into the restroom without breaking stride. I waited for thirty seconds. Then hearing no cries of alarm from the bar or outside, I calmly walked out, descended the steps and escaped into the town to find a taxi.

I disposed of the syringe in San Antonio, as far away from Calle de Mer and the pub as possible. But unfortunately, drug paraphernalia was not an uncommon find around the club capital of the Mediterranean. On my way back to my hotel in Santa Eulalia, I sent mother a text.

'Bellringer silenced.'

The next few days proved interesting. Poor Gavin appeared distraught. A nice cushy number cruising around the Balearics had ended abruptly. I knew I didn't have long before someone arrived from England to claim the body. I called from the hotel lobby to the company dealing with William Hunt's mortal remains.

The embalmer and I rapidly came to a financial agreement. He pushed the older man's name to the top of his list in exchange for a year's salary. I followed him home that evening and dropped the envelope containing the cash off at his shabby first-floor apartment. No chance now of anyone tracing the exact cause of William Hunt's demise.

Two familiar faces arrived in town the next day. Very subdued and with lots of tears. I smiled as I watched them from what had become my favourite spot on the island. It appeared that Erebus was flying home with an escort, and

Gavin was getting things ready to leave the sheltered haven of the marina. As he finalised things with the harbour master, he left 'Elizabeth' unattended. I crept aboard and stowed away until we were well out to sea.

The more people you kill, the easier it becomes. I was so relaxed I slept an hour or two longer than intended. Gavin was fast asleep when I slipped from my hiding place. The crewman awoke a second after my chloroform-soaked cloth pressed over his nose and mouth, but he was too late. He clawed in vain at my strong hands and soon lost consciousness. I tied him up securely and regularly added to his sedative. I sat and watched over him until morning as I read through the manuals for 'Elizabeth' and the rest of her class. By dawn, I was confident I knew which buttons to press.

I dressed in fresh clothes from Gavin's closet, A tight fit, but the ploy was only necessary while I negotiated the narrow channels in the marina. I managed this without mishap and soon motored out into the open seas. From there, three weeks of hopping from harbour to harbour around the coast of mainland Europe lay ahead of me.

Two days out from Ibiza, I got rid of my unwanted passenger. He was alive, if only just. Trussed up like a mummy, he didn't suffer long as he dropped to the bottom of the ocean, unable to move his arms or legs.

The weather remained kind throughout my journey. My GPS and Gavin's technical wizardry at his disposal on 'Elizabeth' were simple enough to master. My birth father didn't pass on many attributes in my genes, but I am always in awe of his innate skill at anything he tackles. Mother had been attracted by it once.

I received more than my fair share of her cold demeanour, which precluded any emotional attachments, male or female. She soon sensed I had inherited her dark side. That was what made us such a formidable pair. There were no limits to what we did to achieve our ends.

I was to deliver 'Elizabeth' to the Lymington Yacht Haven during Cowes Week. I was to arrive within a day or two of the time Gavin expected to steer her into her berth. When William Hunt's friends came to visit from Larcombe Manor, they would find her secure and undamaged.

A note from Gavin showed he had found another post, sailing a yacht in a far-flung Pacific paradise. They had no reason for suspicion. Mother had decided this option was much safer than scuttling the craft in the Atlantic. She frowned at my suggestion of rigging 'Elizabeth' to explode into fragments of wood, glass, and metal when someone from Larcombe entered through the cabin door.

"Far too dramatic, darling, and too remote. I want to be there when they die. Much more satisfying. No, do what they expect Gavin to do, return the yacht to its home, and after that, they can keep it, sell it, whatever they wish. It's of no consequence. We can wait."

Wednesday, August 14th, 2013

Today was the day I left my final safe harbour at Barfleur. I was going to negotiate the English Channel. This journey may seem foolhardy for a novice, if not downright dangerous. That morning I thanked Michael Woodford and the skippers who took me under their wing during that final summer we visited the Isle of Wight together.

In the less frantic weeks that followed the social whirl of the regatta, I crewed for various sizes of boats. Then, my mother disappeared to tour Greece and Italy, so she dumped me on Michael Woodford and his family for the rest of the summer.

I discovered that Michael spent his retirement days drinking cider and chatting about days gone by with locals and incomers. I learned the ropes on the craft that skimmed through the Solent or tackled the busy shipping lanes between the island and the French coast. When I left for home, bronzed by sunny days and balmy breezes, my education for what was to come today was complete.

To make a solo crossing of the English Channel is a daunting prospect. One is sailing out of sight of land, crossing busy shipping lanes and tackling ripping tides. These are stern challenges, but not impossible ones. If your preparation is meticulous – passage plan, weather, tides and boat checks – there's no reason you should fail. Confidence is a hurdle, but not something in short supply as far as I'm concerned; besides, Gavin had already done that work for me in his spare time in Santa Eulalia.

It's the skipper's job to ensure the boat's paperwork is in order. The chances are it won't be needed today, but if it wasn't at my fingertips, I could be in a lot of trouble. I mustn't draw undue attention to myself. Gavin's certificates, licences, and insurance were in order. I had my passport and EHIC.

Gavin meticulously collated the right charts and reference books for easy reference. He even owned one of those handy zipped-top holders full of rulers, dividers, pencils and an eraser. The last time I saw one of those was when I sat my A-Levels.

I had to give Gavin a gold star for his planning. He realised the necessity to use a single time zone and made adjustments for tides and heights. I checked the forecast with our dear old Met Office just in case; if things went wrong, any enquiry panel used their version as gospel on every occasion.

The forecast was southwest Force 3, becoming variable. I could always use the motor if the wind died. Visibility was excellent, and I had a green light. I ensured I was stocked with plenty of easy-to-prepare snacks and drinks. I filled the water and fuel tanks and brought emergency jerry cans of fuel, bottles of water, and odd spares for the engine.

'Elizabeth' possessed a decent toolkit and sail repair kit. I checked engine oil, gearbox oil, fresh water in the header tank, drive belt tension, and saltwater filter. Once I got moving, I ensured I had cooling water in the exhaust.

Gavin's diary confirmed he checked the rig thoroughly a couple of days earlier, and the winches, too, had only recently been serviced. So, a few minutes after five, I eased 'Elizabeth' out of her berth. I focused on every tiny detail. I had courses to steer from buoy to buoy and sails to set — no time left to be nervous.

For that first couple of hours, I found it difficult to judge the range of oncoming ships and altered course very early. Better safe than sorry. I soon settled into the rhythm and spent the next few hours gliding between tankers ploughing majestically on without a care in the world. I took time out for a drink and a bite to eat.

The wind was perfect. 'Elizabeth' skipped along at six knots for a spell; I sensed the wind veering, and we slowed to under four. Finally, it was time to lower the spinnaker and switch to the motor for a while. My nerves endured a severe test for the next few hours, but at last, we emerged on the other side of the shipping lanes without even a near miss.

As we entered the Solent, the wind picked up enough for me to revert to sail. I was in familiar territory now. So

The Price of Treachery

close to the shore, there were dozens of smaller craft. I wondered whether they had someone with the experience of a Michael Woodford to tell them where the dangers lay. It is sometimes hard to manoeuvre through a race in a small boat. How large a race could that little craft ahead cope with and not get mangled?

On my trips alone, close to shore, I avoided races as far as possible. Either by going at slack tide or by staying well out to sea. A very calm sea can give you a false sense of security; the race is cunning and leads you into it; before you know it, the tide accelerates, and you must commit. On the other hand, you can go from smooth calm with a slight swell to a white-knuckle ride in less than a minute.

These experienced kayakers came prepared; it wasn't long before the waters calmed, but I bet their little hearts were beating faster than an excited puppy's tail. A race often forms by headlands where the moving water is compressed, speeding up and causing rougher conditions. If the turbulent waters meet waves in the opposite direction, the water is more likely to break, with short sharp waves collapsing.

Where two streams converge, this results in rough water, as in the tides off Hurst Point, over to my left. I avoided this by keeping close to the Isle of Wight. So I could look up at the cliffs to enjoy the comparative wildness of this part of the island. Occasionally I could see people walking the coast in the early evening sun.

Every so often, the sea became less smooth as I passed a hidden ledge, but the generally calm sea meant it posed no problem. I skirted past Crooked Lake and turned towards the mainland, allowing the stream vector to take me into Lymington port. On the way, I felt the sea become rougher as I passed over the Fiddlers Race. Finally, it smoothed out as I looked for the series of navigation lights leading into Lymington Harbour. It was just before ten when I arrived at the Lymington Yacht Haven.

This last part of the journey took two hours. I had to watch several dangerous rocks and hidden reefs closely. Imagine damaging this beautiful yacht on one of these semi-submerged rocks. I wanted 'Elizabeth' to be in pristine condition when Athena and Phoenix came calling. We didn't wish Athena to be upset, not in her state. She won't know that the mother is aware that she is 'with child'; our colleague is careful not to show their true colours; what a blessing to have someone on the inside these days.

I had to remind myself that I still needed to thread my way alongside the marina and get 'Elizabeth' into her reserved berth. After an exhausting journey, I was losing concentration. Before long, though, everything sat in its rightful place. Time to print off Gavin's note, tidy up, collect my things and get ashore. All that remained was the final paperwork.

With that completed, I set off on the twenty-minute walk into Lymington and the excellent room I reserved at Stanwell House. After ten hours of sleep and a hearty breakfast, I took a taxi to the station. I arrived at London Waterloo before noon. I sent my mother a text while I sat on the train.

'HRH is in residence. Can't wait to meet again.'

My summer break had ended; the business world called me back to its bosom. Deals hammered out, millions made. My phone vibrated as I walked into the atrium that led to my London HQ. Mother had replied.

'Rest. Gather your strength. Difficult days lie ahead.'

Chapter Three

Friday, August 16th, 2013

"We *must* leave for London later this morning Phoenix," said Athena, "you've stalled long enough this week already. My parents will be dashing off for the weekend or boarding a cruise liner before we know it."

"There's a lot of work to be done, Athena. The need for direct action in London is urgent; you know that."

"Could you not delegate? You're supposed to be the joint head of operations here at Olympus these days."

"This one is personal. Rusty and I owe it to the victims to handle matters."

Athena knew the background details of the situation and was sickened by the sheer volume of harassment and intimidation these landlords had meted out. The violence was beyond shocking. How was it that a whole litany of beatings, sexual assaults and far worse could go on under the noses of the authorities without anyone noticing? No wonder Phoenix and the other agents were kept so busy.

She wondered what kind of world awaited their unborn child. It was up to her and the people in her organisation to look for continual improvement. The more they could root out evil, the better. Time was of the essence. Her due date of mid-January was going to be here before they knew it. They had much to do before then.

Phoenix and Athena left their apartment and walked together to the ground floor for the morning meeting. The others were there, waiting. Minos and Alastor sat deep in conversation; Thanatos stood with his back to the window. He looked up when he saw them arrive.

"Good morning," he said, taking his seat. "I have read murmurings in the media this morning that the US will soon begin military strikes in Syria. That matter wasn't on our agenda today; should we promote it to the top of the list?"

"The Yanks are welcome to try to sort out that mess," muttered Henry Case. "I suggest the UK best keep their noses out. The whole region is a powder keg waiting to explode. As for Olympus, we have smaller, less problematic issues to tackle here at home."

"I agree," said Athena, "a wrong move in the North African theatre could easily lead to an international incident. That's the exact opposite of what Olympus set out to achieve. We pride ourselves on working under the radar. We don't want to be caught in the open for the world to see. No, we'll stick to the schedule. We'll be brief today, too, because Phoenix and I are off to London. Minos will finish up proceedings in our absence,"

Minos was surprised by the delegation of responsibility but happy to oblige. Thanatos bit his tongue. All three senior men were coming to terms with Athena being the new head at Larcombe. Erebus had always indicated his wish for the former MI5 operative to be his successor. However, they had inevitably imagined playing a far more significant role because of their seniority.

The rapid rise of Phoenix was something none of them had foreseen.

"Let's get on with matters then," said Athena. She was in no mood to waste time today.

Henry Case and Giles Burke were first in the firing line. The ice-house personnel was developing new systems to improve their intelligence-gathering capabilities. Nobody was allowed to stand still in the modern world of crime fighters. The criminals bettered their operations year in and year out, so Olympus had to stay ahead.

"We have completed the installation, and Artemis and I are testing it thoroughly this week and next," reported Giles. "We will go 'live' from the first of September."

"Will you be able to hack into the BBC and arrange for a decent daytime series in the schedules from January?" asked Phoenix.

"We can achieve the impossible without too much difficulty, Phoenix," replied Giles, "miracles may take longer. Nobody's making decent programmes these days."

Athena tutted. Not so much at the typical light-hearted banter Phoenix always brought to meetings, more because news of her pregnancy was still secret. Throwaway comments like that could get people putting two and two together well before a bump gave the game away. She switched her attention quickly to her chief interrogator.

"Do you have anything else, Henry?"

"As we're limited to time because of your London trip, no, there's nothing that can't wait. I'd mention the recording of several suspicious deaths due to cosmetic surgery. We're investigating whether the same surgeon has been responsible and checking his credentials. There appear to be discrepancies. Finally, a twelve-year-old girl was hospitalised last evening in Glasgow. A rather bad experience after taking an as-yet-undefined narcotic. Artemis has spotted a reduction in the age profile of victims in this region. Not content with targeting young adults and teenagers, the low-life drug peddlers are now waiting at the gates of junior schools to develop a new income stream."

Athena shuddered. She had been correct. There was much to do to lift this world out of the gutter. To make it a better world in which to raise her child. The words of Robert Kennedy drifted up from her memory: -

'Let us dedicate ourselves to what the Greeks wrote so many years ago: to tame the savageness of man and make gentle the life of this world.'

She had lived in the secret service by that philosophy; those words were as pertinent today as ever. Her mind switched back to the meeting as Rusty was speaking: -

"The sooner we can sort out a few slum landlords, the better. We need agents on the ground in every city in the country. This new kit you've got in the ice-house is great, Henry, but it throws up more shit than we can handle at times."

"Always better to be busy than sitting around on our hands," said Phoenix, getting up and making for the door. "I'll see you when I get back, Rusty. We'll begin cleansing the Boroughs of a few of their parasites."

Athena handed the helm to Minos to go through the remaining status reports at home and abroad. She and Phoenix grabbed a bag, and packed clothes and toiletries for a brief stay in her family's luxurious accommodation in Belgravia. They were being driven in a car from the transport section and heading for the M4 within an hour. If the

The Price of Treachery

traffic was kind to them, they should arrive at Vincent Gardens in time for lunch. She rang her mother to tell her they were on their way.

"Things are hotting up, Athena," said Phoenix.

"No rest from the wicked," she replied.

"Very droll," he said and took hold of her hand. "Let's go through our story again to ensure we're singing from the same hymn sheet."

"I shall tell them I'm expecting a baby in January. Then we'll see their reaction and take it from there."

"Terrific, so we're going to 'wing' it? I was hoping we were better than that. If they say this, we counter that; you know the drill. We've done it enough with past interrogations."

"I wish you didn't keep referring to conversations with Daddy as interrogations."

"We don't have much in common, do we? He's bound to be concerned for his little princess. The first time we met, he thought I was a driver ferrying you around London. It's going to be a shock when you tell him I'm the baby's father. He's going to think that you fancied a bit of rough and got caught out. If that wasn't enough, I've been married twice before, and my past has to be a closed book. I suppose I could say I've worked for the charity for the past three years, but in what capacity? Anything related to my role within the organisation, or the skill set I developed as Colin Bailey, must be kept closely under wraps. The conversation will be restricted, making them more suspicious than ever."

"I can see I was right to suggest delaying the announcement of a possible wedding in the future. This is a nightmare," groaned Athena.

"Stick to the basics today," said Phoenix, "tell them our news of the baby. Tell them I work for the charity at

Larcombe as a facilitator. They won't ask what it entails; nobody knows anyway. It's one of those non-job titles that sprang up twenty years ago. I'll say as little as possible, and you encourage them to tell us about their last trip. Get your mother to tell you what medication she's taking and how she's feeling. That should keep things ticking over until we can make our excuses and head home."

"We're nearly there," said Athena.

The car turned into Vincent Gardens and pulled up by the kerb. Athena and Phoenix got out and collected their bags from the boot. The driver gave a wave and headed off to make his way home to Bath.

"Big breaths," said Phoenix.

The door opened before either of them could set foot on the doorstep. Mr Fox ushered them inside and closed the door. There was no hugging and kissing, for which Phoenix was very grateful. Athena always maintained her parents weren't prone to public displays of affection. The coolness thawed when her mother became ill; heart bypass operations tend to make you take stock of your life. To throw your arms around someone that you may never see again if things go wrong doesn't seem like abandoning your principles.

"Annabelle, darling, it's wonderful to see you," said her mother, who joined them in the hallway.

"Let's go to the conservatory; we can have coffee, and you can tell us how things are going at Larcombe," said her father.

"Daddy, may I introduce you to Phoenix?"

"We've met before, I believe? Don't tell me, never forget a name. Pat wasn't it?" said Mr Fox.

"Just Phoenix, sir," replied Phoenix, "my parents were an odd couple."

"Hippies, I imagine?" asked Mr Fox.

"Something along those lines," said Phoenix.

They had arrived at the conservatory. Mrs Fox was in the kitchen. Athena sat on the two-seater lounge sofa and tapped the seat next to her for Phoenix to join her. Her father took his place in one of the armchairs.

"Very subtle," whispered Phoenix as he joined Athena.

Mrs Fox was ready to come through with the coffees; she called for her husband to come and give her a hand.

As he left them alone, Athena gripped her partner's hand tight. Phoenix felt her nails digging into his palm.

"Look, I know you're nervous, but that bloody hurts."

"I couldn't deal with it in the car with the driver listening, but perhaps I fancied a bit of rough and got caught out? Cheeky devil. You didn't imagine you were going to get away with that one, did you?"

She eased the pressure on his hand and kissed him on the lips. Of course, that didn't escape the notice of Mrs Fox as she came through the doorway.

Her husband carried a silver tray with delicate-looking china cups and the trimmings behind her.

Phoenix was more used to non-matching mugs that carried sayings such as Windsurfers do it standing up, or Tree surgeons go out on a limb. But, on this occasion, nerves had rendered his throat dry, so whatever it came in was great.

"How was the south of France this time?" asked Athena.

"Bloody hot," said her father, "too hot these days for your mother."

There was a lull in the conversation as the four started drinking their coffee. Finally, Mrs Fox broke the spell.

"Well, you've come here to tell us something, Annabelle;

you wouldn't drive all this way to ask us how we were. We know how busy charity work keeps you. I think they work you too hard. Are you sure you couldn't find a similar post here in London?"

"Ah, you missed the introductions, darling. This gentleman is called Phoenix. I gather you work for the Olympus Project too?"

"Indeed, I do. Very pleased to meet you, Mrs Fox," said Phoenix.

"Likewise, I'm sure," she replied, "well, Annabelle, are you ready to tell us what's going on yet?

"We're going to have a baby, Mummy,"

"Young people today," tutted her father, "you didn't think to wait until you were married then?"

"I'm old enough to know my mind," said Athena, "we've known one another for three years, and we love each other."

"Don't pay any attention to your father," said her mother. "I think it's wonderful news. I wondered whether I would ever be able to call myself a grandmother. If you ever get around to getting married, I'll be a mother-in-law. If not, it doesn't matter these days. Either way, I'll be Grace to you, Phoenix. Annabelle's father is Geoffrey, for future reference."

"What function do you carry out at Larcombe Manor, Phoenix?" asked Geoffrey Fox.

"I'm a facilitator, Geoffrey," replied Phoenix.

"Really?" said Geoffrey Fox, nodding, "how fascinating."

That broke the ice. Phoenix and Athena heard about St. Tropez, Cannes and Monaco over lunch in a lovely restaurant two hundred yards from the Fox residence. Grace Fox told her daughter what changes she had made to her exercise and diet since her health scare.

At the time, she viewed any proposed minor lifestyle changes with fear and trepidation, if not downright defiance. Now the modifications had become Grace's ideas, not those of Mr Ramanayake, her consultant. Athena thought her mother looked better than she had for several years.

As they walked back towards Vincent Gardens, Geoffrey Fox and Phoenix followed the ladies along the street. Gradually, Geoffrey allowed the gap between them to grow. Phoenix could tell he had something on his mind.

"Where did you serve, Phoenix?" Geoffrey Fox asked.

"I didn't," replied Phoenix.

"I imagined that most personnel at Larcombe were ex-servicemen. It must help if you're dealing with chaps that come home with PTSD. You know, having been in a combat zone yourself. You must have a specialist role if you acquired the grounding on civvy street. What's your game? Psychiatry or something in that field?"

"Far less glamorous; I do a lot of planning to help those leaving Larcombe to achieve success in whatever task they pursue."

Geoffrey seemed content with the answer. Phoenix was happy he hadn't had to lie about the true nature of his role to his prospective father-in-law.

The rest of the weekend passed off without any awkward moments. It was very amicable. Grace Fox questioned her daughter further on the charity and wanted her to consider cutting back on her workload in the months approaching the birth.

"We might not travel quite so much in the future, darling," she said, "your baby will be a blessing. I shall have something exciting to look forward to instead of dragging myself off to Gstaad and god-forsaken places such as that this winter. Been there, done that and got the salopettes."

On Sunday evening, they returned in a taxi from the theatre. Geoffrey walked into the lounge and offered Phoenix a nightcap. Grace and Annabelle Fox were chatting over coffee in the kitchen. Geoffrey poured a generous glass of single malt from a decanter and handed it to him. Phoenix knew this heralded a big moment. It wasn't something her father did very often, according to Athena.

"Welcome to the family, Phoenix. Your parents chose an odd name for you; it rose from the flames, didn't it? It was born again. We worried about Annabelle after the bombings eight years ago, whether she could cope. She found a cause that grabbed her interest. Now she's found someone to grab her interest too. That's good enough for us. Treat her well. Grace was right the other day. Being with the right person is more important than a piece of paper. Maybe you were born again, too, eh, Phoenix? The future is what matters, not the past. So I wish you both good health, good luck and...."

"Good hunting?" added Phoenix.

"Exactly," said Geoffrey Fox.

Monday, August 19th, 2013

The transport arrived bright and early in the morning, and Athena and Phoenix said their goodbyes. Once they were in the car and moving away from Vincent Gardens, Athena breathed a long sigh.

"That went a helluva lot better than we imagined."

Phoenix decided against telling her that Geoffrey Fox

The Price of Treachery

didn't swallow the 'facilitator' tag nor the smokescreen of the charity cover. Her father was an astute man; whatever they were up to at Larcombe was for the greater good. He had brought up his daughter to do nothing less.

"We got through from baby to marriage before we'd finished coffee on Friday lunchtime," he said, "it was plain sailing from there."

"What did you and Daddy talk about last night?"

"He told me to treat you well. Welcomed me to the family; the usual father and son-in-law stuff."

Athena didn't have anything to add. Phoenix let his mind drift back to his father-in-law Tom Smith. He wondered whether he could apply to the Guinness Book of World Records if he and Athena married. He must have a strong chance of being the bloke with the broadest gulf in class between fathers-in-law in the world ever. The only thing they had in common was they both liked a drop of scotch.

They arrived at Larcombe just before eleven, and Athena went to their apartment. Phoenix went to the drawing room. Only the Three Amigos remained from the morning meeting.

"How was your London trip?" asked Minos.

"Very friendly," replied Phoenix, "what's the latest?"

"This warm weather should continue," said Alastor.

Phoenix wondered where Alastor's priorities were sometimes. He didn't comment.

"Any idea where Rusty went after he left here?"

"He was meeting Artemis, I believe," said Minos. "Giles said the new system crashed overnight. She worked on it for several hours and needed a break. So she may be sleeping."

Phoenix thought he'd better not wander over to the stable block to find his colleague. He didn't want to discuss

Hounslow and Ealing when Artemis awoke or if she wasn't asleep and they were doing what came naturally; he didn't want to disturb them. So he headed for the orangery.

It was time to face the next set of horror stories in the 'beds in sheds' saga.

As if the situation in Hounslow hadn't been bad enough, the neighbouring Borough of Ealing had seen fifty thousand more people added to its population. Forget what the census reported only two years ago; many new arrivals are illegally in the country. They live under the radar and never take part in official surveys.

When a council official hires a drone to detect humans on the ground in areas where housing is unauthorised, you know you have a problem. Phoenix was back at work in the orangery. Giles had provided Rusty with additional aerial photographs. They clearly showed that gardens at the rear of streets of pre-war terraced houses contained large outbuildings.

The heat maps for these ramshackle constructions suggested that one street alone could house a thousand people. Rusty's report highlighted one property in Southall where a big back garden held three sheds. He had met and talked with an extended family from India who occupied one of the buildings. They arrived in Britain in 2010 and have lived in Slough.

The elderly grandparents didn't speak English. Their sons lived with them, with their wives and children. The children's ages ranged from three to twelve. One son worked in Reading, the other at Heathrow Airport. Both the wives worked in Southall in convenience stores. They had no complaints. They were happy with their lot.

The Price of Treachery

"We have three rooms and a bathroom," one of the younger women told Rusty. "We are close to the local school. We pay a lot of money, but this way of life is what we've grown up with."

Rusty had found that they were paying around four hundred pounds a month for the property. Ironically, councils had their hands tied with older buildings such as these. If the landlord proved the shed existed over four years ago, they couldn't force the families out and demolish them.

Not everyone Rusty interviewed told the same story. A Moroccan warehouseman went to view what purported to be a studio flat and found a damp, bug-infested, rank-smelling shed. It was available at only seven hundred pounds per calendar month. He had been horrified, but he had no alternative but to sign a contract. He needed a roof over the heads of himself, his wife and their infant daughter.

Rusty had used the information supplied by families such as these to trace the landlords involved. However, one surname kept cropping up on documents and in conversation when there were sad tales to tell. The worst offender was a man named Flynn.

Patrick Flynn was an Irishman in his late forties. He had been a teenager in the mid-eighties, and he and his mates had two primary sources of enjoyment: watching football and fighting. Gangs of vicious soccer thugs leave a decidedly sour taste in the mouth. Paddy Flynn joined one of the most notorious a few miles from where he plied his trade as a landlord.

If you happened to be wearing the wrong replica kit and bumped into Paddy and his colleagues after a League game, you could be spitting out broken teeth before the day's results had been read on the TV. He and the gang he ran with stirred up serious ultra-violence during matches and were responsible for the worst rioting and missile-throwing in British football. However, they were proud of the fact and wore battle scars as a badge of courage.

Patrick Flynn described himself as a businessman these days; he wore a suit and tie. His tattoos were hidden away under crisp white tailored shirts. His knuckles still bore the faded 'Love' and 'Hate' that laser surgery had not entirely removed. It wasn't wise to look too closely to read what had once been there. Under the polished veneer he had adopted in the past decade, the hooligan still lurked as violent as ever.

Two lads from the same sink estate that had run with him back in his youth were still by his side. Eamonn Murphy and Terence O'Callaghan had worked for Flynn as muscle since they received a phone call offering them 'enjoyable' work at the turn of the millennium.

Rusty had uncovered dozens of tenants who had felt the fists of Murphy and O'Callaghan during the past decade. Flynn sent them to one of his properties, and they confronted the twenty-eight-year-old Egyptian tenant about past due rent. Murphy punched the tenant several times and threw him onto a kitchen table, causing it to break. O'Callaghan picked up a chair and hit him repeatedly over the head. The tenant needed medical attention and was off work for two weeks.

A Dutch tenant in his mid-thirties was struck with a baseball bat, choked, and attacked with a broken beer bottle. Tenants in neighbouring flats heard the men yelling abuse at him. They called the police, but by the time they arrived, the thugs had gone. Officers found the victim covered in blood, sitting on the steps outside his building.

They took him to the closest hospital and asked him who was responsible. The tenant said he had slipped and fallen, and no one else was involved. The police could do no more and left. The Dutchman took a taxi back to his apartment and moved out at the end of the month.

Phoenix was half-expecting what followed. The escalating violence was bound to lead to someone's death before long. In November of 2012, a twenty-two-year-old Muslim man, Gibril Khan, moved into a multi-occupancy bedsit on Paddy Flynn's list. He paid six weeks' rent on arrival.

Gibril was a quiet, studious character with few friends in London. He lived next door to a tenant with a noisy dog and tended to play heavy metal music late into the night. He complained to his neighbour to no avail. He went to see Patrick Flynn and asked for something to be done. He ignored him. Mr Flynn told Gibril he was too busy. That night Murphy and O'Callaghan visited Gibril.

They roughed him up and warned him that Mr Flynn didn't stand for troublesome tenants. If he caused any more problems, he faced eviction. Gibril didn't understand why he should be the one who moved out. The two 'heavies' gave him a beating and left.

Gibril was still hurt and upset when he went to work the next day. He told his colleagues at the call centre about his situation. After that, he couldn't concentrate on his job and went home early. His supervisor told him he should report the threats and intimidation to the authorities.

Gibril found he had locked himself out when he returned to his building. He walked to Flynn's offices and demanded a new key. Paddy Flynn exploded with rage. He threw a replacement key at the frightened young man and told him he'd have to move out if there was any further trouble.

The young man walked home in tears. He spotted a police station on the other side of the road and entered. He told the desk sergeant he believed his life was in danger. The officer listened patiently to his story but did not record the details. As far as he was concerned, it was yet another landlord-tenant dispute. They were ten a penny around here these days.

Gibril Khan left the police station and returned to his apartment. It was just his bad luck that Eamonn Murphy pulled up at the lights to allow a group of pedestrians to cross the busy road. He spotted Gibril, realised where he had just emerged from, and later that afternoon, he told his boss, Paddy Flynn.

Flynn told Murphy to get hold of O'Callaghan,

"Get tooled up, the two of you. We need to make an example of this kid."

The three men burst through the door to Gibril's apartment at around ten o'clock that evening. They attacked him with baseball bats. Murphy then produced a knife and stabbed Gibril in the arm and chest. The young Muslim lay on his bed, semi-conscious and bleeding, as the three men smashed up his belongings, emptied drawers and scattered food and clothing throughout the rooms.

"You won't be staying here any longer," shouted Flynn as he left. "We can't have people living like pigs. It stands to reason. So be out of here tomorrow, or we'll be back to finish the job."

A couple from a flat on the second floor were returning home from a local takeaway. The couple saw three men hurrying away, but when questioned by the police later, they said they couldn't identify anyone; they were too far away, and it was dark.

As they passed Gibril's door, they heard him moaning. They called for an ambulance straight away. Gibril struggled to speak while they tried to staunch blood flow from his

The Price of Treachery

wounds. Finally, he told them what had happened and who was responsible. The ambulance arrived and rushed him off to the hospital. Gibril Khan had died at four-thirty the following morning.

Nobody was ever arrested and charged with his murder. Flynn and his colleagues were still terrorising the Borough of Ealing. Murphy reckoned Gibril dying had done them a favour.

"We don't get half the bother we used to get with stroppy tenants. It sharpened everyone up lovely. They're as good as gold these days."

Phoenix closed the files. He had everything he needed. He rang Rusty and asked him to join him.

"Time for some street cleaning, Rusty."

The two friends had much to discuss. It was barely a month since Zara Wheeler had cast off her police persona and joined Rusty at Larcombe Manor. On her arrival, she became Artemis. Zara spent her days and nights with Giles Burke and the rest of the intelligence-gathering team in the ice-house. Artemis spent any leisure time she had with Rusty.

Phoenix missed the easy camaraderie he and the ex-SAS man had developed over the time they had known one another. He could still recall the pain Rusty inflicted on him while he underwent a rigorous training programme three years ago. The friendship that had blossomed from the direct actions they attended together since outweighed that painful memory.

They had stood shoulder to shoulder fighting a common enemy at Eton Wick only a month ago. Rusty had saved his skin near Cropredy when they went to get rid of a couple of rogue agents. Their brushes with the various terrorist cells that had threatened to cause havoc and panic across the

UK would live long in the memory. Their bond relied on mutual respect for their particular skill sets.

Rusty arrived at the orangery and sat opposite his colleague.

"How have you been, mate?" he asked.

"Don't take this the wrong way, but I've missed you," said Phoenix, leaning back in his chair. "These last few weeks have been hectic but strange, you know? Now I've moved out of the stable block; we never get the chance for a quick chat. But, when planning a mission like this one, I used to pop next door, and we'd bounce around a few ideas. It helped get the job done quicker."

"Better maybe, not quicker," quipped Rusty.

"There you go," said Phoenix, "that typified the off-the-cuff sessions we had back in the day. Now everything seems so much more formal. First, I have to ring you up and get you to meet me here in the orangery. Athena limits the amount of banter at the morning meetings to an absolute minimum. Then we're away to our apartment, and you shoot off to rest, train or spend time with your partner. Life's changed. The missions are still full-on and challenging when they happen, but everyone needs light and shade in their life. I'm missing the light, Rusty. Now Artemis is here; I'm scurrying around the place, keeping out of sight. It's driving me mad."

"You reckon your life has changed? What about mine? I never imagined being shacked up with anyone a year ago. You have to remember that one of the reasons for the nature of things lately is because you and Athena are joint leaders of this outfit now. As for Artemis, what can we do to change that situation?"

"Sorry, Rusty, I'm not having a go at you for falling in love with the one woman who could identify me as Colin

Bailey. I guess my past was bound to catch up with me sooner or later. But, with everything ahead of us, we need to find a way forward, or things will get worse."

"Going forward?" asked Rusty. "What is ahead of us, Phoenix? Apart from everything we hear at the meetings."

"Athena's pregnant."

"Congratulations. I'm pleased for you both. Ah, shit, I see what you mean. Do I tell Artemis? She's bound to notice when she sees Athena around the place over the next few months."

"Exactly, sit on our news for now; I'll let Athena tell the others in her own time," said Phoenix. "Our quick visit to London was to tell her parents the news. That went better than she feared, but her father's reaction stunned me. He took me to one side the night before we returned to share a damn good scotch. He's onto things here; the charity camouflage does not fool him. Her mother doesn't know what's happening, but Geoffrey Fox is no mug. So we'll need to tread carefully."

"Artemis knows that you two are a couple. So hearing you are pregnant won't be too difficult to come to terms with," said Rusty. "If you were thinking of getting married and sending out invitations, that might cause ructions. You're not, though, are you?"

"Well, now you come to mention it," said Phoenix, "but we have a major obstacle to overcome first. I don't exist. Not officially. We could manufacture an identity for my passport to get me out to Ibiza, but Athena doesn't want to marry Garry Burns. She wants to marry me."

"Oh, what a tangled web we weave," said Rusty.

"Bit of a nightmare, isn't it? But I want you to be my best man. If we ever find a way to make it happen."

"I'd be proud to, Phoenix. Will my invitation be a plus one?"

"This child of ours is going to be leaving school at this rate before we tie the knot," groaned Phoenix.

"Right, let's get our thinking caps on," said Rusty. "We'll plan this operation, get it sorted, and then find a way to fully integrate Artemis into the organisation. We can't have you skulking around Larcombe in the shadows forever. You need to be free to push that pushchair in the grounds next year whenever you want."

It was time to get serious. Rusty was right. Phoenix forgot his problems for the time being and got his game head in place. For the next few hours, they studied the profiles of the six targets. Giles had provided reports on the patterns of their movements, day to day, week to week. It wasn't long before they had crystallised a method by which they could dispose of each of the landlords and their enforcers.

"OK, then, Rusty. I'll run this past Athena in the morning. We'll ask Giles for the absolute latest on their whereabouts this week and take it from there. Can you drop into the ice-house and visit Bazza and Thommo to order the supplies we'll need?"

"No worries," said Rusty. He left Phoenix in the orangery. It felt good to get back into action; he had been idle for far too long. Eton Wick had been a month ago, for heaven's sake. The next forty-eight hours should see a satisfying conclusion to the hours he had spent researching the landlords' saga. It might take longer to sort out the issues between Phoenix and Artemis.

Phoenix collected the paperwork and walked back to the main building. Athena was reading when he arrived in the lounge.

The Price of Treachery

"Ready to go, darling?" she asked.

"Everything's set for the meeting tomorrow. I'll run through our plan of action for the team's benefit, get the latest intelligence from the ice-house and ask for a green light."

"You can't wait to get back out there again, can you?" asked Athena.

"It will be good to shake off the cobwebs. After losing people as we did at Eton Wick, you start to wonder whether it was your fault. Could I have done anything differently? Then you start to question whether you've still got that edge. I never had the responsibility for teams of people in the old days. I only had to decide who, how and when; then take them out."

"There's no reason to doubt yourself, Phoenix, and there was nothing you could have done to save Jack Mould. That was pure bad luck. As for being responsible for a team? We're a team of two, soon to be three. We'll look after one another and always keep in mind the objectives of the Project. We *have* to maintain our edge, to keep bringing the guilty people to account for their crimes."

"Together, we are stronger, I suppose," said Phoenix, flopping onto the settee beside her.

"We have another Olympus meeting in a month from now. I think it's time I let you in on a secret," said Athena, "in London. I've had Alastor, Minos, and Thanatos carry out in-depth background checks on our senior Olympus colleagues. First, we must identify the elements around the table conspiring against us. Next, we must find the person responsible for the death of Erebus; and whether they connect to any of those conspirators."

"I knew something was going on that you weren't telling me," said Phoenix. "Has anything concrete turned up yet to point to the traitors? Have any of the Three Amigos found confirmation of 'the little black book'? This next meeting will undoubtedly see a list of names for removal coming our way."

"I'll run through what we have so far before you leave for London tomorrow. As for the book, there's very little evidence of what it contains. Nevertheless, it exists; I'm certain of that. I guess its names will combine personal vendettas and significant ministry officials. People who would cause problems if they were still around when the conspirators begin destabilising and overthrowing the government."

Phoenix stood up and walked to the window. He thought for a while; then, he picked up the photograph of William and Elizabeth Hunt. Athena smiled.

"You love that photo just as much as I do, don't you?"

"I miss him every day. I won't stop grieving until I kill the bastard responsible for his death. It wasn't that, though. I was thinking about the yacht. Gavin should have brought her home by now; he hasn't been in contact. Maybe you could call him tomorrow? After Rusty and I finish the job in London, you and I might find time to drive to Lymington and check on 'Elizabeth'."

"Aye, aye, Captain," said Athena, throwing a cushion at him.

Phoenix caught the soft missile and returned it to its proper place. Tomorrow was a day to right wrongs and rid the world of a few of its less desirable inhabitants — people whose hundreds of victims wouldn't mourn their passing.

The day would come when he could take revenge on those who had taken his mentor from him—the man whose vision enabled the Olympus Project to bring undesirables to justice over the past six years.

Chapter Four

Tuesday, August 20th, 2013

The transport section parked the vehicle by the ice-house. Rusty was already below ground, picking up the items they required later today and through the rest of the week. As much as they would have loved to have dispatched six people and been home in time for tea, it was more sensible to pick them off in a manner that didn't attract attention.

Phoenix made his way across the lawns to join up with his friend. He opted to avoid the lift to the armoury on this occasion. It would have been a fun start to the day. A few minutes of banter with Bazza and Thommo always lightened the mood around Larcombe. Things that took your mind off the dangers that lay ahead when you were setting off on direct action.

The possibility of an accidental encounter with Artemis kept him away. He hadn't asked Rusty what time she started work on the first floor this morning. It would be just his luck to bring up weapons and ammunition from the second-floor armoury, and she stopped the lift on her floor to return to the surface. What an uncomfortable few seconds that could be.

Phoenix continued to check out the transport team's work decorating the van they assigned. The ubiquitous 'white van' was complete with a few 'dings' and odd patches of rust. The signage identified 'Scott & Bailey' as a team of handymen perfectly equipped to keep your property in tip-top shape.

"I wonder who the comedian was who thought that one up," mused Phoenix.

He was happy enough with the cover it gave them, but the firm's name sailed close to the wind. At the back of his mind, it rang a bell. While the guys in the transport section filled their downtime watching cop shows on TV, Phoenix spent his leisure time planning his next mission.

Phoenix heard the lift doors open and wandered over to the ice-house entrance. Rusty brought out the first bags of equipment.

"A warm day for it, Phoenix," said Rusty.

"It would be warm indoors painting and decorating, that's for sure. Is this a good idea, using our surnames on the side of the van?"

Rusty looked at their colleagues' handiwork.

"Don't sweat it, Phoenix. Over the next few days, you'll see a thousand vans similar to this in the smoke. They're ten a penny. Of course, nobody takes a blind bit of notice of them. But, if it was a colour or a name that makes it stick out like a sore thumb, that's when you'd need to worry. This firm won't be in business for long. As soon as this job is over, it will be off to the salvage yard and into the crusher."

The Price of Treachery

"Do we need anything else from below, or have you brought everything up now?" asked Phoenix.

"No, this was everything they had on our list. We need to get hold of one more item. The safety and security systems below ground are top of the range, as you know. Everything you would ever need to prevent or fight a fire is on hand, but no mission wish list before has ever called for a fire extinguisher."

Phoenix had studied Rusty's reports carefully. His request had a particular purpose, but Rusty hadn't questioned it. He was comfortable with his friend's selection, as always. With the van loaded, it was time to set off for West London. The radio in the van issued a time-check soon after Rusty turned the key in the transmission. It was seven-fifty a.m.

"We should be leaving the M4 at Junction 3 at around eleven o'clock at the latest," said Rusty, "where do you want to start first?"

"I asked Giles to update me on the latest movements of our targets. He's checking in with us at noon today. We'll leave the M4 at the Chiswick Roundabout and set up a base in our safe house. It's not in current use; I confirmed that last night. It will be just one more layer of camouflage for the house. Evidence of someone carrying out remedial work on the place. It reinforces the neighbours' thoughts; it's just a normal three-bedroomed detached house in the suburbs. As soon as we can put pins on the map to isolate our targets, we'll follow our plans to the letter. We can assemble our device inside the house and store our fire extinguisher until needed. We'll get that delivered after lunch. I'll start sourcing it now en route. What could be more natural than delivering fire safety items to an address going through a home improvement programme? Every multi-occupancy property should have one, as a matter of course. No flags will get raised. The delivery driver will never connect the dots."

"Ingenious, as ever," said Rusty, "this traffic's heavier this morning. Still, we aren't in a mad panic, are we? Are you happy with this radio station, Phoenix, or do you want me to tune into something edgier?"

"We can stick with Heart for a while. You can find Kerrang on 105.2 when we get closer to our destination. That will liven things up a touch. The station's coverage is more restricted these days."

"Is it a fact that most metal lovers are over forty these days? Do any younger kids get that stuff?" asked Rusty.

"It's a simple matter of mathematics, Rusty. How long has heavy metal music been going? Look at the ages of the band members around and still playing. It has broad appeal across the ages, and a disproportionate percentage of the brainiest five per cent of the student population term themselves metalheads. It was the first genre of music that grabbed me when I hit seventeen. Nothing since has had the same effect."

"Whatever works, I guess," said Rusty.

Phoenix checked out the nearest supplier and ordered the largest fire extinguisher and fire blanket combination they stocked. He didn't need the blanket, but it came under the advert for a landlord's special offer, so it made perfect sense. He charged it to the shell company listed as owning Olympus's various safe houses in the UK.

"Same-day delivery cost me an extra five pounds ninety-five, but money's no object when you're not paying," he said to Rusty.

The Price of Treachery

"Time for a change of music," said his friend, "then we're off to Chiswick."

They pulled into the forecourt of the safe-house to the strains of 'Enter The Sandman' at five minutes to eleven. Rusty got out of the van and went towards the back doors.

"Are you going to sit there all day, Phoenix?" he called.

"Just until the end of this track, mate, I'll open up, and we can get started."

In a few minutes, they were inside the house and emptying the bags of equipment on the floor in the living room. There were guns and ammunition. All the ingredients for assembling an explosive device, plus a few tools which, if a policeman ever had cause to check the pair, marked them as going equipped.

Rusty looked through the cupboards and the chest freezer in the kitchen.

"Hungry, Phoenix?" he asked.

"Always," came the reply.

"Well, unless you like fish fingers, baked beans and tomato soup, you might be out of luck."

"I'll pass; there's a pizza place two hundred yards back towards that last roundabout. I'll go there and pick up something. That delivery's due mid-afternoon, so we've got time to get something. How are we off for coffee?"

"More than enough if you drink it black."

"Shall I make a list?"

"Might as well start getting domesticated, Phoenix. Parenthood is just around the corner; it will be nappies and baby food in a few months."

Phoenix went shopping, and the food and drink were gone before Giles got in touch at noon. Phoenix marked the location of each target on a street map showing either

Hounslow or Southall, and then they started manufacturing their device. The front doorbell rang at a quarter past three.

"Package to be signed for," said the Polish delivery driver, leaving the heavy item on the doorstep. He was gone for his next drop-off almost before Rusty could scribble a name.

The two agents spent the next couple of hours manufacturing their device. Giles sent through updates for the target locations at six in the evening. After that, it was time to tour the area to confirm the stages of the plans Phoenix had put together. They got in the van and drove through the suburban streets, studying the specific buildings in which their targets lived. They double-checked the ways in and out of the properties. As they motored back to the safe-house, keeping within the speed limit, Rusty asked Phoenix when they would start work.

"No time like the present."

They paid a brief visit to the safe house. Rusty went upstairs to change. Phoenix collected an item from a medicine cabinet in the bathroom. The usual toiletries were on the top shelf. The lower shelf contained a few drugs useful when interrogating suspects or speeding up the demise of a criminal who refused to cooperate.

On a Tuesday evening, Frank DeAngelo visited Heston Pool for exercise. He wasn't the most proficient swimmer, but he needed to keep as fit as he could now in his mid-sixties. He would arrive at around seven-thirty and leave at just after nine. It was a twenty-minute drive from his house.

Rusty and Phoenix followed him in the van as he travelled across the Borough. DeAngelo parked up, went inside and changed. He emerged from the changing rooms holding a towel and a bottle of water. He wore flip-flops and a sensible pair of swimming shorts. Frank was a man-mountain, and most casual pool users gave him a wide berth. His reputation around the manor meant he always had an outside lane to himself.

Phoenix sat reading a magazine next to where Frank had dropped his towel and bottle of water. Then, finally, Rusty came from the changing rooms. He was over forty, the same as Phoenix, and his SAS training had given him a physique that tempted a few looks from the females in and around the pool.

From watching him swim in the pool at Larcombe, Phoenix knew that a hundred lengths of these baths wouldn't tire Rusty. He could run a half-marathon straight after and not bat an eye-lid. Frank ploughed his way up and down the pool, stopping after every three or four lengths to take a breather. He gave others in the water a stare if they dared look at him.

Rusty was gliding up and down the lane next to Frank. Frank watched him while he rested, but Rusty ignored him. After forty minutes, Frank rested longer than he swam, but Rusty carried on with the same steady rhythm he had started. Rusty was breathing to his left and watching Frank as they swam side by side. Finally, he slowed so that they arrived at the wall together.

Frank was breathing heavily.

"Good exercise for you, swimming," said Rusty. "Do you come here often?"

Frank looked at Rusty. Was that a chat-up line? Unlikely, the bloke looked as if he had served in the forces. Frank didn't care much for small talk.

"Tuesday nights," he grunted.

"Might see you next week then," said Rusty, turning

back to start the next length. Frank DeAngelo watched him go. He thought just a minute or two, and I'll have enough energy to follow you.

Rusty got to the other end of the lane and pulled himself athletically out of the water. He collected his towel and went to the changing rooms. Phoenix sat in the car park in the van's driver's seat. He had finished his magazine; he was listening to the radio. Rusty joined him five minutes later.

"Everything OK?" asked Phoenix.

"He's had enough for tonight. He lumbered into the changing rooms as I was getting dressed. He towelled himself dry and took a long drink of his bottled water. He'll be out later."

"No point in hanging around here then," said Phoenix, "we might as well pick up a takeaway and a four-pack of beers. Then, we can get a good night's sleep and start again in the morning."

In the changing rooms, Frank DeAngelo sat on the bench by the locker that contained his clothes. The man mountain hunched over. As other swimmers wandered in, they looked over, but nobody wanted to trouble him. They didn't need a slap if he had just nodded off after his exertions in the pool.

While Rusty had engaged Frank in a quick chat, Phoenix had emptied a vial into the bottled water container. Frank's heart had stopped around ten minutes after he had taken his well-earned drink. Then, when it was getting near closing time, a staff member realised Frank wasn't sleeping and called an ambulance.

Rusty had been right; he *was* coming out later. On a stretcher, in a black bag. The autopsy would show that DeAngelo died of heart failure. Too much exercise late in life when you're not used to it can be dangerous, so take care.

Wednesday, August 21st, 2013

Phoenix awoke as dawn broke over the capital. He descended the stairs to the kitchen and boiled the kettle for that first cup of coffee. He could still hear Rusty snoring gently upstairs. Today would see a change of direction. He and his colleague were due in Ealing to begin eliminating the Irish murderers of Gibril Khan.

He walked to the lounge and studied the items on the table. Rusty had trained him three years ago to assemble and deactivate the type of weapon they were to use today. Phoenix would defer to his trainer's expertise on this occasion. They weren't looking for a massive explosion that resulted in innocent casualties. It had to be a car bomb that was large enough to kill the occupants of the vehicle, but it must avoid collateral damage.

The car bomb has been a weapon of assassination for decades. More often than not, the desired effect was a far broader impact than the interior of the car itself. Phoenix understood how a variety of methods could activate car bombs. When the doors opened or the key turned in the ignition. The accelerator or brake pedal could activate the explosive device. Many terrorist organisations employ a range of timing devices.

Rusty had a selection of those available this morning from which to choose; he would make his final decision based on today's intelligence from Giles as it was received. Their device would fix magnetically to the car's underside, inside the mudguard of the nearside rear wheel.

It was likely that he'd choose a tilt fuse—a small tube designed of plastic, not dissimilar to a mercury switch. One end of the fuse is filled with mercury, with the other open end wired with the ends of an open circuit to the electrical firing system.

When the tilt fuse moved or jerked, the mercury supply flowed to the top of the tube and closed the circuit. Phoenix remembered Rusty's commentary in the training session. He calmly demonstrated what happened to a remote-controlled toy replica of the Prime Minister's Jaguar as it drove over rough terrain on the grounds at Larcombe.

"The state of the potholes in the roads around the country these days means the IRA, Al Qaeda, or Animal Rights activists could depend on the normal rising and dipping that comes with driving in modern Britain. Then, once the circuit completes, the bomb or explosive is allowed to function. We've done half their work for them by our neglect."

The toy car exploded into the air two seconds after his commentary ended.

Upstairs, Rusty stirred, and a minute or two later, he padded down the stairs in his underwear.

"Morning, Phoenix. Time for a coffee; I'll get showered, shaved, and dressed when I'm awake. I can't wait to get started."

"OK, Rusty, I'll go up and get myself ready now. Giles will be contacting us at eight. He will give us the latest itinerary for our targets, and you can pick which choice to use. I want the victims of these thugs to know someone cared enough to take them out in a spectacular fashion. That's why I plan to attach the bomb inside the rear mudguard. The petrol in the fuel tank will make the bomb's explosion more powerful by dispersing and igniting the fuel."

"We take every precaution to keep the Olympus name out of the headlines," said Rusty. "An assassination such as this will mean the authorities will investigate it thoroughly. My construction will feature elements familiar to them. When they analyse the bomb's characteristics, they will produce a long list of potential suspects, enough to muddy the waters. We could never use this particular method again. It has to be a one-off."

"Understood," said Phoenix, "I know I can rely on you to get it right. Then, we'll pass the design on to Henry Case, who can include it in a 'Do Not Use' section of our standard operating procedures manual."

Phoenix went upstairs and got ready. Rusty followed fifteen minutes later. By eight o'clock, both men were in the living room. Rusty had started to assemble the bomb. Phoenix took the call from Giles Burke.

"Your targets are both still at home. The car is in the driveway of Murphy's house. Their Wednesday routine sees him leaving at around ten-thirty; he then picks up O'Callaghan, and they drive across town to call into Flynn's offices. They leave his place around fifteen minutes later with a list of properties that need to be visited. These aren't courtesy calls; they are visits to tenants who have fallen behind with their rents. These are tenants who complained about shortcomings in the service their landlord provides. Unfortunately, we don't have details of those visits as yet. Artemis is working on that now. She says 'Hi', to Rusty, by the way."

"I'll pass that on," said Phoenix, "he's got his hands full at present. Thanks for that, Giles; we'll hear from you at noon with an update. We can tail them at a distance from Flynn's place in our van in the beginning. Then, if we get the specific intelligence, we can select the optimum kill zone to reduce unwanted casualties and take it from there. It will help, though, if we could plan ahead of time, knowing exactly where they will be and when."

"We'll do our best, Phoenix," replied Giles and ended the call.

Rusty drove the Scott & Bailey van through the streets of Perivale. He watched as Eamonn Murphy parked the car one hundred yards ahead outside Flynn's office building on Fraser Road. Murphy and Terry O'Callaghan got out of the car and went indoors.

"We'll have to find a place to park. That could be a nightmare," said Phoenix.

"If Giles is right, they'll be a while. Don't sweat it. I'll drive around the block and try to look inconspicuous."

Phoenix spotted the car pulling away and into traffic on their second circuit.

"Follow that car," he shouted, "but keep your distance."

Rusty edged into the line of traffic leading them towards Bilton Road. They were five vehicles back from their target. Once they reached the main road, they tracked them to a residential area full of small Drives and Crescent. Murphy pulled up in front of the terraced property. There were many cars and pedestrians on both sides of the tree-lined street.

"I don't like wishing my time away, but I can't wait for noon to arrive. We need that update from Giles. This place is hopeless. It's far too crowded."

The Price of Treachery

"Be patient, Rusty," said Phoenix, "everything comes to he who plans everything perfectly."

The two villains soon left the first building they visited and set off around the narrow avenues. Rusty followed at a discreet distance. Another tenant was quickly ticked off the Flynn hit list for today, and off they drove again. This time, they were clearly bound for somewhere much further away. They headed for Wembley. Heavy traffic around lunchtime meant it took them twenty-five minutes to arrive next to a sports ground.

Murphy reversed into a parking space under a wall, and he and O'Callaghan got out and crossed Marsh Road. Rusty saw Murphy point up to his left, and then they set off for a row of houses to their right.

"They've got two places at least to visit on this estate then Phoenix," said Rusty, as he drove into a parking space next to the car.

"They visit this area every Wednesday and use this car park because the side streets are resident-only parking here. Giles added that information to your files when I read them. It was always a good bet. We don't need the update at noon now."

Phoenix jumped out and opened the rear doors of the van. As he removed the traffic cones provided by the transport section, Rusty slipped around the front of the van. The van door meant he was blocked from view as he attached the explosive device to the rear inside mudguard of the car.

Then he joined Phoenix as they each took a stack of cones and spread them the length of the small car park. Phoenix took a yellow laminated card with 'No Parking' printed on it from the van. He slipped it under the windscreen wiper blade on the driver's side of Murphy's car. In black felt-tip, he scribbled, 'Please remove by two o'clock. Resurfacing.' on the card.

"Our work here is over," said Phoenix.

He closed the van's rear doors and jumped into the passenger seat, Rusty reversed out of the car park, and they set off for Chiswick. They could be home in time for lunch. Eamonn Murphy and Terence O'Callaghan returned to the car around thirty minutes later. They had threatened a Pakistani grandmother with eviction and roughed up a Belgian student who wanted his shower to at least run hot for two minutes in the morning.

"What's going on here," said Murphy. He looked at the card, snorted and threw it on the ground. O'Callaghan kicked over the nearest traffic cones, and they got into the car.

"Bloody council workers," moaned Murphy, "always standing around leaning on shovels or pushing paper."

"Alright, let's get to our next property. We need to report back to Mr Flynn. We don't want to keep him waiting. What did he say this morning when we were five minutes late getting to work?"

"He reckoned I'd be late for my funeral," said Eamonn Murphy with an empty laugh as he started the engine and drove forward. The car park Phoenix had selected did need resurfacing. The first pothole the car encountered was the last.

Rusty and Phoenix returned to the safe house. Giles sent a message with a complete itinerary for the villains today. Phoenix didn't burst their bubble by telling Giles and Artemis they had wasted their time. He remembered what Rusty had said about the added responsibility he had these days as joint leader of Olympus.

He sent a message back to the ice-house team.

The Price of Treachery

"Vital information received. Many thanks for your efforts."

Rusty looked over his shoulder.

"What's that?" he asked.

"BS," replied Phoenix, "what's for lunch? I'm starving."

Back in Wembley, emergency service vehicles were arriving in convoy. They found the wreck of a blazing car, parts of two bodies, and two dozen traffic cones Brent Council hadn't realised they possessed. In his office in Fraser Road, Perivale, Patrick Flynn was fuming.

"Where are those useless boys now?" he yelled at his receptionist. "Keep trying their mobiles. Then, tell them they're out of a job when you get hold of them."

At the safe house, Rusty was polishing off a fish finger sandwich. Phoenix had resisted the temptation and settled for two slices of buttered toast.

"Do we wait a while before we move on, Phoenix?"

"No, we're going to do the same as last night; visit a keep-fit establishment. Read goes to the gym three nights weekly to train for his mixed martial arts fighting."

Rusty groaned. "Does this mean I'll be busting a gut lifting weights to distract his attention?"

Phoenix smiled. "There will be lifting involved tonight, but we'll do it together. So you can spend the rest of the afternoon relaxing. I'll run through things for tomorrow and finalise our plans for dealing with the two landlords."

In Hounslow, Sylvester Read finished work for the day at half-past five. Oscar Friedman didn't need his services this evening. Read was off to a gym in Staines Road for a training session. He needed to keep sharp for the cage fighting, and he owed it to the city's females to keep his body in shape. Sylvester had a high opinion of his appearance; most women he abused held a very different view.

He changed into shorts and a cutaway vest that showed off his over-developed upper body. He looked at his reflection in the full-length mirror he had installed on his locker door. He liked what he saw, except for his legs. They needed work. Compared to his torso, they lacked muscle and definition. He went into the gym and began a series of sets and reps; he did standing, and seated calf raises. Then he moved on to barbell squats and dumbbell lunges. After several items of equipment, he needed to take a breather.

Sylvester Read towelled down and took a swig of his energy drink. He scanned the gym, searching out the female talent. There were several young women here tonight. Most of them were regulars, and he either discounted them or they had knocked him back. He wasn't worried; there were always plenty of choices. Anyway, if he went short for a while, he could always find a willing tenant after a bit of persuasion.

Sylvester started to think about Frank DeAngelo. Odd that he hadn't turned up for work today. Frank hadn't rung in to say he was ill. He thought he'd finish his workout with a few bench presses and drop in on the old bugger on his way home. The bench presses should impress that young blonde over on the rowing machine. He could see the reflection of her breasts fighting to escape from her top in the mirrored wall she was facing. She was a new face. Maybe Frank could wait until the morning.

He began adding weights to the bar on the guillotine press. He wanted to give the newcomer a show. He loaded one hundred and forty kilos onto the bar and laid back on the bench.

The blonde had finished her routine and moved away to the opposite corner of the room. Sylvester didn't notice her leave, nor did he realise that he was out of sight of most of the other gym users at this time of the evening. Using a medium-width grip, he lifted the bar from the rack and held it over his neck with his arms locked to achieve his starting position.

As he breathed in, he lowered the bar slowly until it was an inch from his neck. After a second pause, he brought the bar back to the starting position, breathing out and pushing the bar using his chest muscles. He locked his arms, squeezed his chest in the contracted position, held it for a second, and then started coming down half as slowly as he had risen. Sylvester Read knew how important it was to control the barbell at all times.

He had seen the safety notices on many occasions but rarely read them. They were for pussies. He was ready to repeat the movement for a further eleven repetitions. As he breathed in, he sensed movement. Two shadows hovered over him in shorts and t-shirts.

"I don't need any spotters, guys; thanks for the offer," he said.

"We just wanted to help you out," said Rusty.

Sylvester carried on his repetitions; on the seventh, when he locked his arms out, he felt something had changed; this was wrong. The bar had drifted too far forward; he couldn't control the weight. Why had he been so ambitious and put too much weight on the bar to impress that bloody girl?

All these thoughts flashed through Sylvester Read's mind as the bar fell onto his upper chest. His two tormentors stood and watched as his life ebbed away. It looked painful, but neither of the Olympus agents was overly concerned. Instead, they kept an eye on the other gym users to see whether anyone had heard anything amiss.

They needn't have worried. Anyone who used the

Staines Road gym and knew Read kept out of his way. He was a nasty piece of work. Well, he had been. Phoenix and Rusty slipped quickly and quietly away when they were satisfied he was dead. They changed and went outside to retrieve the van. It was time for a bite to eat and a good night's sleep. They still had two more names on their list for tomorrow.

Thursday, August 22nd, 2013

In the morning, the news was encouraging from Giles in his eight o'clock update. The death of an overweight senior citizen after a strenuous session in a local swimming pool had raised no suspicions.

The local radio station reported the death of a former estate agent, Sylvester Read, in a tragic accident. Mr Read, in his late thirties, had died from crush injuries while lifting heavy weights. It seems he was alone at the time of the accident. A female member, Hanti Cronje, a twenty-six-year-old financial analyst from South Africa, said she saw Mr Read working out aggressively earlier. She had been on the other side of the gym when the accident occurred. The police have questioned the gym owners and are satisfied; no safety issue contributed to Mr Read's death.

Police identified the bodies of the two men killed in an explosion in a car park in Wembley. They worked in the security business for a local landlord. Their employer, Patrick Flynn, forty-eight, had offices in Perivale. He was unavailable for comment last evening.

Police enquiries were ongoing. They appealed for witnesses. Detective Inspector Adebiyi Cisse said that the

The Price of Treachery

police kept an open mind at this stage. "It bears the hallmarks of a terrorist attack, but the victims had no links to terrorism, nor is there any apparent reason for them getting targeted. However, we are looking into the possibility the business they were involved in might be significant. Anyone with any information should contact Crimestoppers."

"It looks as if we've created enough of a smoke screen there, then, Phoenix?" said Rusty after Giles had completed his report.

"Yeah, Giles will keep tabs on the situation, though. He's ready to sprinkle disinformation here and there if it's needed. Then, of course, we can nudge the police further into the murky world of slum landlords later when we remove the 'unavailable for comment' Mr Flynn."

"Has that altered your plans?" asked Rusty.

"It won't be an accident; that goes without saying," Phoenix replied.

"Who do we pay a visit to first, Oscar Friedman or Patrick Flynn?"

"Oscar will be working in the grocery shop this morning. He takes the afternoon off on Thursdays to take his wife to the hairdresser. She has a two-thirty p.m. appointment every week at a salon in Hounslow. He fetches her over from their home in Richmond. She's been going to the same place for over forty years. While getting her blue rinse tidied up for the weekend, Oscar goes to a local park to sit on a bench and people-watches."

Later that day, the two agents sat on a bench in a park in Hounslow. On the other side of the walkway sat an elderly Jewish gentleman. He was people-watching. The two men were each studying him over the top of a daily newspaper.

"Off you go then, Phoenix," said Rusty, "time to collect the equipment from the van."

"I'll leave you to get Friedman to the rendezvous point," said Phoenix, getting up and walking to where they had parked the van. The next step would be the most audacious part of their mission, but in many ways, the most satisfying.

Phoenix collected the heavy fire extinguisher. Rusty walked Mr Friedman to his car. Phoenix checked nobody in the park was noticing what was happening under the trees where the grocer's car was parked. Rusty had identified himself as a council official. He informed Oscar Friedman it had come to their attention that a safety inspection had raised issues at one of his nearby properties.

The elderly grocer protested his innocence, but Rusty was adamant that a quick ten minutes of his time could save him hassle. So Friedman got in, and Rusty sat in the front passenger seat.

Phoenix put the fire extinguisher in the boot.

"My colleague will be joining us," said Rusty.

Oscar Friedman looked even more nervous as he saw Phoenix appear in his rear-view mirror.

"Reverse out and turn left, then second right, please, Mr Friedman. It won't take long."

Oscar did as Rusty asked. He didn't want any trouble with the council. Oscar was racking his brains, trying to think of what could be causing any 'issues'. He would have had stern words with poor Sylvester Read if he hadn't killed himself last evening trying to blow his muscles up like balloons. His death was very inconvenient. So who was going to do the dirty work now?

"This is it, No. 148, Manor Road," said Rusty. Friedman parked in the driveway.

Phoenix got out of the car and opened the driver's door.

"Come with me, Mr Friedman," he said, taking a firm grip on the old man's arm.

The Price of Treachery

Rusty went to the boot. He waited until the pavement was clear and a car had passed. Then, he removed the fire extinguisher from the boot, slammed it shut, and followed Phoenix into the house. The ground floor flats had name tags on the wall outside to identify the occupants.

"You might remember this place, Mr Friedman," said Phoenix. "The first floor will be ready for use in a week, but the top floor won't be in a fit state to let out for ages."

Oscar Friedman felt a chill run down his spine, even though it was a hot afternoon in August.

Phoenix had chosen this property for a purpose. Friedman had crammed ten people into this house.

The evil landlord risked his tenants' lives by neglecting to ensure an adequate fire safety system was in place. It was a typical example of the properties in his empire where he put greed before his tenants' welfare.

Following an investigation by the council last year, Friedman had to limit the maximum number of people at the property to six. In addition, he had to install a fire warning and protection system. A later visit revealed the same number of tenants, inadequate fire doors, and a lack of smoke and heat detectors. Also, no emergency illuminated exit signs were on the stairs or to the fire escape at the rear.

Phoenix knew the courts had imposed a hefty fine when the case went to court, reflecting the seriousness of the offences. However, the landlord and his employees didn't change their ways.

A young family of illegal immigrants got the key to a box room designed for single occupancy. The husband was at work while his wife and young child were home. Sylvester Read and Frank DeAngelo regularly visited No. 148, Manor Road, intimidating tenants on all three floors.

They found the wife trying to dry washing over a radiator that didn't work on their last visit. Frank DeAngelo had gone outside and retrieved an old tumble dryer that someone had thrown into a skip.

The consequences were fatal a week later when the tumble dryer burst into flames in the tiny flat. The mother couldn't speak English and was scared to call for help in case their illegal status was exposed. Instead, she removed the child from the flames and covered him with her clothing. Both died from smoke inhalation. There was severe damage to the apartments on the top floor, and debris fell into the flats below.

Read had been on the ground floor, hassling another couple when this occurred. People upstairs, who were at home, ran downstairs to raise the alarm. Read rang for the fire brigade. DeAngelo went upstairs.

By the time the brigade arrived to put out the fire, any evidence of human fatalities had disappeared. Frank DeAngelo had wrapped the bodies in a carpet from the landing and taken them out by the rear fire escape. Read had waited until the husband returned from work, told him his wife had started the fire deliberately and run away. He threatened to hand him over to the authorities if he didn't salvage any belongings that hadn't been destroyed and make himself scarce.

"You see, we do our research, Mr Friedman," said Phoenix. "My colleague here talked to the husband at a hostel where he was waiting to hear about his deportation. He now knows what happened to his family. My colleague also heard from people who lived in flats on the first floor. They told him of the dryer's noise and that they heard the child running around on the wooden floors above them that afternoon. They noticed the missing carpet from the landing. The debris the firefighters removed went into the skip that still stood in the street at the time. They piled the debris on top of an old carpet."

"I didn't know; they never told me. So you can't blame me for what happened," whined Friedman.

"But we do, Mr Friedman," said Rusty. "If you had limited the multi-occupancy building to six as ordered and carried out the safety instructions to the letter, this would never have happened."

"What are you going to do to me?" asked the landlord.

Phoenix looked at the fire extinguisher.

"I think the punishment should fit the crime," he replied.

Chapter Five

As they drove towards Perivale for their final appointment, Rusty wondered how Mrs Friedman would get home to Richmond this afternoon. Her husband should have turned up to collect her by now. She would be getting worried. If she wanted to continue her regular Thursday afternoon trips to chat with her old friends, she needed to book a taxi in future.

Oscar Friedman lay dead on the floor at the top of No. 148, Manor Road. A fire extinguisher lay beside him. It would be the next day before workers discovered him as they continued to refurbish the flats. They recognised his car in the drive and thought he had called around to complain about how long they were taking.

The police would attend the scene. It appeared to be a bizarre accident. In the past, the landlord received fines for issues with fire regulations. How ironic then that when visiting one of his many buildings, he dislodged a fire extinguisher from scaffolding. It was left behind by the builders in the high-vaulted ceilings of the upper floor. The elderly grocer had died from a crushed skull.

The builders denied any knowledge of the fire extinguisher. The police assumed that Sylvester Read or Frank DeAngelo must have been responsible. Sadly, neither was available for questioning. A male and female officer were sent to Richmond to inform the grocer's widow of his demise.

As the first officer on the scene left to return to the station, he reflected on the recent deaths of three men associated with the building he had attended. All very sudden, nothing suspicious about either of them. It only went to show; you never knew when death came calling.

At least he could draw a line under it now. As his old Mum used to say, these things come in threes. So that was that.

Patrick Flynn was a worried man. The police had kept him at the station for hours, asking about Eamonn and Terry. They wanted to know if they had links to the IRA or another terror organisation. They kept probing into the work they did for him around the properties he rented. Could any other landlords be trying to take over the business? Had he been threatened?

"Leave it out." he had told them, "I'm an honest businessman trying to earn a crust. We have difficult tenants and old buildings that need loads of maintenance. Those two helped me keep my head above water. But unfortunately, the red tape I have to battle with daily from the council makes it hardly worth the effort."

Flynn didn't think they believed him. When they let him go, they told him they might need to talk to him again. He had returned to the office and jumped every time the phone rang, or his receptionist slammed a filing cabinet drawer shut. Was someone trying to do him over? Who could it be? He opened the bottom drawer of his desk and helped himself to a mugful of whisky.

Chantelle, his receptionist, was filing her nails in the outer office. Two men walked in through the door.

"Do you enjoy working here?" asked the tall ginger one. He looked cute, Chantelle thought.

"Not really," she replied, smiling, "he can be an awkward sod sometimes. I'd prefer my own mobile nail business, but I don't have the start-up cash. I've got the designs and that. I studied at college, didn't I?"

The dark, quiet one threw an envelope on the desk. Chantelle could see lots of fifty-pound notes. She'd seen them on the telly but never held one in her hand.

"Good luck with the business," the ginger one said.

Chantelle didn't need to be told twice. She gathered up her things, the envelope first, and tottered out of the office on her four-inch heels. Mr Flynn must have upset some dangerous people. She knew enough about London criminals to know that she would forget everything if she wanted to keep breathing. It was best to have a complete blank about ever working for the Irishman and who had come to call on him this afternoon.

Patrick Flynn never got to finish the whisky. It wasn't mixing well with the dregs of the coffee in the mug. He knew there was someone outside chatting with Chantelle. It was probably someone asking for a list of flats available. He suddenly remembered he needed to find two new assistants. Get them to start asking around to find out who was out to get him.

The door opened. A tall, dark stranger entered. He was holding a gun. Patrick Flynn took two bullets in the chest and slumped back in his chair. The coffee mug fell to the

The Price of Treachery

floor. Phoenix closed the door behind him with a gloved hand and joined Rusty outside on Fraser Road. The late afternoon sun was warm on their backs. Their London trip was at an end.

"Time to get home to Larcombe Manor, Rusty. First, we contact the transport section. Then we can tidy up the safe-house ready for its next occupants. The transport guys will send a car to collect us and someone to take the van to the scrap yard. It's served its purpose."

"I can't think of anything we've forgotten, can you?" asked Rusty.

"We'll debrief the mission with Athena in the morning. Olympus will need to find a way to handle the fall-out from two landlords' businesses unable to continue trading. Their properties and tenants need to be absorbed by reputable operators. So they don't suffer the same intimidation and abuse as they did from these two. We will do what we can to facilitate the transfer without revealing our hand. It will be a challenge, but not one we haven't faced many times."

Rusty nodded. He had to hand it to Phoenix; he planned these missions well. Six nasty pieces of work were disposed of without any clues leading back to Olympus. Three accidental deaths for the Hounslow crew and a big hint that the slaughter of the Ealing gang was part of a turf war. They should be home by nine tonight. If Artemis had finished her stint in the ice-house, they might be able to celebrate sleeping together again for the first time in a week. Happy days.

When they had sat in the back of the car that picked them up from the safe-house, Rusty nodded off before they reached Reading. Phoenix listened to his gentle snoring and thought about 'Elizabeth'. He wondered whether Athena fancied a trip to the south coast tomorrow.

Friday, August 23rd, 2013

Phoenix and Rusty met up again at the morning meeting. Athena listened to the debrief.

Giles updated her on the latest from Hounslow, Ealing, and Wembley. So far, there was nothing to concern Olympus. However, he would watch the situation closely over the weekend.

"Excellent work, you two," Athena said. Phoenix had received his reward for his efforts last night. He checked out how his mate looked. Yes, the smile on his face suggested he had also enjoyed a night in his bed for a change.

"I think we can draw a line under this matter now," said Athena. "I'll set the wheels in motion to ensure the tenants are well treated."

The meeting continued with short, sharp case evidence and decisions for action. Their bogus doctor still attracted attention, with several female patients posting comments on social media sites concerning their treatment for cosmetic surgery. So far, the police didn't seem to be involved. Or they failed to act when they were. The two deaths he may be linked to appear to have faded from memory. Athena logged the matter for future discussion.

By eleven o'clock, the meeting came to a close. The Three Amigos appeared disconcerted. As Athena and Phoenix made to leave, Minos spoke: -

"I hoped we three might have had a meeting with you, Athena."

"One of our regular face-to-face meetings," said Alastor.

"Of course, if personal matters are taking priority these days, we understand," added Thanatos quietly.

"Phoenix and I are going to Lymington to welcome 'Elizabeth' home. We need to decide what to do with her. We hope to talk with Gavin; to see if we missed any clues that will lead us to the person who killed Erebus."

"Don't worry about the work you've been carrying out for Athena in secret," said Phoenix, "it's still essential. Yes, I can see by your faces that you didn't realise I was up to speed. Eton Wick and other matters made it perfectly reasonable for Athena to shield me from your investigations for a while. But, as a co-leader, I need to be aware of everything in which Olympus is involved. We'll update you when we return with whatever information we can gather. As for the meetings regarding the trustworthiness of the people with us at top-level Project meetings, I'll be happy to discuss your progress with Athena at any time. Will there be anything further?"

He and Athena returned to their quarters with nothing but silence from the other side of the room.

"You certainly told them what's what, Phoenix," said Athena, giving his hand a squeeze when they were behind closed doors.

"It's time to be assertive," he replied. "Now Rusty and I have completed our direct action; we need to concentrate one hundred per cent on internal Olympus matters. Hunting Erebus's killer and any link to our so-called colleagues in the hierarchy. I want our priority to uncover the group members conspiring to disrupt the democratic process. What we have may not be perfect, but a dictator put in place by a group of....what's the word?"

"Plutocrats?"

"If that means a small group of the wealthiest people in the land, then yes, that's what I mean."

"I'm with you totally," said Athena, "let's start by driving to Lymington; to see if we can find Gavin."

Two hours later, they had negotiated the A36 and arrived at the Lymington Yacht Haven. Phoenix soon located one of the Haven Masters and was shown where 'Elizabeth' sat.

"She arrived on the fourteenth, sir, at around ten in the evening. There's been no one aboard her since, as far as I know. The young chap who brought her hasn't been back, that's for sure. The berth has been a long-time home for craft belonging to the Hunt family. We receive an annual fee every January via a standing order Sir William set up years ago. We've not heard from him since he retired to Ibiza. Is everything alright?"

"I'm afraid he died last month," said Phoenix, "his crewman Gavin was bringing the yacht home. Sir William's estate has passed to my partner, who's sat in the car. We're here to check on 'Elizabeth'. We need to decide on whether to keep her or sell her."

"Oh, I see. I'm sorry to hear about the old gentleman's death, sir; he was a lovely chap. He always had a smile and a kind word when he came here. He loved the sea, and coming from a family with such a famous naval background, well, when he talked about the sea – you listened, didn't you?"

"We both miss him very much," said Phoenix. "So you haven't seen Gavin since the fourteenth?"

"Gavin? I haven't seen him since he sailed away to Ibiza to await Sir William's arrival, sir. But, no, the gentleman who moored 'Elizabeth' here was a different character altogether. A bit obnoxious, full of himself, if you don't mind me saying so."

The Price of Treachery

"Many thanks for your help," said Phoenix and Athena joined him as they walked to the mooring.

"Interesting," said Phoenix. "Gavin didn't sail her home."

Once onboard, Athena and Phoenix began checking the items that remained. They found the note almost at once.

"Typewritten. Even if we didn't already know better, that should have rung an alarm bell," said Athena. "Gavin would have called Larcombe as soon as he got home."

"That suggests that either Gavin didn't leave Ibiza, or he died on the way home," said Phoenix. "More likely the latter; he was probably buried at sea."

Athena sat on a bunk.

"Right; that's another death to be avenged. Who could it have been who sailed her back?"

"An obnoxious young man who was full of himself," said Phoenix, "if the Haven Master pegged him right."

"We'll get Henry Case and the team to start drawing up a list of likely suspects. Let's continue here for a while, checking for any clues the killer may have left."

The killer had done an excellent job. There was very little to suggest anything sinister had occurred on board. Then, just as they would lock up the hatch and drive back to Larcombe, Phoenix spotted a slip of paper tucked into Gavin's charts and brochures when planning to sail the yacht. He had talked Phoenix through his routine when they chatted on 'Elizabeth' in the marina at Santa Eulalia. He slid it out and scrutinized it.

"Hang on, this receipt is for food and drink from a store in Barfleur. It's dated the thirteenth. Whoever it was, they paid cash. Things in the toolkit looked brand new. Did you notice that? This guy knew what to buy; he was sensible enough to take precautions against engine failure. He must have good knowledge of the sea and boats. Unfortunately, there are no cash receipts for those more substantial items. We need to get Giles to trace credit card payments in the area on the thirteenth. I wonder whether there's any CCTV in the store or the local ship chandlers? If we're in luck, we may get a visual. Someone we recognise."

"Let's get back home," said Athena, "you drive. I'll call Henry and set the wheels in motion."

They left 'Elizabeth' safely secured at her mooring and travelled back to Bath.

It's over a week since I got home, and not a dicky-bird from Larcombe about Lymington. So they must have a busy schedule. Ah, well, there's nothing on board to give them a hint as to my involvement. Long may that continue.

If my mother has her way, then it won't be that long, of course. If I stay in her good books, perhaps she'll let me dispose of Phoenix and Athena. Once you chop off the head of the snake, the rest of the body will wither and die. That's the way of the world.

Mother will be in London next week. She'll be checking into the Chelsea Harbour Hotel for three weeks. No doubt she'll want to get together before she leaves. She'll bore me to tears, no doubt, with what she's doing until the first week in October. We'll meet again in London then anyway. I'll probably get a re-run of the whole sorry saga.

At least she's never asked me to accompany her on holiday or one of her trips since I was eighteen. God, what a drag that would be. To watch her drool over her latest flame or suffer one of her legendary tantrums over the most straightforward thing would be dreadful. I prefer to be in my office, making lots of money during the day and then spending it on the high life in the evenings; that's more my style.

We always keep in touch while she's away. I have many staff around the country who are prepared to work overtime. They tell me what she said, and I interpret it using our secret code. I've received many messages telling me to do something illegal on her behalf without anyone being wiser. The public is so gullible that a superior mind will outwit them every time. I owe my intellect to my mother.

Rusty and Artemis walked across the lawns from the far end of the estate. They had been for a swim. Before Giles Burke needed Artemis in the ice-house for a twelve-hour shift, they had a few hours of leisure time. They arrived at the stable block and walked along the corridor to their quarters. Rusty's phone rang.

"Damn," he said, "it's Phoenix; they're back from Lymington. They need me in the main house. I'm sorry."

Artemis kissed him hard.

"Just in case you forget what you're missing, mister," she said with a chuckle. "I'll have to make do with the memories of last night, won't I?"

"Do you know what Giles has got in store for you?"

"Not a clue; we've completed the installation of the new system. We need to have something meaty on which to test it. I'll see you tomorrow."

Rusty was leaving, but then he doubled back.

"Look, I'll talk to Athena and see whether she can give you access to a few more places at Larcombe. You've become invaluable to Giles from his comments at morning meetings. Athena might have intended to review matters after three months, but she may bring things forward."

"I'm happy with things as they are, Rusty, honestly," said Artemis. "I could do with spending more time with you, but we see each other more now than when I was still in the police force."

"Do you miss it?"

"Like a hole in the head. Why?"

"If Athena does agree to you becoming more integrated, then there's no going back. You will learn facts that can never leave Larcombe in possession of someone who isn't one hundred per cent committed to the cause."

Artemis blinked rapidly. There were traces of her past that she couldn't forget. She pushed her glasses back up her nose and breathed a huge sigh.

"Gosh," she said, "does this mean I'll uncover the truth about the identity of Phoenix?"

"Do you want that?" asked Rusty.

"As long as we're together, Rusty; his secret's safe with me, I promise."

Athena had come to accept the hectic nature of things at Larcombe Manor since Erebus had retired. Phoenix and her agents had carried out mission after mission, sometimes overlapping, so it concerned her when the lull after the landlords' action stretched into September.

After she and her partner had returned from Lymington, everything had become less frantic. She recalled the words that Erebus had used a year ago. He compared it to the 'phoney war' his father had experienced in WWII. She knew something was coming that would challenge them more strongly than anything they had ever faced; she didn't know where or when.

Giles Burke had followed up on the till receipt discarded

by the killer on 'Elizabeth'. The store's CCTV history was located and analysed. Giles also identified the chandler in Barfleur that supplied engine parts and tools for the cross-channel journey. Their CCTV was limited and concentrated on the stock shelves' high-value parts and the car park. Giles only discovered one image to fit the time frame they sought.

If their image was indeed that of the man who killed Erebus, their assassin was a well-dressed young man wearing a baseball cap.

"He's aware of the camera," said Artemis as she inspected it with Giles.

"The angle of his cap covers his face, and he's turning away as much as possible to avoid a clear picture. So we can only confirm what the Haven Master told Phoenix. Our man is in his thirties and of average height and build."

"Why don't I go to Lymington?" suggested Artemis. "I can find the Master that Phoenix talked with and confirm this to be the man who delivered the yacht. Then I could use our new system's updated EvoFIT package. I used it at Durham in its infancy; it's improved since then. We reckoned at Portishead that our picture led us to the criminal three times out of four."

Artemis had driven to Lymington on Friday, August the thirtieth. She introduced herself as a colleague of DI Hounsell of Avon & Somerset police. The Haven Master confirmed the CCTV image from the Barfleur store was indeed the yachtsman who delivered 'Elizabeth'.

He wasn't overly concerned that she hadn't given him a name or shown an ID card. She had been a colleague until September, and Phil Hounsell was still officially a policeman. So Artemis crossed her fingers and hoped it didn't count as an actual lie.

"That's him, miss. He looked the part, didn't he?" said the Haven Master. Artemis took him step-by-step through the process of getting a good likeness using the application on her laptop.

"You're going to see dozens of images. I want to rebuild your memory of the few minutes you spent together dealing with the paperwork after this man moored the yacht. This programme is a new system of facial composition that's revolutionising the way we analyse witness descriptions and assemble images of suspects."

After nearly an hour of working through countless screens of faces, they had managed to reach an approximation of the killer by 'evolving' a face relying on his hidden memories. Traditional facial composite systems asked victims and witnesses to remember critical features such as the nose and eyes in isolation. However, EvoFIT was underwritten by research indicating that we unconsciously remember faces as a whole rather than features in isolation.

"That's the chap, I reckon," said the Haven Master, pleased with his work, "what happens now?"

"I'll report back to my superiors. We need to put a name to this yachtsman. He may be able to help us with our enquiries. We want to know why Gavin didn't sail the yacht home himself as scheduled and to discover his present whereabouts. There have been no confirmed sightings of him for two months,"

"Right you are, miss, good luck, and if you need anything else, just call me."

With that, the Haven Master gave her a card and trotted off to welcome another boat into the Lymington Marina.

Artemis had driven back to Bath and shown the likeness to Giles Burke on Saturday morning.

The Price of Treachery

"I know who it reminds me of, but I must admit it's a surprise," he said.

"Who does it look like?" asked Artemis.

"That chap off the TV, the one who does those cheesy ads for the mobile phone company."

"Does that mean we've hit a dead-end Giles?" said Artemis, deflated. "The Haven Master may have watched TV before I spoke with him and caught a commercial break. But, on the other hand, he might just be projecting the freshest image in his head."

"We can search through the data banks we have for a close match to this image. More credible suspects are likely to be out there. You said yourself that the system is seventy-five per cent accurate at best. It's all we've got at present."

Giles and Artemis tried to match the image to faces over the next two weeks from the vast database held by the ice-house. They had found eleven close matches by Friday, the thirteenth of September. They discounted three straight away as they had been in prison at the time. Six more went because of their height and weight.

The two that remained were a thief who specialised in antiques from country houses and a former soldier — a thug who had just completed seven years in Winchester prison for manslaughter. Neither man had any sea-going experience.

"We're not making much progress, are we?" asked Artemis, "maybe we need to get today out of the way. I always hate Friday the thirteenth, don't you? I'm not superstitious about thirteen as a number on its own, but over the years, if something was going to spoil my day, it happened when those days and dates coincided."

Giles grimaced.

"I used to carry a lucky charm, but it never did me any

good. As for making progress, it appears not," replied Giles. "I suggest we run what we've got past Henry Case. Then, if he thinks it's worth taking to the morning meeting, we'll let him carry it forward. There's very little more we can contribute, I'm afraid."

"Are you feeling okay, Giles?" asked Artemis.

"Frankly? I'm feeling shit," replied Giles. He looked as white as a sheet and clearly in pain.

"You're in the right place," said Artemis, with a grin, "who would have thought I could ever be saying that? We're several metres underground in a highly confidential environment. The best place for you is the medical centre. I'll get someone to collect you straightaway. We need to diagnose at once. If you have something contagious, everyone on this floor is at risk. If it's specific to you, they can treat it without waiting weeks for a doctor's appointment; or hanging around for hours in A&E in Royal United. Olympus needs you back here, fit and well, as soon as possible. Where does it hurt?"

"Here," groaned Giles, holding his lower stomach as another severe twinge gripped him.

"Did you have your appendix out as a kid?" asked Artemis, recalling her time in a hospital in Durham at the tender age of thirteen. Very tender, from what she remembered.

"No," moaned Giles, "just my tonsils. It's easing off now. I'll be alright."

Artemis wasn't going to back down. She adopted her Mother Hen persona and gave it to Giles Burke with both barrels.

"Look, Giles, if you don't get treatment for it, the appendix can rupture. That's a life-threatening situation. You should always seek immediate medical attention if you think you have appendicitis. Which of these symptoms have you experienced or are you suffering from now? A dull ache in the middle of your stomach? Severe pain on your right lower side? Are you feeling sick? Do you have a fever?"

Giles nodded like a toy dog in the back of a car. It took his mind off what he had ignored for the past two days.

"All of the above," he admitted.

"Right, I'm going to alert the medics; they'll whip it out in no time. After surgery, most people recover quickly and without complications. You're relatively young and fit; you'll be back on your feet in no time."

"Thanks," said Giles, "I think."

"How long have you been getting pain?" she asked as she left for the medical centre.

"Since Saturday morning," replied Giles.

"You are an idiot. Let's hope you haven't ignored it long enough for it to be peritonitis."

After the doctor had seen Giles and conducted tests, they scheduled him for an immediate open appendectomy. First, they removed the affected appendix and cleaned the abdominal cavity. Then, they closed his wound with stitches and allowed Giles to recuperate. There were no complications. When Henry Case heard, he decided that this was a good time for Giles to take a well-earned holiday.

He dropped in to see him the morning after his operation.

"Crikey, old chap, this was a turn-up for the books. Just as well that Artemis was on the ball. The doctor says you'll stay here until your pain is under control and you can consume liquids. Then I want you to get off on holiday for a week or two. Lie in the sun and have complete rest."

Giles protested. He wanted to be back at his desk in the morning.

"Not a chance, Giles," said Henry. "Athena agrees with me. You deserve a break. Things are quiet now, but they're bound to kick off again soon. We need you to be one hundred per cent when it does."

Giles realised when to give in; he sunk back into his pillows and relaxed for the first time in months.

When Henry left, he bumped into Rusty and Artemis. They were Giles's next visitors.

"Just the young lady I need to see," said Henry. "Giles is *hors de combat* for a while, Artemis. I'm sure Rusty will agree this will be an ideal opportunity for you to step up to the plate. You will attend the morning meetings with me from Monday morning. I'll clear things with Athena and Phoenix first, of course."

Rusty looked at Artemis. She looked surprised but happy. They had discussed her full integration into Olympus at a meeting only two weeks ago, on the second of September. However, Athena had wanted to wait until Artemis had completed three months' service with Giles's intelligence section before that happened.

Perhaps, Henry was right, it was only two weeks later, but this could be an opportunity to bring matters forward. Maybe he could talk to Phoenix before Monday. To sound him out, to see whether he was ready to face the former policewoman, Zara Wheeler, across the table in a meeting.

Monday, September 16th, 2013

No matter how much they wanted it to stop, the clock continued to tick around to nine o'clock. In the stable block,

The Price of Treachery

Rusty and Artemis were getting ready to walk to the main house together for the first time.

In their apartment, Athena and Phoenix were nervous too. Athena had agreed to Henry's request last evening that Artemis attend in Giles's absence. She was still concerned at the prospect of such a rapid promotion before really getting to know Artemis and understanding what made her tick. Her background didn't suggest that an ex-detective could fall in line with everything Olympus did, not without a few doubts. She had wavered in her early days at Larcombe. Erebus had guided her gently through the darker moments; he showed her the ends justified the means.

As for Phoenix, he received an urgent message from Rusty yesterday. They met in the orangery, and his friend made him sit while he told him the news.

"How do we play it?" asked Rusty.

"Stay cool?" Phoenix had replied. "We let Athena chair the meeting as usual. She will introduce the newcomer, tell us who she is and why she's there for the next two weeks. After that, we run through the schedule, make our contributions and get out. I don't think they'll ask us to stand up and introduce ourselves as we did when we went on courses back when we were youngsters."

"Are you okay, darling?" asked Athena, bringing Phoenix back to the present.

"Never better; can't wait to get this over with," he replied.

The couple held hands as they walked to the meeting room. This outward display of affection was not typical. It was just nerves. Athena opened the door and, taking a deep breath, walked in. Alastor, Minos, and Thanatos sat together as usual. Henry Case had arrived from the icehouse with an armful of folders. Once she and Phoenix were seated, Rusty and Artemis slipped through the door at the far end of the room and joined them around the table.

"Good morning, everyone," said Athena, "welcome to another week. Giles is progressing well after his emergency appendectomy. We have Artemis to thank for her prompt actions. Giles is a typical man; he soldiered on until it was nearly too late. Henry asked if Artemis could fill in for Giles while he recuperates fully. I agreed. I'm sure we will extend her a warm welcome. Artemis, you appreciate why you needed to relinquish your past life and the name you were born with when you joined us at Larcombe. As for the rest of us, you work with Henry in the intelligence section. Rusty, you know, on a more personal level. The others are also known by a code name to protect their past identities from the outside world. Alastor, Minos, and Thanatos have been with Olympus since its conception. They are my senior colleagues. Phoenix is my partner and joint leader here at Larcombe. Whatever we discuss within these walls is classified. At no time can you share what you learn with anyone outside the Olympus family. Is that clear?"

"Absolutely," said Artemis. She blinked furiously, her face reddened, and despite herself, continued staring at Phoenix.

Athena made the lightest contact with her fingers on the back of her lover's hand for reassurance over what came next. Phoenix was glad of the chance to look her way; he was well aware of the attention he received from the other end of the table.

"We wish to share our news with you. Around the middle of January, we will welcome a new arrival at Larcombe. I am expecting our first child."

Rusty tried to appear surprised. Phoenix had told him

The Price of Treachery

earlier and sworn him to secrecy. Athena had warned Phoenix she was going to let everyone know today. She was four months into her pregnancy, and the evidence would be in front of their eyes before many more weeks had passed.

Once Henry mentioned Artemis, she seized the opportunity; she thought it might help to have another female on the team. Breaking the news in an otherwise male environment was daunting. Just having Artemis in the room made it more comfortable.

"That's wonderful news," said Artemis, "congratulations."

"That goes for me, too," added Rusty.

The Three Amigos and Henry Case muttered encouraging platitudes. Finally, Athena was ready to move on with the agenda for the day. Phoenix was still absorbing the 'first child' titbit. He hadn't realised there could be more little ones on the horizon.

"Will you be getting married?" asked Thanatos.

Phoenix gave him a stare.

"One thing at a time," said Athena, "now, let's get cracking. I know things have been disrupted in the past two days, Henry, but what's new from the ice-house."

Henry gave a summation of everything the team had gathered over the weekend. Intelligence gathering was time-consuming and never-ending. He referred briefly to the hunt for Erebus's killer. He informed Athena that he couldn't pin the image from the Barfleur store to a definite suspect.

"Of course, this chap may never have been arrested."

"Can we trace the card transaction he made at the chandler's?" asked Phoenix.

"We tracked it to a company based in the Cayman

Islands," said Henry, "from there, the trail has gone cold. Someone has done an outstanding job of hiding the person, or persons, behind it."

"Keep at it; we don't have any more to go on," said Phoenix.

Athena continued to tick items off the list. The final matter was to tell the meeting of the upcoming Olympus hierarchy meeting.

"Phoenix and I will be attending the next meeting on Wednesday, October the ninth; I received a text message over the weekend. It was coded, as usual, and read Locksley; Black."

"Nottingham is the venue then," said Minos, "but why black?

Phoenix understood the reference; it was the black book, in whichever form it existed, containing the names of targets chosen by Zeus and the other nine Olympians. That list was likely to be heavily influenced by the faction working to gain control of Olympus.

The names were sure to be of people who stood in the way of any proposed overthrow of the democratically elected government. He and Athena had suspected a future coup since their first board meeting in Knightsbridge. But, so far, they were only scratching the surface in determining who was involved with that faction.

"Whereabouts in Nottingham is this one, Athena?" he asked.

"In a suite just around the corner from the Theatre Royal," she replied. For the benefit of Minos and the others, she added, "the 'black' refers to a list of targets Zeus and the others want to eliminate. We touched on it at the meeting in Curzon Street, but clearly, it's moved up the agenda now. We shall have to see what it means for us at Larcombe."

It was time to bring the meeting to a close. The Three Stooges left together; Phoenix and Rusty chatted amicably. Henry waited for Artemis to join him to get back to work in the ice-house.

"Thank you for letting me sit in on the meeting today, Athena," said Artemis. "It was fascinating, and your news was wonderful. You must both be thrilled."

"We are," replied Athena. "My parents were surprised but pleased. I think they had given up hope for grandchildren. You're still young. If you and Rusty think of starting a family, you've got time on your side."

"I've no idea what he's thinking half the time," said Artemis with a chuckle.

"I wasn't sure how Phoenix would react to becoming a father again. To lose his teenage daughter must have left horrible scars."

Athena stopped herself from going further. She may have said too much already. It was the dilemma she knew they faced. How much does Artemis know of Phoenix? Does she think he's Garry Burns or has she made the leap back to the man rescued by Erebus from Pulteney Weir? The man whose fifteen-year-old daughter was raped and smothered by Neil Cartwright. A deed that was the final straw sparking a killing spree where nine villains died within two hours, only miles away from where they stood.

That night started him on a journey that brought them together at Larcombe. Unfortunately, he had been responsible for many more deaths since then.

Phoenix and Rusty moved across the room to join the two ladies. Henry waited patiently by the door.

"You can go on, Henry," said Phoenix, "we'll see she gets to work on time."

The four were left alone in the room.

"What did you make of your first meeting," asked Rusty.

"Brilliant," replied Artemis, "I've learned so much."

"It's a shame you haven't been able to put a name to the Barfleur customer," said Phoenix.

Artemis looked at him and swallowed hard. Phoenix thought his voice or a mannerism had triggered a memory.

"With the fuss over Giles being sick, I'd forgotten," she said. "When I showed him the EvoFIT picture, he put a name to it straight away. We discounted it because it seemed so absurd. We never checked where he was at the time of the murder, nor did we delve into his background to see whether he had any yachting expertise."

"Who was that?" asked Rusty.

"The mobile phone CEO who takes part in his company adverts on television."

Athena gasped.

Rusty looked to Phoenix, "Is that likely? What's his name?"

"No idea, mate," lied Phoenix, "but we'll find it and check him out. Thanks, we'll be seeing you."

The two couples left the room. Rusty and Artemis went outside to walk across the lawns to the stable block. Phoenix and Athena climbed the stairs towards their apartments.

"That's one name identified on the list of our adversaries at the top table," said Phoenix. "Hermes is our killer."

Athena stopped on the top stair. The view that stretched to the stone-pillared gateway to Larcombe Manor was stunning.

"We must do whatever it takes to protect this place and

what it represents. I fear we have more unpleasant discoveries ahead of us. We will avenge the deaths of Erebus and Gavin in time. One identity is a step forward, but we shouldn't act before we understand who we're up against; our meeting in Nottingham will give us answers."

Chapter Six

Monday, September 30th, 2013

Giles Burke returned to work in the ice-house. He had enjoyed his holiday in St. Tropez. Giles thought of it as having been his first complete break in over two years. But, in reality, it was ten days of sun, sand and texting Artemis to ask if anything unusual had happened back home.

At this morning's meeting, he resumed his place alongside Henry Case at the table. Artemis left Rusty at the stable block door and turned left for the first time in a fortnight to head off for a shift in the intelligence section.

"I'll see you tonight," said Rusty. "You made a great impression filling in for Giles. It won't go unrewarded. Phoenix and I will keep chipping away at Athena to let you join the elite operatives in your own right."

Artemis kissed her partner on the cheek.

"I can be patient when it suits me," she said.

Rusty made his way over to the meeting room. He was the last to arrive.

The Price of Treachery

Athena wanted to keep the proceedings where everyone was present as brief as possible. She and Phoenix decided that individual meetings with Alastor, Minos and Thanatos were the order of the day. First, they needed to collate the information the three men gathered from the photographs Athena issued. One-third was from the Olympus hierarchy; the others merely camouflaged the real purpose of the exercise.

Athena wanted to understand her enemy. Of course, they must deal with those against her, but they must preserve the protection afforded by the faithful gods' code names. There may be several bad apples alongside Hermes, but the rest of the barrel was trustworthy.

Athena welcomed Giles back, but he hardly had time to get comfortable in his chair before Henry left. Phoenix handed him a folder with instructions on proceeding with the Barfleur suspect.

"Alastor," said Athena, "we'll begin with you. If you two gentlemen could leave us, we'll call you back in individually when we're ready." Minos and Thanatos filed out of the room.

Major Michael Purvis, ex-Blues & Royals, had lost his wife, Jenny, nine years ago last Monday. She had been stabbed several times by a burglar in her parent's home. The intruder was a young addict stealing to feed his habit. Unfortunately, the police never caught Jenny's killer. Michael Purvis joined Olympus from the beginning in 2006.

"Right then, Alastor," said Phoenix, "let's have the data you've got on the nine photos we allocated you."

Alastor slid the folder across the desk.

"I haven't got a clue which of the people you gave me are candidates for the genuine Olympians. Those with stacks of money from backgrounds suggest they might favour the methods we adopt. You chose it very well, Athena. Their secret is safe with me, that's for sure."

"Good," said Athena. "I do try. Are you happy this contains a complete record of these people?"

"Yes, I have traced family lines back several generations where possible. There were no blocks to prevent me from investigating them in full."

"That will be it, for now, Alastor," she said, "can you tell Minos we'll see him in forty-five minutes, please?"

"What about Thanatos?" asked Alastor.

"Tell him to take an early lunch," muttered Phoenix, already leafing through the folder. "We'll get to him eventually."

Alastor left them alone. Athena and Phoenix sorted through the photographs.

"It's a shame because he's done a lot of work on the people I gave him. We're only interested in these three - Zeus, Hera, and Poseidon."

"That's interesting," said Phoenix, "we wondered about these two, didn't we? Zeus and Hera are husband and wife then, and older than I thought. The country air must agree with them." He read Alastor's summary aloud.

Duncan (67) and Celia Eliot (66) of Barley Mill, Kent (code name Zeus and Hera)

Married in Canterbury Cathedral (1973). Their children are Simon (39). Georgina (37) and Mungo (29). The Eliot family have occupied the Mill for centuries. The family home stands on many acres of rolling countryside. Their bank statement indicates they are 'rolling' in old money.

"What do you think?" asked Phoenix.

"I think they're an odd couple, but they've stuck together no matter what. So I put Zeus and Hera in the Olympian camp."

"I agree," said Phoenix, placing the two photographs into a folder. He set it on the table to his left-hand side.

Leopold Andrews (69) of Elmbridge, Surrey (code name Poseidon) He's unmarried, educated at Trinity College, Cambridge, in the mid-Sixties and retired from the City aged fifty-five after a career in banking. His financials show him getting by on a pension pot that would make Donald Trump jealous.

"He lives in 'Beverly Hills, UK' then? Just up the road from Elton by the look of things," said Phoenix.

"Did Alastor find out who he mixed with during his time at Trinity?" asked Athena. "He may be a 'cold fish' emotionally, but several extreme societies existed back then. Did he associate with any political groups?"

"Alastor has highlighted one telling link. Young Leopold contributed to the long-running anarchist paper '*Freedom*' from eighteen. By 1966, he had severed all contact with them and worked hard in a private merchant bank in Moorgate. Odd that someone so anti-establishment followed the profession he did as soon as he left university."

"I think we need to look into Leopold Andrews more closely, Phoenix," said Athena. "Place his photograph in a separate folder. Please put it on top of the folder containing Zeus and Hera. We're due to see Minos in a few minutes. I'll take that large folder Alastor prepared and keep it from prying eyes. You and I can continue to dig into the detail of our suspects later. The Three Amigos aren't stupid. If they see their work segregated into discrete groups, the penny will drop, and they will realise we are dividing the actual Olympus hierarchy into factions. I want to shield that knowledge from them for as long as possible."

They made their final preparations and removed evidence that might have triggered concern in the mind of Minos, their next guest. A knock at the door heralded his arrival.

"Come on in, Minos," said Athena.

Sir Julian Langford, QC, was sixty years old. He retired in 2005 after a lifetime in the legal profession. His time as a judge saw a steady rise in crime and a steady decline in the degree of justice meted out, something he regretted and tried to rectify.

Minos, the judge of the dead in the Underworld, met Alastor at Larcombe on their first day with Olympus.

"Thank you for your efforts, Minos," said Athena. "You and I have discussed one of the people I asked you to investigate. Perhaps we can see everything you covered, so Phoenix can get up to speed."

"Certainly, Athena," said Minos, handing over his bulky folders for inspection.

"That will be all, Minos," said Athena, "we'll be in touch if we need any clarifications. If any of these people deserve deeper study, I'll brief you after tomorrow morning's meeting."

"Understood," said Minos.

Athena opened the folder and isolated the relevant items; she discarded the 'dummy' photographs and their backgrounds; then she placed the data on the true Olympians on the desk – they were for Apollo, Dionysus, Heracles and, of course, Demeter.

Troy Gardner (50) of Salisbury, Wiltshire (code name Apollo)

The Price of Treachery

He was born in the East End of London to a low-income family. Troy left school at sixteen with very few qualifications. A former boxer who was world champion for three years in the Eighties. He used the fortune he amassed from the fight game to build a considerable property portfolio that expanded his wealth to an estimated four billion pounds—twice married—several children inside and outside those marriages. He lives with a thirty-two-year-old model at present. His sporting pursuits following his retirement from the ring are golf and shooting.

"Any views?" asked Athena after she finished reading.

"Was there anything in his youth that might point us in the right direction?" asked Phoenix, "before he found a way out of poverty with his fists."

Athena scanned the details once more. She shook her head.

"I'm wary of placing Apollo in the 'all-clear' camp just yet; I'll add him to Poseidon's folder and get Minos to keep digging."

Sir James Grant-Nicholls (62) of Musselburgh, Scotland (code name Heracles)

Educated privately in Edinburgh and attended St. Andrew's University. He worked in various management positions in industry. He became Chairman of a conglomerate spanning merchant banking, financial services, recruitment, marketing, business services and stockbroking in 1984. James received a knighthood for his services to industry in 1988. He won the title of "Industrialist of the Year" on three occasions. Frequent television appearances. Pilot's licence. Married to Fiona for the past thirty-one years. No children.

"Loads of money and no one to leave it to," said Athena, thinking how lucky she was.

"Not a motive for overthrowing the government, though," said Phoenix. "I reckon Heracles is one of the good guys."

There was no argument from Athena, and Heracles joined Zeus and Hera. Then, they moved on to the next name on the list.

Sir Malcolm Reginald Montgomery Dunseith (58) of Bromham Grange, Moreton-in-Marsh (code name Dionysus)

He attended Harrow School before going up to University College, Oxford. Double First in Classics. He married Louise Anne Frobisher in 1978. They have a son Gerard (31), and two daughters, Corinne (29) and Madeleine (27). Dunseith had a high-profile career in the Civil Service from 1977 to 1997, serving as Private Secretary to three Prime Ministers. He took his seat in the House of Lords in 1997 and attended no more than half a dozen times a year.

"He's from the upper classes, and no mistake," said Phoenix. "A very swift climb up the ladder and a nice soft landing once John Major got the elbow. Could he hold a grudge over being put out to grass at a relatively young age, do you think?"

"Civil servants are devious by nature," said Athena. "Looking through his background, there's not a single red flag that suggests he's more than a nob worth a bob."

"We're not finding the rotten apples as easily as we hoped, are we?" said Phoenix.

Athena read out the following account: -

Philomena Victoria Jacinta de Beauchamp Alexander, (code name Demeter)

The Price of Treachery

"Has anything been added to the information I read here since I left for Chiswick?" asked Phoenix.

"Only that she's on tour now until a day or two before the next Olympus meeting."

"She may call herself Honey B these days, but in my book, she's Queen Bee," said Phoenix. The photograph of the sixty-three-year-old pop singer went into the folder with Poseidon and Apollo.

"I won't ask what the B stands for; let's break for lunch, darling," said Athena. "I'll contact Thanatos, and we'll meet him at two o'clock."

"He'll love hanging around," said Phoenix. "At least he's well-balanced with a chip on each shoulder."

"You're too dismissive of those three," Athena said as they returned to the apartment. "They do considerable work behind the scenes here at Larcombe. They beavered away here for four years before you suddenly appeared, don't forget. So it's only natural they might resent your promotion over their heads."

"Let alone be miffed that Erebus picked you to succeed him."

"Possibly," Athena admitted, "but they had longer to get used to the idea; Erebus announced that ages ago."

"That doesn't mean they accepted the decision with good grace, no matter how long they had to come to terms with it."

Athena called Thanatos and said they would see him after lunch. At two, all three met in the meeting room, ready to start. Thanatos slid his folder forcibly across the table.

"Not much here, I'm afraid. A bit of a mixed bag. High-flying people and ex-debutantes."

He sat back in his chair, waiting for Athena to pass a comment on his hard work.

"That will do, Thanatos," said Phoenix, "we'll take it from here."

Christopher Rathbone, ex-SAS, served in Northern Ireland during the Troubles. He spent too long undercover. After thirty years of loyal service, the Army threw him on the scrap heap. They gave him no protection from any future reprisals.

When he arrived at Larcombe Manor, he was in the safest place he had been for over a decade. Every day he had expected a knock on the door from an IRA assassin.

Thanatos gave Phoenix and Athena a thunderous look and stormed out of the room.

"He took it well," said Phoenix.

"Let's see what he's got before we judge him too harshly," said Athena.

She separated the three Olympians from the others and set them on the table. The photographs were of Aphrodite, Hermes, and Nemesis.

Elizabeth McLaren, Duchess of Lochalsh (54) of Glenfinnan Castle in the north-west of Scotland (code name Aphrodite)

Elizabeth was tutored at home and then attended finishing schools in Geneva and Paris. She's way down the list in the line of succession to the throne of England. However, vast family fortunes have never discouraged her from finding charitable works to occupy her time. She's a widow with one son, Rory (32), who travelled at twenty and lives on a commune in the Brecon Beacons.

"I've seen enough," said Phoenix, "one rebel in this family is probably the limit."

"Agreed," said Athena, "let's move on to the next person."

Dominic Perkins (31) of Knightsbridge, London (code name Hermes)

He was born in London. Parents travelled extensively. He attended boarding schools in various parts of the Home Counties. Very bright. Dominic moved to London at eighteen. Successful entrepreneur. CEO of the third-largest mobile phone company in Europe. Popular media personality.

"Is that it?" asked Athena.

"Well, that's the synopsis Thanatos has provided. We need to dig further into the data to glean more. Do you know how this reads? Hermes struck me as the type of young businessman who trampled on dozens of people in his scramble to the top of the pile. He's in a market that's cutthroat and highly technical. I bet he was among the first in the queue when this European right-to-be-forgotten legislation became a hot topic. His history seems to have been scrubbed clean."

"There is another explanation," said Athena. "Thanatos has deliberately sanitised the data for Hermes."

"That's a possibility," admitted Phoenix, "either way, we've been alerted to something suspicious in young Dominic's past. Let's ask Giles and Artemis to take his file to pieces. I want to learn who his parents are and where they live. Where did Hermes get his start-up money to set him on a journey resulting in him being so filthy rich? Hermes was always the easy one to allocate. We know he's a killer, but who is he working with and why?"

"Only one Olympian left," said Athena, "the curious character, Nemesis."

Lady Primrose Alice Louise Charmbury, (52) of South Kensington, London (code name Nemesis)

She studied at Broomwood Hall, Grey Coat Hospital School and Lady Margaret Hall, Oxford. She lives alone in a mews house with her cats. Shut herself off from society after leaving university. Her wealthy father lives alone on the edge of the New Forest. Lady Primrose is an only child. In the 2011 Census, she listed her occupation as 'Artist'. Lady Primrose has never exhibited her work. Instead, she delivers a painting to Lot's Road Auction House every few weeks. Her work reflects a very dark and tortured image of the world. Prices fetched have ranged between six hundred and a thousand pounds.

"I wonder what happened at Oxford that turned a refined young lady into a recluse?" asked Phoenix. "Why does she need to sell a few paintings? She can't be short of money. Her contributions to the Project were substantial back in 2007 when she joined. There's no sign Daddy disowned her. They live separate lives."

"I'll double-check, but I couldn't spot any reference in the file on what happened at the university. The woman gave me the creeps. I don't remember her speaking in Curzon Street. She just twitched at the mention of the little black book."

"Another one to hand to Artemis to hunt the real truth," said Phoenix. "It's going to be busy in the ice-house."

Athena got up and walked around to the side of the table where Phoenix sat. She took hold of the top folder.

"Demeter and Poseidon; and maybe Hermes, Nemesis and Apollo."

Phoenix opened the other folder.

"Zeus, Hera, Heracles, Dionysus and Aphrodite. The O Team."

The Price of Treachery

"I'm happy to run with that for now. We need to trawl for more detail on Hermes. I agree that Apollo and Nemesis leave room for doubt. I'm not going to speculate on which camp they will finally fall into. Time is of the essence. Our meeting is only nine days away. I want to be aware of the make-up of the Titans when we sit around the table with them in Nottingham."

"Dolos - the spirit of trickery and guile," said Phoenix, "a master of cunning deception and betrayal. Erebus left a significant clue as he sat dying in Ibiza. With a single word, he told us of the existence of the Titans. Moreover, he intimated that one of these names was his killer. Could it have been a woman, though, not a man? Is it possible a woman sailed 'Elizabeth' home with Hermes, and they both disposed of Gavin?"

"Don't go there, Phoenix," chided Athena. "Several names are embedded in our nation's sailing history, demonstrating how perfectly capable a female yachtswoman can be. We mustn't assume anything. We must delve deeper into each of our suspects and find the truth. Something ties these suspects together. We need to trace that very quickly. Whether Hermes sailed alone or with an accomplice is of little importance. Hermes is aligned with the Titans and will pay the price."

Phoenix closed the folders and thought for a while.

"Everything we ask Giles and Artemis to investigate has to be done in secret. We cannot discount a link between the names in this folder and at least one of our own. When trying to find that missing link, we need to see whether any other names fit into the chain."

"I hope you're mistaken, Phoenix," sighed Athena, "but I fear we have more enemies than we first thought."

"We only have just over a week to get *all* of their

names," said Phoenix, "we must not strike until we are sure of the extent of their treachery."

"We must clean our own house first. We must get Olympus back on the right track, the track Erebus set us on at the beginning. Then Olympus can uncover how many more Titans are there if they exist across the country. How far along the road towards a dictatorship is this nation of ours?"

Athena appeared more concerned than Phoenix had seen her in the past three years.

"Things look dark at present, Athena," he said, trying to comfort her, "but we won't stop. There's too much at stake. I won't let these people achieve their goals. Our child will be born into a country free of the evil the Titans wish to impose on it."

Chapter Seven

Tuesday, October 1st, 2013

Phoenix and Athena chatted over a quick coffee before going to the meeting room.

"Every second is vital," said Athena. "Giles and Artemis need to be working on these files twenty-four seven."

"I can rely on you to speed things along so that Henry and Giles don't hang around too long."

"What do we do about Thanatos?" she asked.

"Nothing yet. We must be certain who is with us and against us. I'll ask Rusty to keep an eye on things for now."

When they arrived in the meeting room, the three senior agents were already in position. Alastor and Minos acknowledged their arrival; Thanatos hurriedly finished a text message on his mobile phone and sent it.

Giles, Rusty, and Henry barged through the door together. Everyone appeared to be in a good mood; that was about to change.

"Giles, I want you to go with Phoenix to the orangery.

He has a job for you. Henry, please go back to the ice-house and ask Artemis to delegate tasks on her desk to another agent. Then I want you to find people on this list and interview them. Those interviews can take place in their own homes or places of work. It won't be necessary to bring them here for interrogation. We need answers to a few questions, that's all. So be gentle with them."

"Of course, Athena," said 'Head' Case, "may I ask what we're looking at?"

"I can't tell you at this stage. However, it's of the utmost urgency, so please take this folder and get cracking. Don't discuss the contents with anyone except myself and Phoenix."

"Yes, Athena. I understand," said Henry. He took the folder and headed off for the ice-house.

"Is there something we can do to help?" asked Minos.

"Follow the agenda I gave you for today and keep your reports brief, please," said Athena.

Rusty sat alone on his side of the table and held his tongue. He had never seen Athena so focused. Although Alastor, Minos, and Thanatos gave their reports, it was clear their hearts weren't in it.

They were all wondering what was happening, just as he was.

The Three Stooges soon disappeared, and Rusty was alone with Athena.

"Rusty," she said. "My apologies for the mad rush and the secrecy, but we have a mountain of work to get through before next Wednesday. Phoenix and I have uncovered a faction with the Olympus Project we believe is plotting to take the organisation in a far more sinister direction. What is definite is that they are planning to eliminate a significant number of important people. The Project has a so-called 'black book.' Members of this faction have persuaded Zeus to add names to the dozen, or so it contained to date. The original list emanated from Yewtree. Olympus identified former MPs, celebrities, and priests who carried out dreadful acts against children in the distant past. We had no doubts over direct actions against these despicable individuals. This extended list, though, is of concern. It now includes people we believe have been added by members of the hierarchy to settle personal scores. Several new names they have added are harder to fathom when taken individually. However, if your ultimate aim was to overthrow the elected government, these people could be a huge stumbling block if you wished to be successful. We believe these killings are a precursor to an eventual takeover."

"What do you want me to do?" asked Rusty.

"Phoenix is telling Giles who we suspect; Artemis will be helping him day and night for the next week, getting every last grain of data on our targets. Henry will be travelling around the country, talking with individuals who knew these suspects in their younger days. We have to build up a complete picture before next week. There's a common bond that links our conspirators. Henry will be instrumental in finding that bond. We trust you implicitly, Rusty. We have had doubts about at least one of our numbers in the past few days. The faction working against the organisation's best interests know details they shouldn't."

"A mole? Here at Larcombe? That's incredible," said Rusty. He was shocked.

"I want you to keep a close eye on my three senior colleagues; plus, be aware of anyone on the general staff who is acting suspiciously. There may be a single traitor in our midst, but we must try to find his fellow rats before we take action."

"Understood, Athena," said Rusty. "I'll be on my guard and report morning, noon and night."

"Good hunting," said Athena, and with that, she left.

"Bloody hell," said Rusty.

He sat alone in the meeting room for a few moments. Shit. Fan. Here we go again.

There are only a few days before the next meeting. I must attend to matters in the basement before I leave home. The blood draining from my latest victim should now be complete—such a satisfying death. Not for him, of course, but when you are a serial abuser of young people, you should expect retribution to be swift and inevitable.

Maurice Kingston became an associate professor in the music department of a nearby college in 2011. During the following school year, Kingston began grooming his female students, inviting several to drink alcohol at his home. In October 2012, Kingston invited a nineteen-year-old student to his house for dinner and wine. She said he kissed her without her consent. Kingston threatened her, telling the young girl that if she didn't sleep with him, she wouldn't graduate, and it would end her hopes of a musical career. Instead, she let him have sex with her on the sofa in his lounge.

Throughout 2012 Kingston routinely put other female students in compromising situations. Kingston even visited a twenty-year-old student on campus, plied her with alcohol and had sex with her against her will.

By spring 2013, music department staff were aware of Kingston's behaviour, placing him on gardening leave in April. Kingston denied any inappropriate sexual conduct or harassment of students. The college advised him they were

The Price of Treachery

to start a full investigation into the matter. He resigned on June 30, 2013. The college decided to take no further action.

My investigations discovered Maurice Kingston resigned several times from other educational institutions across the country. These girls were the last in a long list of victims.

I slipped out of my home two days ago and drove across the city to his house late at night. He didn't expect a visitor — especially not one who entered his bedroom without him noticing. I injected him with a neuromuscular blocking drug. The drug soon affected his voluntary muscles. I was careful to administer a dose that didn't paralyse his respiratory muscles. Maurice Kingston was conscious and able to feel pain but paralysed and unable to speak.

I left him in bed and went downstairs. My colleague had reversed his van to the front door; the rear doors were open. We collected my guest and placed him in the back, securing him with the four restraints bolted to the floor. But of course, one can never rely on traffic at night. Any unforeseen delay might have resulted in the delicately prepared dosage wearing off before we reached my basement.

I drove carefully home in my car while the van followed at a safe distance. Once my guest had been transferred from the van to his final resting place, my colleague wished me goodnight and left. Maurice Kingston lay on a stainless steel table in the centre of my basement floor. Chest freezers surround the four walls. The ceiling lights are far brighter than is necessary for a typical household, but I need to be able to see what I'm doing.

Maurice Kingston weighed around twelve stones. We arrived at this conclusion when we carried him downstairs. We were grateful for him not being as overweight as the others. I removed his nightclothes and fetched my knives. When I first used this method of killing rapists who had escaped conviction, I warned them what was about to happen would hurt.

I rarely bother these days. I had become proficient in collecting their blood for as long as possible. I thought of it as a kindness. One slash of the aorta and they would lose consciousness within seconds. The heart stops beating before all the blood can pump out.

Hundreds of tiny cuts allowed me to extend the time the heart continued to pump blood before stopping, and then the table could be tilted ninety degrees. The remaining blood then drips into containers and can be salvaged whenever I need it. My latest donor should offer ten pints. Finally, it was time to descend to the basement to dispose of the empty shell hanging from the table.

The containers need to be stored away for later use. The table has to return to its normal position. The thick basement walls will mask the sound of the saw.

I've earmarked the chest freezer on the end wall for this skeleton. My freezer cabinet at the bottom of the stairs will find a home for the bagged-up flesh and internal organs. In time my cats will receive a treat mixed in with their regular food.

Just look at the clock. So much to do and so little time.

Phil Hounsell stood a few yards along the corridor from Honey B's dressing room. He could still hear the commotion coming from inside. They were coming to the end of this UK tour, and the singer's nerves had started to shred. He and Wayne Sangster had stumbled upon a lucrative first gig for HSS. Who and what they might provide security for in the coming weeks and months was anybody's guess.

The Price of Treachery

"At least it's the management of the Alex that's getting an earful, and not us," thought Phil, as he edged further away from trouble.

The Honey B roadshow was to appear at the New Alexandra Theatre in Birmingham for three nights. However, the singer was hugely disappointed at ticket sales and placed the blame fair and square on the shoulders of the poor manager. So far, they had sold only between seven hundred and eight hundred tickets for each performance. As a result, the auditorium would be less than two-thirds full each night.

"Why didn't you advertise it better? How many 'walk-ups' do you generally get per performance?" she yelled. She punctuated each question with another glass or bottle smashing into a wall. Finally, the manager tried to tell her how much effort they had made to soothe her with promises of potentially hundreds of her fans making a late decision to attend.

Honey B didn't listen. "Don't you know who I am?" she screamed.

A celebrity should be aware that they've lost the argument once they resort to that plea. Honey B waited for a reply. Nothing was forthcoming from the young manager. He was scared stiff to tell her the truth. No, I don't have a clue who you are. He thought it best to keep that information to himself, but his silence infuriated Honey B further.

"I've had enough of these provincial theatres," she said, "I'm leaving."

The manager suddenly grew a pair and reminded her of her contract. Then, he walked out of the dressing room, having told the former Sixties pop idol that she was due on stage at eight-thirty and not to be late. He closed the door just in time to avoid the bottle of champagne hurled at his head.

Phil spoke to Wayne through his wireless headset. The other two HSS personnel were on a break until later this evening.

"Wayne, I'm going into her dressing room. Please send a rescue party if I'm not out in ten minutes."

"OK, boss," said Wayne. He was in the wings, watching the support act doing a soundcheck. The girl singer looked tidy, and Wayne wondered whether she liked a man in uniform.

Phil waited thirty seconds, took a deep breath, and knocked on the dressing room door.

"What?" yelled Honey B.

Phil opened the door and entered. It was a mess. Broken glass, vases overturned, flower petals everywhere and water dripping from the dressing table onto the carpeted floor.

When she saw him, Philomena Victoria Jacinta de Beauchamp Alexander gave him one of her half-smiles and pouted like a spoilt teenager.

"I've been a diva again, haven't I, darling?" she purred.

"Nothing a cracking two-hour performance can't put right," said Phil. "Keep your eye on the prize. After next Monday night in Nottingham, you'll be able to put your feet up and rest until you spend the winter in Australia and New Zealand."

Honey B knew that there would be very little rest. There was much to be done if she and her colleagues were going to achieve their goals. Over the past two weeks, she travelled from one luxury hotel to another. She moved to and from the theatre courtesy of an HSS driver. Her security cordon had been perfect on every occasion.

Honey B had no complaints about someone she

employed for the first time in years. That was why she had flown off the handle earlier; she had something to get angry about, and the manager was the nearest person at the time. No, employing Phil Hounsell and his team was her best decision in ages.

Honey B would cast aside the pop star image after next Monday. She then became Demeter, Queen of the Titans. The meeting in Nottingham would set in motion a string of events that would change the course of British history forever. Phil Hounsell would unwittingly provide help in getting things moving. On the first date of this tour in Bristol, he spotted the photograph showing Phoenix and Athena.

Only recently, Demeter had met these two leaders from the Olympus HQ at Larcombe Manor. She now possessed background information on both of them from her inside man, but Phoenix remained a mystery. Erebus brought him on board three years ago and promoted him rapidly. Who was he, and from where did he come? Demeter believed that Phil Hounsell knew. That was the clincher; she was not giving her security contract to anyone else. No matter how experienced they might be in comparison to this new outfit. She wanted to keep Phil Hounsell close by her side.

They had chatted before and after shows in her dressing room. She had to be patient. She couldn't risk revealing the real purpose behind wanting to unmask the mystery face in the photo. She used glasses of champagne and feminine wiles to prise snippets of information from the former policeman.

Phil Hounsell was a happily married man. A younger woman had tempted him on one occasion, but Demeter wasn't aware of this fact. She was sixty-three, with a very young partner, and despite expensive cosmetic surgery, she couldn't disguise the fact she was several years older than the security consultant. She had to concede that as far as Phil was concerned, 'her mojo wasn't working.'

As for Phil Hounsell, he knew Honey B was coming on to him. He wasn't stupid. He was flattered but unprepared to risk the contracts that might come his way with the singer's glowing references after this tour ended. After all, if he could stay in her good books for three weeks, he would be a diamond and much coveted. So he needed to tread with care so he didn't alienate her by sidestepping her advances.

She kept that photograph in plain sight in the dressing room of every theatre she played so far, a beautiful woman with a man who reminded him so much of Colin Bailey. Each night she entertained him after the show; she handed him a glass of champagne; because she said, I hate drinking alone. Then the questions began.

New Theatre, Cardiff: -

"I think you know these people, am I right?"

"Never met *her*, but the man seemed familiar."

"Your paths met while you were a policeman, I suppose?"

"I was a copper for thirty years; I met many people. Not all of them criminals."

Swansea Royal Theatre: -

"Why do you say the man only *seemed* familiar?"

"He reminds me of someone who died."

"He has a striking face, hasn't he; surely you wouldn't forget it?"

"I bumped into him at Glastonbury in June; he was with the lady."

"You said you'd never met her."

"You asked if I knew her; I don't."

Llandudno Venue Cymru: -

"How did he die, the man who looked like the man in the picture?"

"He drowned."

"You saw this woman with this man at Glastonbury Festival?"

"Yes, when he bumped into me."

"Go on," urged Demeter slipping from behind her mask, "I find this *most* interesting."

As the shows in Manchester, Liverpool, and Belfast got ticked off the list, Phil gradually told Honey B his history with Colin Bailey.

Finally, in Usher Hall. Edinburgh; after the second glass of champagne: -

"When he bumped into my shoulder that day, I spun around to apologise. Facially, he hadn't registered. Something triggered a memory as I watched the two striding through the crowds of festival-goers. The way he walked, carried himself, and his shoulders. It was him, yet he was so different from the man I knew."

"They never found the body?"

"No, but that's not unheard of in those situations. Bailey was under the water for so long; it's inconceivable he survived. I only escaped, thanks to a colleague diving in to drag me to the wall. When they got me up onto the towpath, I'd stopped breathing. A female colleague carried out mouth-to-mouth and got me back."

"Lucky girl," said Honey B, back in her on-stage persona.

"Another minute and I would have died. Bailey never surfaced. The rescue services stayed on site until night fell. That's why it's incredible that this man makes me think he's Bailey. It can't be him."

"What a shame," said Honey B, "but it's a great story, isn't it?"

Demeter had thought, but it was him; it made perfect sense. So that sly old fox Erebus named him Phoenix. What else do you call a man who rose from the dead?

They played more theatres after that, working their way towards the Midlands. The questions kept coming, and the details of Colin Bailey's former life altered from a briefly sketched outline to become a fully-fledged oil painting,

Demeter had everything she thought she needed to bring down Phoenix. She looked at Phil Hounsell. Wayne stood in the corridor, ready to ride to the rescue. Instead, the pop singer glided across the room and stood next to her security consultant.

"Thanks for everything you've done for me on this tour," she said, standing on tiptoe to brush an ice-cold kiss across his cheek, "I won't forget you. You are my hunter, my Orion. When the time comes, I shall contact you. I want you to work for my colleagues and me. You'll find it very rewarding. What do you say?"

"We're always ready to talk business," said Phil. "You only need to tell us who we're hunting for, and we'll trace them."

"The chase has begun then," whispered Honey B. "I'll see you after the show."

Phil left the dressing room. Wayne leaned against the wall.

"Everything OK, boss?"

"A little chilly," said Phil, rubbing his cheek, "but the future sounds promising."

Chapter Eight

Honey B performed to just over a thousand adoring fans in the end. The young manager had his 'I told you so' face as he strutted backstage. He was smart enough to steer clear of the top of the bill when she made her way to the stage. There was no point in rubbing her nose in it.

Wayne was backstage, deep in conversation with the pretty singer in the support band. He had no chance, but Phil didn't want to spoil the moment. It filled in time until Honey B had finished her two-hour set and retired to the dressing room. He would then interrupt Wayne and get him to have Dusty and Leggo on standby, ready to whisk their charge off to her five-star hotel.

How long they hung around depended on how much champagne she wanted to use to loosen his tongue tonight. She was an extraordinary woman. She was attractive and yet cold. She exasperated him when she pouted and stamped her feet over the slightest glitch, yet she could be sweetness and light with her audience.

As an interrogator, Phil reckoned she could have made an excellent detective.

Their after-show conversations were pleasant and covered many subjects that demonstrated her high level of intelligence. She sensed at once when Phil was off his guard, and he found himself answering an innocent question without realising its importance. Her follow-up questions came rapidly, leaving no time for filtering out things he didn't want to reveal.

He knew he had told her far too much about Colin Bailey, but what difference did it make if he was dead?

Phil stood in the wings listening to Honey B going through her greatest hits for the umpteenth night in a row. But then, he heard something that caused him to listen more carefully. He shook his head. Well, she was sixty-three, and his late mother-in-law Mary started forgetting things in her late sixties.

It struck Phil as odd for a knowledgeable lady who couldn't recall the lyrics to one of her chart-toppers. He noticed it on a couple of occasions over the past weeks. But, of course, if his mother hadn't owned a copy of the original single and played it non-stop that summer, he wouldn't have spotted the changes. But, odd or not, Phil would not raise the matter with her. He wanted to keep HSS in business to bolster his pension, and he had the wages of three employees to satisfy.

A rewarding future with Honey B would be right out of the window if he mentioned her minor memory lapses.

Wednesday, October 2nd, to Tuesday, October 8th, 2013

The Price of Treachery

In the ice-house, the general intelligence-gathering still carried on in the background. Agents hacked and retrieved, logged and recorded. They captured any small grain of data that might aid Olympus in the next few hours or at an unknown point in the future. While other agents performed these tasks, Giles Burke and Artemis worked alone.

After meeting in the orangery with Phoenix, Giles returned underground and took Artemis to one side.

"Henry has told you that you will be working with me on a special project, I understand?"

"Yes, Giles," replied Artemis. "He's told me to drop everything, and what we'll be doing is top secret."

"If there was a higher level, this qualifies," said Giles.

They occupied a secure room where they could work, isolated from the rest of the team. Henry had additional equipment delivered within the hour. As he looked around, Giles was happy everything they needed was at hand. The two agents set to work.

The calendar flipped over from day to day. As they uncovered potential leads, Giles assessed them. If he thought they were worth following up on, he contacted Henry Case. Henry had based himself in the Chiswick safe house to visit and interview people who had known their targets earlier in their lives. Four of the five concerned lived in London, while Troy Gardner lived only two hours away in Salisbury.

Henry and Giles agreed once the London leads were exhausted, he would do a sweep of any interviewees within a one-hundred-mile radius. Then, they handed anyone who fell outside the ring to more local agents. Henry had set aside the weekend to sift through the dialogue these conversations produced.

Artemis was searching through social media sites to

find school friends of the teenage Troy Gardner. She noticed several male contemporaries, ex-girlfriends, ex-wives and his older children. Troy's father had worked in a flower market a mile away from their home in Bethnal Green. His mother had stayed home looking after her six children. When Troy brought home a school report, which wasn't very often, it showed he struggled with reading and writing.

Troy was handy with his fists and enjoyed sports. He was bullied by older boys when he first got to secondary school, but they regretted tangling with him when he had grown. Only a few of his fellow students had left the area north of the Thames, so Henry located them quickly and interviewed them.

The stories he heard from the ex-wives and girlfriends were similar. He was good-looking and fit; he made them feel special. He was a bastard because he had a roving eye. No, he never hit me. It appeared he paid his alimony dues every month, where required. Henry wondered where this was going. He thought he saw a sign to nowhere.

Giles tracked down two men from Bethnal Green who remembered Troy from a local youth club. He flagged their profiles up for Artemis to scrutinise.

"This is something different, Artemis," he said.

Artemis read through the details and gave a low whistle.

"Bingo, this explains why Troy guards his younger life so closely. His image could take a battering if it became public knowledge."

Henry Case visited a bar in Shoreditch that evening. The two men he was looking for sat at a corner table. Henry almost missed them at first. The more glamorous one in the sparkling red cocktail dress waved a black-gloved hand and patted the stool next to him.

The Price of Treachery

"You're a big boy, aren't you? What was it you wanted? Drinks are costly in this place."

Henry wedged two folded fifty-pound notes into the man's cleavage.

"You knew Troy Gardner back in the days before he became famous, I hear?"

Both men laughed.

"We remember him, alright. Troy was experimenting back then. We were fifteen when we met. We both already knew which way our bread was buttered, but Troy couldn't decide, poor boy."

"What happened?" asked Henry.

"We started leaving the youth club once we hit sixteen and going uptown. We'd hang around on street corners and wait for a car to stop. Troy came with us a few times and waited until we returned; he didn't get in a car with anyone. Then, when he saw us with ten or fifteen quid each time, he joined us. We were making forty to sixty quid a night."

"How long did this go on for?" asked Henry.

The other man spoke. "Troy got out of that game as soon as he found a boxing gym. We worked with him for nine months, a year maybe. We carried on into our twenties."

"We had started using crack," the other man broke in, "we were a mess. We cleaned up and started working in nightclubs as a drag act."

"Did you ever see or hear from Troy again?"

Henry spotted a glance shared between the two. He waited.

"How much did he pay for your silence?" he asked.

"Enough to buy this place, sweetheart," came the reply.

Henry drank up and left the bar; Troy Gardner had a secret. He relayed the result of his interview to the ice-house. They could decide what to do next. It was time to move on to a new location, but first, back to Chiswick for a good night's sleep.

Giles Burke had taken the file containing the life of Leopold Andrews and dissected it. Many of his former work colleagues and schoolmates were dead. Those that survived were living in every corner of the world. Giles found it tough to trace anyone who remembered Leopold well enough to give them anything useful. It was his time at university that held the key. While at Trinity College, Cambridge, he joined or dabbled in the fringes of several radical organisations. Leopold was anti-democracy, anti-monarchy, anti-blood sports, and anti-vivisection.

"I don't think this chap was in favour of very much when he was a student," exclaimed Giles.

Artemis took a look over his shoulder at the data on the screen.

"He's never been married. Was there ever a woman in his life apart from his mother? How does he spend his leisure time? Is he gay? Is he among the one per cent of the population that's asexual? There has to be something that fires him up, surely? Whatever the elusive spark is, that has to be what links him to the others. But, unfortunately, nothing we've uncovered gives us the slightest clue."

"Well, you've given us several new lines of enquiry. So let's divide those between us and get searching."

At midnight on Thursday night, Artemis found something. Leopold Andrews had bought a poster on eBay three years ago for a rock festival held in June 1981. It seemed so bizarre when held against the image of the rest of his life. Yet, the price he paid was so insignificant that it would have been easy to overlook.

The Price of Treachery

"Why did someone like Leopold Andrews buy an old poster? What memories did it hold for him?"

Giles scooted his chair across to where she was working. He was getting nowhere and feeling weary.

"Where was it?" he asked, stifling a yawn.

"It was Summer In The City, Crystal Palace; it featured bands such as Ultravox and Madness."

"It's odd, but how does it help?" asked Giles.

"It doesn't," admitted Artemis, "but it will. So let's take a break; come back at six, refreshed, and take another look at this Philomena Alexander, the singer."

On Friday morning, they skimmed over the singer's early career. They noted the very brief marriage to her record producer. She married her actor in 1971 and ditched him in 1981. She was single for a period and married her international footballer in 1985.

"It's starting to fall into place," said Artemis, with more enthusiasm than Giles could justify.

"Really?" he said, scratching his head.

"Look at the synopsis that we have. After the divorce in 1981, Honey B took a career break for several months in 1982. What does that suggest?"

"She was drying out in a clinic for drink or drugs, perhaps?" said Giles.

"We're both too young to remember how things were for pop stars from the Sixties; their publicity machine hid things from their adoring fans. John Lennon was married when The Beatles hit the big time, but they kept that fact from the public for as long as possible. Their management wanted them to appear as the boys next door and be available to the ordinary fan. What if Honey B had a child during that career break? She wasn't married, and the dates don't fit for it being her second husband. It's unlikely they were sleeping together. Even though it was 1982, her publicity machine had been weaving its magic for fifteen years. They would have convinced her that an illegitimate child could harm her career. We can see from all past evidence how closely she fights to protect that."

"Where was she in mid-June 1981?" asked Giles, starting to get interested in where this was heading.

"Near the bottom of the bill at Summer In The City," said Artemis, "look, her name's mentioned in this festival report. The Croydon Guardian's write-up reported her as a token establishment name among the rising stars of modern music. A weak sound system and various technical problems bugged her twenty-minute performance. Later in the evening, while Madness smashed it, she was seen drinking champagne straight from a bottle at the venue."

"So, we have Leopold and Philomena potentially in the same place at the same time," said Giles. "She's drunk; he's available. Why he was there, we may never know. Maybe Henry can find out for us. They have a one-night stand. A child is born, a child who would now be thirty-one. The same age as Dominic Perkins. That wasn't the name of either of her husbands, though, was it?"

Artemis thought about how Giles had joined the dots. He could be right; stranger things had happened. People had fallen into bed with the wrong people for various reasons. Then she had a brainwave.

"We need to look at her third husband. Nobody has ever delved into his history. So why should we, or whoever put together this original file for Athena, check him out? It hasn't been the husbands who have been under the microscope. Let's see what his record shows."

Giles pulled up the profile of Anthony Grant, an international footballer. The clubs he played for were listed, the number of caps he won and the goals he scored. There were statistics and news items everywhere. But unfortunately, Giles couldn't find a birth certificate that matched the available information.

Artemis pointed at the screen.

"Scroll down the page. There he is, Anthony Grant Perkins, born February 28th, 1965, in Peckham. He dropped his surname when he signed on for the Arsenal youth team. There wasn't room for another player with the nickname 'Psycho' in the game."

"You've lost me there, Artemis," said Giles, who wasn't a great football follower, "but I remember the film. You've cracked it; Dominic Perkins is Philomena's child, quite possibly fathered by Leopold Andrews, and the third husband was happy enough for the boy to take his name. The mother always hid her surname, whatever her marital status, and in public, was always known as Honey B."

"Now we appreciate Philomena Alexander's devious; it makes sense she persuaded her husband to allow Dominic to take his name. It reduced the chances of anyone linking them together as mother and son. What time is it?" asked Artemis.

"Half-past eight; brilliant, I can take this gem to Phoenix and Athena before their morning meeting. They need to see this. We've found our missing link for three of the photographs. Troy Gardner is the odd one out so far. I don't believe he's connected. So that leaves us with Lady Primrose Charmbury, her paintings and her cats. I wonder how Henry's getting on with the names I sent him from her university days?"

Giles hurried over to the main house to pass on the news. Artemis continued to list questions for Henry Case.

Finally, satisfied that she had exhausted the possibilities, she rang him.

Henry was ready for action. He had been up since seven. As soon as he ended the call from Artemis, he left the safe house and drove towards his first contact. It was going to be a long day, but Henry could see the winning post. There were only a few loose ends to tie up now, and Olympus would be prepared to face whatever lay ahead.

Henry was pleased with their progress. He was a little disappointed he wasn't inviting any of his interviewees to Hotel California, but one didn't always get things one wanted in life.

As he drove back to Larcombe Manor late that evening, he reflected on the answers he received. He didn't understand how they fitted into the jigsaw, but he thought Phoenix and Athena were in for a surprise.

Catherine Morris studied Russian at LMH, Oxford. She and Lady Primrose Charmbury had been fellow students. As 'freshers', the two girls attended various events together. Although they weren't close friends, they were young, single girls away from home for the first time.

"She was so 'posh' I never understood why she latched on to me," Catherine told him. They met in a tea shop in Notting Hill. She was plump, married with children and working as a translator. Her native Yorkshire voice had never softened over the years. Henry idly wondered how Russian sounded with a Bradford accent.

Over two cups of tea and a plate of Rich Tea biscuits, he heard from young Catherine about the changes she'd observed in Primrose.

"Our professor was Russian, the youngest don at Oxford. He was so handsome. When we were in his rooms, he was a god to the girls in our group. He didn't look twice at me, of course. A couple of the girls were pretty, and he flirted with them. Prim was beautiful and had class. Professor Sokolov was smitten; I could tell. When Prim and I talked about him, he obviously frightened her. We were nineteen years old. Neither of us had any experience with men. Not even men of our age, let alone a sophisticated, intelligent foreigner like Anton Sokolov. University life can bring you out of that innocence pretty quickly. I soon found male undergraduates who didn't mind learning things outside the curriculum with a fat lass from Barnsley. These liaisons tended to keep me from seeing Prim so often as the years passed. When I saw her during our finals, she was pale, thin and withdrawn. I hardly recognised her. I grabbed her when we were leaving our final exam and dragged her off to my room. She was a mess. When she told me her story, I felt dreadful. If I had been a better friend, I could have saved her. Instead, I left her to fend for herself while I went off drinking and partying. I thought she would find friends of her kind, the Hooray Henrys and Henriettas who populated Oxford. It turned out that Sokolov started to see her in his room alone. He was an animal, and Prim was raped repeatedly for two years. He subjected her to all manner of abuse. Prim was so shy; she was scared and ashamed. You can guess the rest. A beautiful first year caught his eye, and Prim got thrown aside. I told her she had to speak out; tell someone. We should both go and warn this girl. Prim wasn't having any of it. She fled from my room, and we never met again."

"What happened to Sokolov, do you know?" Henry had asked.

"He left Oxford four years after I graduated. He moved to Winchester. No doubt, he carried on abusing the young women he tutored. The police found his car abandoned on the edge of the New Forest in 2004. Parts of a skeleton were eventually uncovered and identified as belonging to him a year or two later. Animals and insects had devoured everything to show how he died. It might have been natural causes or suicide; it was impossible to tell. The coroner recorded an open verdict."

Henry had waved goodbye to Catherine Morris as she shuffled off to her Honda Jazz in the car park. He then drove to Esher in Surrey to talk to Paul Trevelyan. Now a successful restaurateur, Paul had been at school with Dominic Perkins. They studied together for two years from the age of fifteen. Paul knew how it was for Dominic, moving home and schools regularly; his father had been in the RAF.

"We weren't best mates or anything. Dominic wasn't easy to get close to; now and then, he'd let something slip about his parents fighting. He always thought he would be moving again soon. The only constant he had while in his teens was the Isle of Wight. Once the holidays came and we went home to our families, Dominic took the ferry across to the island from Lymington. When we met again in September, he would be full of the sailing he had done. No doubt, he was brilliant. Annoying. Some people seem to be able to turn their hands to anything. I can cook, and I'm proficient at running a successful restaurant, but that's my limit. Dominic was multi-talented. I laughed at his mobile phone adverts; I was surprised he didn't pick a more difficult challenge. That line of business feels too easy for him."

It was mid-afternoon when Henry had left Paul Trevelyan's place and headed back into London. Reading the menu and the specials board had made him hungry. So when he reached Peckham for his last appointment, he invited his contact to dine with him.

The Price of Treachery

Mick Reynolds looked as if he could do with a good square meal. He was in his early sixties, with a thin, unshaven face. The bags under his eyes gave him the look of a world-weary greyhound. Henry took one look at his shabby clothes and uncombed hair. Fine dining was out, but plenty of pubs served acceptable food. Henry fetched a pint of lager and a soft drink from the bar. They chatted while they waited for the food to arrive.

Henry asked Mick to tell what he remembered about the Anti-Royalist and anarchy groups active in the early Eighties. Mick Reynolds looked around the bar furtively, expecting a hand to fall on his shoulder at any moment.

"I've finished with that nonsense. I'd left school eighteen months before, only a rubbish YTS stint in a bakery, and then I was on the dole. We were angry young men. We had to find something to do to let off steam."

"Who recruited you?" Henry had asked.

"A bloke who called himself Leo; he must have been pushing forty. A bit arrogant. Leo turned up in a suit and tie. Marcus joined up the same week as I did."

"Marcus?"

"Sarjeant, he was sentenced to five years the next summer for firing blanks at the Queen in The Mall, remember? We were just kids, messing around. Do you get me? I spent the rest of the summer handing out leaflets and hanging posters."

"Did you hand out leaflets at any big public events?"

"Loads in London; music festivals and concerts, that type of thing."

"Summer In The City?"

"Yeah, places similar to that every weekend. Leo took us around in a van, then paid us to hand out leaflets."

"So Leo was with you at Crystal Palace?"

"Yeah, he was there throughout the day. Then, he ran us back home at the end of the gig."

"When did you last see Leo?"

"During the Peckham riots in '85. He was stirring things up from the sidelines as usual. He never got his hands dirty. He was too posh for that, but he spread his money around to get a few of us tooled up, so we could cause trouble."

The food had arrived, and it was still repeating on Henry as he continued to make his way to the M4 and home.

Chapter Nine

Saturday, October 5th, 2013

Phoenix and Athena were up early. Yesterday had been a day full of revelations. They had fifteen minutes before they were due to start their scheduled meeting with their senior agents. Giles had arrived from the ice-house. They now had a far better appreciation of who comprised the Titans, what the links were between them, and why they were plotting to overthrow the democratic government.

They didn't have all the answers, but they had enough to arm them when they confronted the conspirators in Nottingham the following Wednesday. Of the ten others who sat with them around the table, they knew eight of them were true Olympians. Only three were against them. One name was still under investigation.

There was no meeting this morning. Rusty had called Athena yet again to ask for a get-together. He wanted to report what he observed during the past twenty-four hours.

Athena hoped Artemis could have had time off to keep him occupied. Giles was loading more of the general surveillance back onto her now the top-secret investigation was ending.

"Let's get along to the meeting room to hear what Rusty has discovered," said Athena. "Then we need to start preparing our strategies for Nottingham."

"Three hours up the M5 works for me," said Phoenix, receiving a dig in the ribs for his light-hearted remark.

The couple walked hand-in-hand downstairs and met Rusty and Henry in the hallway.

"Henry," said Athena, "welcome back. How was your trip? I hope you picked up news that could be helpful?"

"I'll show you mine if you show me yours," said Henry.

Once in the meeting room, Athena summarised the latest information for Henry and Rusty's benefit.

"Philomena Alexander had an illegitimate child, Dominic Perkins, in 1982. We believe the father was Leopold Andrews. The boy took his stepfather's real surname, confirming a tangible link between three of our main conspirators. We're happy that Troy Gardner is no danger to us, although he does have a skeleton in the closet. One he would not wish to be allowed to escape."

Henry added the details he gathered yesterday.

"Leo Andrews was at Summer In The City in the summer of 1981. He was involved in an anarchic organisation and the Anti-Royalist Movement at the time. He employed local unemployed lads to distribute leaflets at public events throughout the summer. That's why he was at Crystal Palace that day. It cements your belief that he met Philomena there, and a one-night stand resulted in young Dominic. Another gem I uncovered was that Perkins is a highly accomplished sailor. According to one of his school

The Price of Treachery

chums, he's a modern-day C. B. Fry. My first interview yesterday revealed the tragic reason behind Lady Primrose and her transformation from a beautiful young girl into an oddball recluse. She was the victim of a randy Russian professor. She was too scared of him at the time to report it to the college or the police. An interesting footnote was that his abandoned car was discovered on the edge of the New Forest nine years ago, and they found his body in 2006. When we check this fact, we'll discover it lies within a short distance of the Charmbury family home. It wouldn't surprise me if Lady P took her revenge."

"The only link we haven't established then is between Lady Primrose and the others," said Phoenix.

Nobody could come up with a suggestion based on the data they had gathered.

Rusty took advantage of the lull.

"I've continued to watch the general staff and the others on your list, Athena. The past twenty-four hours have been the same as the earlier part of the week. There's nothing to suggest more than one mole at Larcombe."

Henry sat up and took notice.

"We have a traitor in our midst? Who do you think it is? Bring him to me in the ice-house. I haven't had a visitor book into Hotel California for weeks."

Athena tried to diffuse the situation.

"Rusty meant we don't have an infestation of moles. We need absolute confirmation of a single mole's existence first; then, we will take action against that person."

Phoenix gestured to Athena for permission to bring Henry into their confidence. She nodded.

"Look, Henry, this can't go outside this room. Not even to Giles and Artemis. This group, we suspect, is plotting to take control of Olympus to appear to know more than they should. In particular, things we've only discussed here at HQ. That implies they have someone on the inside. We have a suspect. Rusty watched them closely and made sure they acted alone. That now appears to be the case. After the meeting on the ninth, we shall know how to proceed. We'll keep the lid on things here at HQ for now. The time for action, though, is fast approaching."

"Understood, Phoenix," said Henry.

Athena decided there was little more to gain from Henry and Rusty.

"Enjoy what's left of the weekend; we'll see you first thing on Monday. Phoenix and I will stay here for the rest of the morning to prepare for Wednesday. Olympus's business continues despite this internal friction. There are other missions to plan and undertake. We must not take our eye off the ball. I can rely on you to ensure that doesn't happen."

"I'll pass on the reminder to Giles and the others in the intelligence section, Athena," said Henry and briskly marched out of the room.

"Artemis is working, I guess?" asked Phoenix.

"Another long day with Giles. They're catching up on surveillance reports that came through while she was on 'special ops'. We're hoping to get together tomorrow."

Rusty left them and wandered off to the stable block.

Athena and Phoenix started planning. Nottingham was only four days away.

Sunday, October 6th, 2013

The Price of Treachery

Athena and Phoenix were in their apartment, enjoying a late breakfast.

"If you're feeling up to it, why don't we take a trip to the coast?" asked Phoenix. He was feeling hemmed in by the four walls of Larcombe Manor. The London mission seemed so long ago.

"To Lymington, do you mean?" Athena replied. "Well, we need to decide, one way or another, whether to keep or sell her. Perhaps a day aboard her without leaving port might help us make up our minds."

"I just want to get away from here for a while," said Phoenix.

Athena's phone rang. She sighed. "This might scupper our plans."

It was Henry Case. Athena switched to speakerphone, so Phoenix heard what he had to say.

"Good morning. I have an interesting update. My interview with Paul Trevelyan was rewarding, as you know, and revealed a good deal about the schoolboy Dominic Perkins. On the other hand, his work colleagues in the city were very backward in coming forward. What they told me was vague and of little use when they did. I began to suspect that his business style included payments to secure non-cooperation with any visiting reporters. However, I received a call back from one such colleague this morning. She was most insistent none of what she told me ever got back to Perkins. Just over three years after his company acquired a major contract, it virtually doubled the business's size overnight. He invited a small group of his senior staff back to his flat after they had been for a meal in Knightsbridge to celebrate. She said, 'The penthouse apartment was ultra-modern and must have cost an absolute fortune. Dominic lived there alone. I don't think he entertained very often, if ever. It felt empty as if we were in a showroom. He's cold and calculating by nature; those who worked for him would tell you that. He wouldn't have made his fortune unless he had that hard edge, but that flat was creepy. He showed us around the rooms. I believe he had drunk more than he was used to because it was unlike him to be so friendly. The walls were an off-white colour. All the curtains were black. The only hint of decoration was in the paintings on every wall. You know when you look at a face in a picture, and the eyes follow you around the room? I couldn't wait to get out of there; I wanted to get into the lift and find a taxi. They were so gloomy and disturbing. Every painting featured dark colours and heavy use of, what's that colour called? Carmine, that's it. Everything had this dark red background. Glimpses of it appeared everywhere. Every door Dominic opened, you saw another slash of red across the wall. When he closed the door to move on to a bathroom or another bedroom, it wasn't the same as when the eyes followed you. It was as if someone was screaming, 'Don't leave me here alone.' It was horrid. We left after an hour, leaving Dominic half asleep on a black leather settee. I don't think any of us wanted to stay any longer. Nobody spoke in the lift. There were many hugs on the pavement outside, and we each made our way home. I always thought the hugs were for reassurance more than anything else. I left the company a month or so after that night. I couldn't see Dominic without remembering those paintings. I quit the mobile phone business altogether. I'm a wedding planner these days.'

"We didn't need to hear the last bit, Henry," Phoenix called out, "but the rest was pure gold. Thanks."

Athena thanked Henry Case for the update and ended the call.

"Another piece of the jigsaw. I can't see where it fits, can you?"

Phoenix scratched his head.

"So you're saying that Nemesis is the artist? She sells her stuff to Hermes, and whoever bids on the items she takes to auction. That's a leap, isn't it?"

"Why so? Lady Primrose paints dark and depressing paintings she sells at auction. She's a recluse, yet she *is* the person we know as Nemesis, one of the original financial backers of the Project. She sits at the top table beside Hermes. His former work colleague's description of the paintings is too similar not to be a tangible link between them, surely?"

"We haven't found a link between Nemesis and Demeter, nor between her and Poseidon," said Phoenix introducing a note of caution. "The artwork could be the link between her and Hermes, but what ties her in with his parents? So let's get off to the coast. We can chat as we drive, find somewhere for lunch, and then do our final planning for Wednesday on board 'Elizabeth'."

"You're on," said Athena.

As the sun was setting, they drove home towards Larcombe Manor. They had spent a pleasant day discussing the paintings, the meeting, and the future in the autumn sunshine. They had agreed to hold onto the yacht. Olympus might have a use for it one day. Agents joined them from each service, so men with the same skills as Gavin could sail her. She could prove to be a useful acquisition on a direct action that required men to be brought ashore under cover of darkness.

"As we're driving through the New Forest," said Athena, "why don't we drive over to where Lady Primrose's family live? Call Giles and get the address, then ask him where the police found the professor's abandoned car."

With Phoenix at the wheel, they drove through Lyndhurst and headed for Brockenhurst.

"There's a dark van behind us," he said, "three cars back. I think it's been with us since we left the Boat Haven."

"Why should anyone be following us?"

"Maybe they're out on a quiet Sunday drive the same as us," said Phoenix.

Her phone rang, and Athena jumped out of her skin and swore. It was from Giles.

"Leave this road at Cadnam," she said after he'd rung off. "Turn right towards Bartley. That's where Lady Primrose's father lives. Then, a little further on, we'll find Netley Marsh, where they eventually found the mortal remains of Anton Sokolov. Once there, we can join the A36 near Totton and shoot up to Salisbury. It will be quicker."

Phoenix checked his rear-view mirror as he turned off onto the narrow road through the Forest.

"He's turning to follow us," he said, accelerating away as soon as he rounded the corner.

As Phoenix concentrated on the road ahead, Athena called Giles and relayed their position. The closest Olympus cell was in Southampton. Giles immediately alerted that crew; he sent a detailed road map to Athena's laptop. She removed it from her handbag.

"How long?" shouted Phoenix as the car bounced along at sixty miles an hour. Too many potholes, blind corners, and bends needed careful negotiation. The van behind them was closing despite his best efforts. The van's headlights were getting more prominent in his mirror.

"Twenty minutes at a pinch," said Athena, hanging on for dear life with one hand while trying to access the file.

The Price of Treachery

The van rammed the back of their car. Phoenix tried to remember everything Rusty had taught him. Unfortunately, the second collision came before he had a chance to react. The car slewed from side to side. He thought he had lost control on the grass verge, but he managed to correct it. Phoenix accelerated again, even though it was a risk. This guy meant business and was trying to force them off the road.

"We must keep them occupied long enough for the cavalry to arrive, Athena," he shouted. "I don't suppose you brought a weapon?"

"Don't shout at me, but it's in the boot. In a recess under the carpet by the right rear wheel. It's a Smith & Wesson MP Shield; and it's loaded."

Phoenix looked in his rear-view mirror again. The van was closing in for another hit. These humps, bumps, and bends were a hindrance to their pursuer. One trick Rusty had taught him three years ago surfaced from what remained of his scrambled brain. All he could think was that Athena sat beside him, carrying their unborn child.

He could hear Rusty's words as they careered along a windy track in a wooded area on the Larcombe estate. "One of the best ways to distance you and the chasing vehicle is to reverse directions after a curve on a narrow road. Either the pursuer will miss a place to turn and back up or need to go a long way to another one."

Rusty had manoeuvred perfectly. They were soon speeding back along the track in the opposite direction. If there had been a chasing car, it would have been history. But, of course, Phoenix was a novice driver back then, and he struggled to master it. Phoenix could remember the sequences, but could he get them in the correct order this time?

"What's ahead of us, Athena?"

"One hundred fifty yards, a sharp right-hand bend, a concealed farm road on the right at ninety yards. No more exit roads for a mile."

It was their only chance. Was the van far enough back? How many passengers was it carrying? How could he protect Athena? He pressed the accelerator to the floor. He had no idea how he took that bend; he heard the car's squeals of protest ringing in his ears. Then, finally, his headlights caught the edge of the angled circular mirror on the left that identified the presence of a concealed turning.

Phoenix stood on the brakes and wrenched the wheel to aim the car for an unseen farm road. Instead, the car shot into the entrance to the narrow track. He killed the engine and his lights and then looked in his mirror and saw the van's lights catch the circular mirror opposite. It wasn't slowing. The van shot past the entrance and barrelled along the road towards Bartley.

He leapt out of the car and opened the boot. The gun felt good in his hand despite it being relatively small. At least the first part of that turn had worked okay. Now they had to reverse out of the hedge and follow the van. He jumped back inside, and they set off in pursuit.

"Why are we going this way?" asked Athena.

"It makes more sense to head towards the cavalry as opposed to extending the gap between us," Phoenix replied, "have you heard from them yet?"

"If the van keeps travelling at the same speed as when he passed us, they'll meet head-on in seven or eight minutes,"

"We don't have that long, I'm afraid," said Phoenix grimly. He could already see the van's headlights in the distance. The driver realised they had turned off and turned back.

"Get down," he shouted.

The driver's side window was open.

As the two vehicles drew closer, the driver's right arm appeared from inside the van. Phoenix saw flashes from the muzzle of a gun. He slammed on the brakes, throwing the car into a spin and dived for cover, throwing his body across the cowering Athena. They left the road and ploughed up the verge into bushes on the opposite side of the road.

Phoenix drew the handgun from his waistband and got slowly out of the car. He had the bushes at his back as he stood against the driver's door. Athena was still in the passenger seat; she appeared uninjured but winded. Their car faced back the way they had come, which exposed the passenger side to the gunman.

The windshield on his side had taken two shots to the bullet-resistant glass fitted to vehicles from the Olympus transport section. The glass had broken but hadn't flown apart, the energy absorbed by the layers. Phoenix watched the road ahead and waited.

The van headed back their way.

He stood with his gun in the fighting stance adopted by the special forces. He was square to the target, his feet slightly wider than shoulder-width and his right foot a little behind his support left foot. His knees were bent to absorb the recoil. The shooter needed to realise he wasn't up against an amateur.

The van stopped. All Phoenix could hear was the rhythmic pulse of the van's engine above his breathing. The driver must be alone. No gunmen were piling out of the van to finish them off by the sheer weight of numbers.

The lone would-be assassin was weighing up his

chances. If he identified the nine-millimetre Smith & Wesson at that distance, he knew it only held a maximum of eight rounds. He would understand, too, that his opponent would use every shot sparingly. It was a stand-off.

One minute passed, then two. Each minute felt like an hour. Phoenix controlled his breathing, ready to react to any movement. In the passenger seat, Athena stirred; her phone was ringing. She managed to answer it; the Southampton cell members were thirty seconds away. She whispered the information to Phoenix.

The van suddenly reversed onto the grass verge and drove off towards Cadnam at speed. It was unclear whether the driver heard the ringtone and realised someone was on their way or heard a van approaching. Either way, Phoenix was able to breathe normally again and checked Athena. She was in discomfort but thankfully uninjured.

The Olympus van pulled up beside them. Four armed men in dark clothing jumped out. Their leader approached Phoenix.

"Are you alright, sir?"

"We're fine, don't worry. Get after that bastard."

"He'll be long gone, sir. It would be safer if we escorted you to Salisbury. Giles Burke has dispatched a unit from Bath to pick you up from there. When you're ready, we'll deal with your car."

Athena and Phoenix walked to the van. The team punched in the car windscreen to remove any signs of an armed attack. Its presence halfway into the leafy undergrowth might explain the damage to the front and rear of the car. It could be picked up by the transport section tomorrow.

"A single assassin suggests it was our friend Hermes," muttered Phoenix when he sat in the back of the van.

The Price of Treachery

"We'll handle Hermes in good time," said Athena. "What concerns me is how Hermes knew exactly where we would be today and when? We spoke to no one before we left."

Phoenix rang Larcombe Manor.

"Henry? Institute a total lockdown; nobody must come in or go out. I don't care what time you finish. Then, sweep the entire site for hidden cameras and listening devices."

Chapter Ten

The armoured vehicle from Larcombe Manor picked them up near the cathedral. Two heavily armed agents escorted Phoenix and Athena from the Southampton van. There was no sign of the dark van.

Their driver slowed for the barrier to lift at the gates. The car rattled over the cattle grid into the estate just after midnight, and Henry Case met them at the front door.

"Thank God you're both okay. Lockdown has been effective since you rang at twenty-one fifty hours, Phoenix. Guards are in position. We've cleared over eighty per cent of the buildings for bugs. The sweeps will continue through the night. We started in your apartments. I'm afraid we found several listening devices. Nowhere was safe."

Thank you, Henry," said Athena, keen to lie down. She was exhausted and concerned for the baby.

"Where's Thanatos?" asked Phoenix.

Henry paused as he absorbed the weight of the first words Phoenix had spoken since his arrival. He passed no comment and continued with his report. If he were to receive orders regarding Thanatos, or any other person living at Larcombe, he would carry them out with his trademark professionalism.

"Because of the late hour when you instituted lockdown," he continued, "many people were already in their rooms. We didn't advise them of what had happened. We didn't intend to make enough noise to disturb their beauty sleep. Everyone on the estate will still be here in the morning."

"As soon as you're satisfied the entire site is clean, you can get to sleep, Henry," said Athena. "We'll start on our action plan for a response to this direct attack at six. But, first, take Thanatos to the ice-house for interrogation."

Henry left them to supervise the rest of the sweep. He determined to lead the arrest party later this morning himself.

Athena and Phoenix reached the doors to their apartment.

"I can't bear to think how long Thanatos was able to listen to everything going on behind these doors," said Athena.

"Henry will get the truth from him in time," said Phoenix. "I wonder how long his treachery has been going on? What turned him? These listening devices may have been in place when Erebus was alive."

"I can't believe that," said Athena as she opened the door and steeled herself to walk in. "There's no evidence to suggest Demeter and her companions impacted upon operations before we assumed control here. I thought back over the past months while we drove home. The only logical explanation is that he was more displeased with your promotion than we imagined."

"I consistently said the three Amigos had an axe to grind," said Phoenix.

"I know you did, darling," said Athena, "well, it is what it is. If Thanatos were so bitter, he contacted our enemies and offered his services; he must pay for that lapse in judgement."

"Let's sleep on it," said Phoenix, "you look shattered."

"Today has taken a lot out of me emotionally and physically. I'll see my doctor as soon as possible to check everything's fine. But, as I waited, crouched in the car, wondering if the gunman would start firing again, I could think of nothing but you and this baby. I couldn't bear to lose either of you."

"Athena," said Phoenix grimly, "it *had* to be Hermes in that van. If for one second he thought he could have attacked and killed both of us, he would have. The fact he saw I was armed, and prepared to fight, held him back. Discretion was the better part of valour back there in the New Forest on his part. You went over things in your mind as we travelled home. So did I. Why did he strike this evening? Where were we headed? Unless there were bugs onboard 'Elizabeth' or in the car we drove, he couldn't have known our plans. It was a last-minute decision to visit the scene of Anton Sokolov's mysterious death. It was on a whim we wanted to check how close the Charmbury family home was to the place where they discovered his body."

"So you're saying Hermes was involved in Sokolov's death? I assumed he merely planned to follow us from Lymington back to Bath. Perhaps he might have rammed us somewhere in the Forest to send a message. To try to stop us from attending the meeting on Wednesday. How can you be so sure he wanted to kill us?"

Phoenix listened to Athena's reasoning. However, it was

evident that she still struggled to come to terms with the extent of the treachery that confronted Olympus.

"The stakes are too high for them to be playing games. The attack was to take both of us out of the picture. Our removal would greatly enhance their cause. Wednesday's meeting would rubber-stamp the proposed assassinations in the black book. When we turned off towards Bartley, Hermes realised where we were going and struck as soon as possible. It was no accident that he ran us off the road before we reached Bartley. He was hell-bent on us never getting there. Ask yourself why?"

Athena considered what Phoenix said.

"It implies that he and Nemesis have more things connecting them than a penthouse full of disturbing paintings."

Phoenix smiled.

"By Jove, I think she's got it," he said. "He couldn't risk us finding out how close the abandoned car had been to Lady Primrose's home. That was his first mistake. We managed to avoid being killed by the skin of our teeth. That was his second mistake. It revealed his role in the Russian's death, and we can now add that link to the chain connecting Nemesis to the three family members."

"Let's call it a night," said Athena.

"It's too late for that," said Phoenix. "It's morning, and we need to be awake in only a few hours."

Monday, October 7th, 2013

At six o'clock in the morning, Henry Case and two armed stewards entered Thanatos's rooms in the main building.

There was no sign of Christopher John Rathbone, MM. He hadn't slept in his bed. It appeared he only took a change of clothes and his wash kit. He was travelling light.

"Our mole has gone to ground, Phoenix," said Henry when he contacted his superior.

"He must have received a warning," said Phoenix. "Can we check if he left before nine-fifty last night?"

"Giles is checking," said Henry. "We'll put out an alert for our Olympus cells to warn them of the situation. We want him taken alive and returned to Larcombe for interrogation."

"Okay, Athena and I are in the meeting room. Keep us updated and join us as soon as you can."

I thought I had them. I anticipated Phoenix would protect the car to a degree. I didn't expect the gun. It's not the first thing one would pack for an afternoon on the coast. I won't make that mistake again. Without it, I would have killed both of them.

Mother sent me another message. She scolded me for my failure, like a ten-year-old child who has scuffed the toes on a new pair of shoes. We wanted those two dead before Wednesday. But, unfortunately, it will be impossible to get to them while they're on full alert at Larcombe.

Our man on the inside is on the run. I called him as I watched Phoenix aiming that MP Shield towards me. I couldn't risk his capture. But, he may prove helpful in the future; if he can hold himself together. His past is always only a short distance behind him in his head.

I'm positive my original plan to strike near Lyndhurst would have been successful. It threw me for a while when

The Price of Treachery

they changed direction. Why do people never do what you expect them to do? It makes life so much simpler.

I knew where they were heading, of course. I had to stop Phoenix from talking to Prim's father. The old codger hasn't many brain cells left, but he could have told him how much time she and I spent together that summer.

There has never been anything physical between us; of course, neither can give nor receive affection. Prim's desires were torn away by her seducer and were replaced by a zeal for revenge. Mine never developed. Not surprising when you look at my parents. I admired Prim's tenacity and enthusiasm in pursuit of her goal.

A chance meeting near my underground car park one early spring evening showed us we were near neighbours. She appeared from nowhere and quite startled me. We chatted over trivialities for a few minutes, as one does. I fully expected her to disappear as soon as she came, never to see her again.

On reflection, I believe she was searching for someone. She had been living alone in the heart of the city for twenty years — two decades of festering and plotting. We bumped into one another often after that, and she became less withdrawn. She sensed we were kindred spirits.

Later that spring, she invited me to her house, just a few minutes away. We talked through the night. We shared our secrets. Our relationship evolved; we were never to be friends or lovers. We had become one.

Mother disapproved when she found out we saw one another. She thought I should be mixing with girls of my age. A titled lady twenty years my senior didn't suit her image of a dashing entrepreneurial son. Mother never did understand me.

Prim and I found we had so much in common. She

asked me how far I would go to be a success in business. There were no limits, I told her. She almost clapped her hands in glee. My muse and I talked about books, music, art, and how best to use the wealth at our fingertips.

One evening she showed me a photograph of a handsome professor. Prim then uncovered a painting she had just completed.

It was the same man stabbed to death; it was awe-inspiring. This man was to be her first victim. Prim explained her reasons.

She outlined her plans, and I knew instantly that this was what I had been searching for — an outlet for my frustrations. Not only would there be the pleasure of the act itself, but the memory of it would always be there for me to look at whenever I wished.

We resolved to work together. Prim visited her father near Bartley. I drove to Winchester and called on Anton Sokolov. I succeeded in convincing him I was interested in learning Russian. He didn't sound that keen on tutoring me. I mentioned my younger sister wanted to learn, too, and his interest rose. I suggested we drop in on our parents to arrange details, and we took his car to Bartley.

Thirty minutes later, Prim met us in the lane near her home. She wore a hooded jacket. Sokolov wasn't able to see her face. She slipped into the seat behind him, and I told him to drive deeper into the Forest. He had no idea where our so-called house was or what we intended to do to him. Prim injected him in the neck with something she had concocted. His death had been a long time in the planning.

Prim had waited for this moment for over twenty years. We watched him die. She was disappointed she hadn't been able to make Sokolov suffer more. We buried his body in a quiet spot away from any tracks or pathways. We left his car a distance further on, and she drove me back to Winchester.

We met at her house the following night. She took a knife to the painting of the professor. It wasn't long before she found our next victim. By the time my Mother joined the Olympus Project to amuse her in her leisure time, Prim and I had killed half a dozen rapists who escaped prosecution.

We modified our method to match Prim's vision.

I helped in her basement with the layout and the furnishings.

The paintings were a bonus.

My parents were both now involved with Olympus. Mother persuaded me to contribute to the cause, and after a heated argument, I could add Prim's name to the principal financial backers of the organisation.

Since 2008 we have sat together on the Olympus top table. My parents are still unaware of our secret. Mother imagines I'm sleeping with Prim. My father barely acknowledges our existence and couldn't care less what we were doing.

I carry out Mother's orders when she needs dirty work done. She knows I enjoy killing people. Her requirements are so bland. A shooting, a car crash or yet another murder staged to resemble a suicide. They are so dull, so clichéd. She has no idea how satisfying Prim and I find it when we chat into the early hours in her house. Below us, our latest victim is bleeding to death.

I become aroused during those conversations—Odd, the things that turn people on.

Chris Rathbone was alone and nervous. He had constructed his hide hastily in the dark. Even though it had been years since his SAS days, Chris retained enough knowledge to survive in the wild. He was confident nobody could see him from the nearby road. He knew, too, that he had rested for too long already; his pursuers would be on his trail. It wasn't so easy to cover the ground rapidly and unnoticed at fifty-five years of age. He had needed time to recover.

The call came at around nine forty-five last night when he was in his room watching TV. It had been his handler. He told him to get out while he still could. The assassination attempt failed.

Chris had snatched up the bare essentials and left his room. He took one final look. He knew he was never returning.

He descended the back stairs to the kitchen and the stewards' quarters. From there, he skirted the side of the lawns, keeping an eye on the main building and the stable block. Everything was quiet. He reached the far end of the grassy areas and darted among the trees. He shuddered as he passed the pet cemetery on his left. That was where he would end up if they caught him now. He carried on through the woods until he reached the edge of the estate.

A steady mix of jog and walk across open farmland and country lanes followed until his legs couldn't take him any further. Finally, he arrived at his current location at four o'clock. He lay in a wooded area on the Longleat estate; it was almost nine o'clock.

He snacked on an energy bar and took a sip from his water bottle. It was time to pack up and move. Daylight brought risks, but he couldn't stay here. He felt in his backpack for the reassurance of his Sig Sauer and survival knife.

Items were stored in his bag for weeks for such an emergency.

At Larcombe, his name had been Thanatos – the demon personification of death, rarely seen in person. That was how he lived for years after the regiment had unceremoniously dropped him — hiding away, afraid to be seen outside his house. Every knock on the door brought visions of an IRA assassin sent to kill him for his covert work with FRU during the Troubles. Olympus offered protection, a purpose in life, and he grabbed it with both hands.

He and his colleagues, Alastor and Minos, worked tirelessly for Erebus. Almost from the outset, it was inevitable Athena would assume control at HQ when Erebus retired. He swallowed that bitter pill, hoping she might foul up, so Erebus had to look to him to take on the mantle. He was ready. Alastor was weak, and Minos was too old. A younger man was needed to guide Olympus.

Then Phoenix arrived. A man with a dark past never revealed to them. Erebus had watched his career closely and spotted something in him that Olympus might use. Within months he proved to be an efficient killer. His promotion to the elite group at Larcombe was swift.

Chris Rathbone warmed to him for a while. He injected a lighter note to meetings. The occasional digs at him and his colleagues were harmless enough, even if Alastor took umbrage. As the months and years passed, it became clear that Erebus had grown to admire the newcomer.

The next bombshell came when Athena and Phoenix got together. Her traumatic experiences in 2005 had made him believe she would be single forever. Look at things now. She was expecting their baby. They kept it secret from everyone for weeks, but Chris knew. He heard everything. When Erebus announced he was retiring and Athena and

Phoenix were to assume control, it crushed him. Yet another slap in the face.

He couldn't sit back and do nothing, not this time. Erebus initiated Olympus through an entry in the personal column of The Times almost a decade ago. Chris entered his plea weeks after Erebus flew to Ibiza.

The man who was to be his handler contacted him within twenty-four hours. They had never met in person. He asked Chris to install listening devices in the couple's apartment and report what he heard.

Money wasn't the motivator. Chris Rathbone had enough money to last; it was the power he craved. When the people represented by his handler assumed control of Olympus and eliminated both Athena and Phoenix, he would take charge at Larcombe Manor. That was his right; that was his reward.

Chris Rathbone collected his belongings and set off towards his final destination.

Honey B relaxed in her hotel room. She had one more performance left, then, tonight at the Theatre Royal, Nottingham, her brief UK tour ended. After that, she would return to the hotel to while away the hours until the meeting on Wednesday.

Her son had called with the news last night. He missed an excellent opportunity to get rid of their main adversaries. She knew she could count on him in normal circumstances. He had never failed her, but Phoenix proved a more than worthy opponent. He may have escaped last night, but it was only a matter of time. She would prevail in the end.

There was a knock at the door. Honey B lay back against the pillows and adjusted her dressing gown. She knew it showed more than was decent for a woman her age, but her visitor intrigued her. She wondered whether an older man might prove more adept than the young man she had been living with lately. Her latest flame had become tiresome.

She called out for her visitor to enter.

Her Orion, former DS Phil Hounsell, CEO of Hounsell Security Services, was the man she had been using for this tour. She used him not just for her security but for information on her enemies. Mainly information on Phoenix and who he was, and where he used to live.

"Good morning, ma'am," said Phil, keeping things on a formal footing. He was aware of Honey B's tempting pose. He stared at the photograph above her bed as he took her through the routine they planned to follow later.

"We'll collect you at four-thirty this afternoon, then transfer you to the theatre to meet the local press. Four loyal fans have asked to have their photo taken with you. You then donate a cheque to a local representative from the animal charity you support. We'll be on standby while you run through your soundcheck; then, we'll have you back here at six o'clock. Wayne will collect you at eight to deliver you to the stage door. I've checked your dressing room. Everything will be to your satisfaction."

"You're so commanding, Orion," whispered Honey B. "Can't I persuade you to stop calling me, ma'am?"

"My wife would get suspicious if I started calling you Honey, ma'am," said Phil. "Perhaps I should learn your real name?"

Philomena Alexander roared with laughter.

"I think we've established over the weeks that I ask the questions. Call me B if it makes you more comfortable."

She sat up and patted the bed.

"Come and sit here. Don't be shy. This B doesn't sting. Tell me again what I have to do today."

Phil walked over to the bed. He sat just out of Honey B's reach.

"You're no fun, Orion," she tutted.

"You're my boss," Phil replied. "I've liked working for you these past few weeks. So much more enjoyable than my last few years with the police. But, to continue this business relationship, we should try to stay professional. No matter how hard that might be."

"Ah, your heart is melting, Orion," simpered Honey B. "I believe there's hope for me yet."

Believe what you want, thought Phil. The things a bloke has to do to keep their boss happy. He wasn't falling for Honey B and her wiles; he had seen those smiles that never reached her eyes. He had felt her ice-cold hand on his arm and her breath on his cheek. Her kiss stung like frostbite.

Honey B was a generous employer, but Phil never wanted to get on the wrong side of her. He imagined she would be deadly.

Chapter Eleven

Phil Hounsell patrolled backstage at the Theatre Royal. Honey B sat in her dressing room. He spotted Wayne, Dusty and Leggo gathered in a corner, chatting with a group of stagehands. His crew was winding down towards their last gig with Honey B.

Wayne and the lads were returning to Bath to the HSS office. They were going to follow up on valuable contacts the singer had provided. He was remaining with her in an as yet unspecified security role. The money she promised was silly money. No one in their right mind would refuse it.

Phil grinned to himself at the shenanigans in the hotel earlier today. Honey B had thought it would be easy to seduce him. He hoped he had sidestepped her gently. She wasn't one to give up easily, though. After he repeated her itinerary for the day, sitting on her bed, he got up and walked towards the door.

He heard the bathroom door slam. He thought he had blown it; he would surely get fired. He turned back as he reached the door. Honey B hadn't gone into the bathroom.

Instead, she got out of bed and shut the door to attract his attention. As she stepped into the shower, she removed her gown to give him a glimpse of her naked body.

"I just wanted to show you what you were missing," she purred.

Phil thought, 'You got what you paid for, Honey B; those cosmetic surgeons can work miracles. I still prefer my Erica, though. Thank you all the same.'

He asked Dusty to collect their client for the soundcheck and social engagements this afternoon. Dusty told him Honey B never said a word on the way over and back.

"Saving her voice, I guess," he added. Phil had smiled.

There was a good crowd in for this final night of the tour. Honey B emerged from her dressing room when the stage manager called her. Her two-hour concert flew by. As usual, Phil listened to his favourite songs as he watched her from the wings. He listened.

There it was again. A change in the lyrics, different once more from last night. Just what does she think she's doing? Is it deliberate? The final curtain call ended. Honey B headed for her dressing room. Phil knew he would have to put in an appearance.

He found Wayne and told him to get ready to ferry the singer back to her luxury hotel at a moment's notice. Phil walked back to see what she wanted to do tonight. He hoped it wasn't going to be a late night. He tapped on the door.

"I'm busy; go away," called Honey B.

"It's me, Orion," Phil said, hoping her pet name for him would humour her.

"I know. I have company. Come and collect me in five minutes."

Phil called Wayne and passed on the news. Wayne soon

The Price of Treachery

had the limousine ticking over by the stage door, waiting. Phil hoped they could soon get off home to Bath, and he would sleep in his bed with Erica again. But he couldn't wait to see the kids in the morning.

Five minutes passed; Phil wandered across to the dressing room. A young man was leaving. He looked familiar. Had he seen him on TV? He didn't even look towards Phil. Instead, he rushed along the corridor and disappeared from the theatre by the stage door.

Honey B swept out of the dressing room a minute later. Phil held the door open for her, and she darted inside the limousine and drove away in seconds. Not a word passed between them.

Phil went in search of his other two lads. They stood outside, having a smoke.

"As soon as Wayne returns, we'll drive back to Bath, boys. Have a lie-in tomorrow."

"Thanks, boss," said Jake Legg. "No champagne tonight, then?"

"No, thank goodness. A cup of hot chocolate when I get home will have to do for tonight. Our taste of the good life is over for now."

"It was a good crack, though. Especially for our first job," said Dusty.

"You've helped HSS gain a good reputation as a reliable security firm. That goes a long way, especially when you add in a personal recommendation by someone as hard to please as Honey B. There will be plenty more gigs after this one, I reckon."

"You won't be around so often, though, boss. Is that what Wayne said?" asked Jake.

"I don't know how long it will last, but Honey B wants me to help her find someone."

"A missing person type of job, you mean?" asked Dusty.

"Something like that," said Phil with a smile.

Wednesday, October 9th, 2013

A van left Larcombe a few minutes after eight o'clock in the morning. There were armed agents on board. Rusty Scott was at the wheel. Phoenix and Athena were safely seated inside and *en route* to Nottingham.

Three hours later, they arrived at their destination. Rusty and his squad were to wait outside the building. Phoenix wore a concealed microphone in case of an emergency. Athena had persuaded him they should not attend a meeting with Zeus and the others expecting a gun battle. So neither of them was armed.

"Why did we need to use this venue? I thought the Curzon Street place was the most central location for the twelve of us?" asked Phoenix as they headed for the lifts.

"This apartment is tailor-made for a group of our size. We've used it before, once or twice. I believe Demeter asked Zeus if it could be booked on this occasion to fit in with her work schedule."

Phoenix was already on the alert. To hear that Demeter had influenced the choice of venue made him even edgier. When they reached the venue, they discovered the set-up was highly professional. Phoenix and Athena entered to find a similar traditional boardroom layout to the one they used in London.

Twelve comfortable chairs were in place around a large circular table.

The Price of Treachery

"We'll be able to look our enemies in the eye this time, Athena," said Phoenix, checking the name cards.

The table held the facilities Phoenix anticipated. Yet again, there was a complete lack of any equipment. They were not the first to arrive.

Apollo, Aphrodite, and Dionysus were already chatting over coffee by a side table. Phoenix walked over to get a cup for himself; Athena stuck to a glass of water. She poured it from one of the carafes on the main table and joined the others.

"Hello again," she said. "I hope you are well. We're looking forward to an interesting meeting today."

The replies were much expected from these three; they were Olympians, after all. There were no hidden agendas. What you saw was what you got.

One by one, their colleagues joined them. Heracles bustled into the room. He had flown into the City airport and been brought here by taxi. After greeting everyone, he said: -

"When my cab pulled up outside, I thought I saw an Olympus van parked to the side of the building. That's rather unusual. Is there something I should know?"

The other three had been inside the building when Rusty dropped off Phoenix and Athena. They shook their heads. Phoenix looked to his partner for a lead.

"We had a transport problem at the last minute," she replied, "there were no other cars available at short notice."

The conversation stalled; the six leaders took their seats and awaited the rest of their party. Phoenix watched the door intently to see who arrived with whom.

Zeus arrived with his wife, Hera. They, too, collected refreshments before sitting. Hera sat directly opposite her husband. Phoenix and Athena were side by side to her right. To her left were placed Aphrodite and Apollo. Heracles joined Zeus on the opposite side and took the chair two places to their leader's right.

Poseidon arrived next. His demeanour was unchanged from that afternoon in Curzon Street. Phoenix watched him as he strolled behind Zeus and sat beside him.

The final two pairs arrived seconds apart. Phoenix imagined this was deliberate; it was clear that Demeter and Nemesis were uncomfortable companions. The pop singer went directly to Zeus and kissed him on the cheek, and then she flopped onto the chair beside him. Phoenix allowed himself a brief smile. Zeus was a rose between two thorns.

Hermes walked in with Dionysus, chatting to the former civil servant as if they were bosom pals. However, Sir Malcolm Dunseith's expression told a different story. Hermes sat next to his mother. Dionysus seemed happy to be taking the final seat next to Phoenix. He turned his body very slightly to catch his neighbour's eye. He didn't want to engage in further chit-chat with Dominic Perkins.

"Hello, Dionysus," said Phoenix, "good to see you again." Dionysus nodded.

"Time to get our meeting underway, ladies and gentlemen," said Zeus.

The following two hours passed quickly, with reports of facts and figures concerning the operations with which Olympus was involved. Phoenix was punch-drunk. Zeus ticked off the items on his list with military precision.

"Donations continue to flow into our accounts," said Zeus. "We have sufficient funds to cope with the rise in criminal and terrorist activity we have experienced worldwide. More of that later. Let's break for refreshments."

"So far, so good," said Athena as she and Phoenix waited for the rush for refreshments to ease. They stood by the main table and watched the Titans. It was fascinating to see them today, knowing their relationships and something of their connection. It was so much easier to interpret things once you know.

Zeus and Hera each slipped into the role of host with practised ease. Poseidon hovered close to Zeus but said little. His ice-blue eyes darted from side to side. He didn't miss a word, a glance or a gesture. Hermes and Nemesis kept as far away from one another as possible in the relatively small apartment. They mingled with other leaders. Phoenix lost count of the number of times their eyes met as they searched each other out across the room. Where was Demeter?

Athena grabbed Phoenix's sleeve.

"She's slipped outside, Phoenix," she whispered. "I need the Ladies, so I'll check what she's doing."

Phoenix watched her go, then walked over to the side table. As he collected a plate full of items from the buffet, he heard a familiar voice. It was Hermes.

"Will you be staying in Nottingham? Maybe we can meet up for that night out in town we couldn't arrange in London."

"We'll be returning to Larcombe straight after the meeting," said Phoenix.

"Ah, I suppose Athena has to take things easy these days. I should offer my congratulations."

Phoenix knew very well that Athena hadn't told any of the leaders of her pregnancy. So if they needed proof of who Thanatos had betrayed them to, there it was.

"There are enough able-bodied men at Larcombe to make sure she comes to no harm," said Phoenix.

Hermes gave him a disdainful smile and moved on to chat with someone else.

Athena returned to stand beside Phoenix. She grabbed one of his sandwiches.

"She's outside in the corridor chatting on her mobile phone to someone she called Orion," she whispered.

"Orion? Is he one of ours, someone I've never heard of?" asked Phoenix.

"No," said Athena. "I couldn't hear much of what she said, not without making it obvious that I was eavesdropping. She had her back to me when she mentioned; I've seen your old friend. I bet you wish you were here. Who do you think she meant? Could it be one of the others, or you, perhaps? If so, to whom do you think she could have been talking?"

Phoenix had an idea who it was. It wasn't something he wanted to consider. Zeus and Hera circled the others, guiding them back towards the table. The break was over; they had to discuss the rise of new terrorist threats. They reached the final item on the list an hour later. It was Yewtree.

Zeus expertly steered them through the minefield that investigated historic sexual abuse allegations, predominantly the abuse of children. The efforts of the police had identified hundreds of potential victims.

Olympus believed there were still dozens of predatory sex offenders who had slipped through the net. They had compiled a list of MPs and celebrities that warranted direct action. A few of these abusers would get protection from the consequence of criminal activity by friends in high places. These so-called friends' names went on the list.

"The guilty must pay for their crimes," he concluded.

"We need your agreement to sanction these direct actions," said Poseidon, suddenly addressing the room. "We are keen to take action."

The Price of Treachery

Zeus turned towards Poseidon. As chairman, he always organised any votes that were needed. He was aware there were now many more names in the 'black book' and the scope of the action far more extensive than those connected to the Yewtree scandal. The other leaders needed to be aware of that to consider their opinion.

Demeter joined in from his left-hand side.

"You are aware of the worst offenders Olympus tagged for punitive action. At our last meeting in Curzon Street, one of our members referred to it as the little black book. I don't think anyone here can object to that going ahead, can you?"

Zeus started to protest, but Poseidon insisted.

"Are there any objections to us going ahead?"

Phoenix and Athena raised a hand. Aphrodite joined them.

"It's so final. How many will you be eliminating?" Aphrodite said. "How can we be sure that the authorities won't identify Olympus as their executioner?"

"We are experts in what we do," said Hermes, glancing at Nemesis, "we will take every precaution not to leave any clues. The numbers are unimportant. We have to remember their victims. As Zeus said, the guilty must pay for their crimes."

Nobody else felt strongly enough to object. Zeus relented. He stood and announced: -

"The direct action against the names on the list is duly sanctioned."

Poseidon looked at the three leaders who had opposed him.

"If you don't have the stomach for the fight, perhaps you should consider your positions."

"Don't make the mistake of underestimating me, Poseidon," said Athena. "When we have to make tough decisions, I can make them."

Phoenix wondered why Athena hadn't told Zeus and the other Olympians of the scheming behind the scenes carried out by the Titans. No doubt she had her reasons. He merely added: -

"The best way to make the right decision when confronted with a tough situation is to have all the facts available, Poseidon, wouldn't you agree?"

Poseidon gave Phoenix a cold stare but passed no comment.

Zeus was keen to bring the meeting to a close. He could see Hera getting agitated. She hated it when the leaders argued. She preferred everything to remain on an even keel.

"We will meet in London three months from today," he said. "Good afternoon, everyone and have a safe journey home."

"Amen to that," said Phoenix.

Aphrodite and Hera said their goodbyes. The Duchess then came over to Phoenix and Athena.

"I was concerned at the haste with which we dealt with that last item. Why did Zeus allow Poseidon to railroad him? Poseidon is generally so quiet. We were the only people to stand up to him."

"We have our concerns too, Aphrodite," said Athena, "the black book is fast becoming a series. The likes of Poseidon, Demeter, and others are adding names that were never the subject of a Yewtree investigation."

"Why haven't we been told this?" asked Aphrodite.

The room had thinned out considerably; only Apollo and Dionysus remained. They gathered around them.

"Did you have concerns?" asked Dionysus, "we thought we were clear to proceed. We were all shown the scope of the operation during our meeting at Curzon Street."

Phoenix knew Athena couldn't show their hand just yet. They might believe they knew who they were facing. Proving to the other leaders that four of their number were plotting to take the organisation on a different path would not be easy.

The majority of the leaders were still faithful to the Olympus cause. They might decide that eight votes in a fair fight would always win the day; it was business as usual. After that, the four dissenting, more strident voices could come into line.

"Everything is not as it appears, Dionysus," said Athena.

"It never is, Athena," said Apollo.

"Do you have news of your own, Athena," asked Aphrodite. "I can often sense things, you know."

Athena sighed.

"I'm expecting a baby in January. I didn't think it showed in this outfit."

"How wonderful," the Duchess said with a sad look. "I often wish we had had more than just one child."

"Congratulations," said Apollo and Dionysus. The five remaining leaders left the apartment together. They travelled to the ground floor in the lift. Rusty was standing inside the foyer waiting.

"All clear, Phoenix," he said.

The others went off to their cars. Rusty led Phoenix and Athena to the van. Once safely inside, they drove back to Larcombe.

"An uneventful trip," said Phoenix when they were back in their rooms, "if not an uneventful meeting. We'll have to watch for the first strikes on the black book targets."

"We need to get Giles to start hacking into phones and

computers belonging to the Titans," said Athena. "We must know more about what they're planning. They're poised to take action against Olympus as well as her targets. So we must protect ourselves, Zeus and the others, and the innocent people they've added to their hit list."

"No time like the present," said Phoenix. "Artemis has met me face-to-face; it should be alright for me to revisit the ice-house. I'll talk to Giles tonight. We must not delay. I want to hear where we are with tracking Thanatos."

Phoenix walked across to the nerve centre of the intelligence section. He took the lift to the first level and sought out Giles Burke. Artemis was on duty at a terminal on the far side of the room. She looked up and acknowledged his presence.

"Giles, what have you got for us? Any news on Thanatos?"

"Your timing is uncanny, Phoenix," he replied, "one of my lads found him on CCTV footage. So we know where he was twelve hours ago. Where he headed after that, who knows?"

"Show me?" said Phoenix, sitting beside the chief intelligence agent.

"This was our man at nine a.m. this morning. He had just left a convenience store on a garage forecourt near Tidworth. As you can tell, he's carrying a backpack. Look at this image. When he lifts it to slip his left arm through the strap."

"It's heavy," nodded Phoenix, "when we checked his room, it appeared he left in a hurry and took very little. So what has he got now, and where did he get it? A handful of chocolate bars wouldn't create that bulk."

Artemis joined them.

"I may have discovered something. Thanatos was ex-

SAS when he arrived here to join Olympus. He left school at sixteen and joined the regular army in 1974. Several years before, he underwent the rigid selection process to join the elite regiment. He was a young soldier at Bulford Camp on Salisbury Plain for three months. He had received training at the School of Ammunition at Kineton, Warwickshire."

"Training in what?" asked Phoenix.

"Everything a boy should know about explosives," said Giles.

"Exactly," said Artemis.

"Good work," said Phoenix, "so we think Thanatos made his way from Larcombe to Salisbury Plain. How did he get hold of any explosives? Or does the Army have a one-stop-shop for would-be terrorists these days? We had better start checking. There will be traffic between the Plain and the MoD reporting any shortages. Find it. We need to know what he took. Our next task is to work out where he was heading after he left Tidworth. An educated guess, you two?"

"London," said Giles.

"Given what you know of him, would he be acting alone?" asked Artemis.

Phoenix considered their comments. London was his favourite. The Titans' initial targets in the black book would be individual strikes. The methods might vary. None would include massive explosions that were far too theatrical. They didn't want to raise suspicions around Olympus. They might be planning to take control; they certainly didn't want to risk losing access to the funds Olympus offered.

No, this was an event intended to follow the removal of their opposition within Olympus. An event that was so big it rocked the country's foundations to the core.

Chapter Twelve

Thursday, October 10th, 2013

Chris Rathbone knew he would create headlines that allowed the Titans to grasp control. A blast that left a vacuum in the corridors of power they could attribute to any one of the extreme terrorist groups out there. With the democratic government crippled, the Titans would surface and step into the breach. They would establish a plutocracy.

Of course, there would be temporary resistance, but the former Olympus agents would soon fall in line to help the armed forces bring order and control. There may be dissenters among them, but the vast majority were mercenaries. They'll work for the highest bidder.

Chris Rathbone was on the outskirts of London. He travelled at night exclusively now. His handler had a safe house for him in Knightsbridge. 'I'll stay there until the next two phases of the coup are complete', he thought. 'Tonight, I'll be indoors in the warm instead of lying in a hide on this damp grass'.

The Price of Treachery

In the ice-house, Giles, Artemis, and the other members of the intelligence section were analysing data collected from the four Titans. Poseidon's activity by phone or email was negligible. His home had been under surveillance since Phoenix returned from Nottingham. There was no sign he used handwritten letters to communicate with his colleagues.

Hermes was a different kettle of fish. As CEO of a mobile phone giant, his activity was immense. It would take a long time to sift through the grains of sand to find the nuggets of gold.

"I'm noticing a trend here, Artemis," said Giles, "there's irregular and limited communication between Hermes and Demeter. Neither of them communicates directly with Poseidon. As for Nemesis, she's a recluse, so maybe it's no surprise she doesn't have a large digital footprint."

"Let's look at this another way, Giles," said Artemis, "we can eliminate eighty per cent of this paper trail if we stick to the personal calls he receives. His business line is unlikely to be used for the darker dealings in which he's involved. Now let's see where these personal calls are originating. There are a few repeat calls. OK, looking at that number, that's Demeter's phone. We can read what she was saying later. In the past month, there have been several one-off calls. Our system tells us they came from right across the UK. We need to list the locations in date to see if it might tell us something."

"Good thinking; have you done something like this before in your police work?"

"Funnily enough, Giles, yes I have," said Artemis. "It was over three years ago. A series of murders coincided with the visit of a Canadian tribute band to several northern cities."

"Did you catch the killer?" asked Giles.

"Sadly, no, I don't think I ever will now," replied Artemis. "Well, what do you know?"

"Have you spotted a link already?"

"This GPS data from the system pins the location tighter than just to a town or city. Each call I've highlighted came from inside or near a major theatre. It's that concert tour once more. These are messages to Hermes from people who went to a concert that night. Honey B, his mother, has just finished her UK tour. Why would these people be contacting Hermes during or after a show?"

Giles read the first text message sent from Belfast.

"It doesn't make sense. It rhymes, I suppose. What could it mean?"

"It's not poetry; might it be song lyrics?" said Artemis.

Giles scanned the subsequent few messages from different nights and different venues.

"They're all from the same song, by the looks of it. But the words keep changing slightly."

"We'll have to Google her hits."

It didn't take long to find the song in question. Then Giles struggled with the variations and tried to make sense of what he was reading. Finally, Artemis listed the callers' names and found they were employees of the mobile phone company run by Hermes.

"Very clever," said Giles, "they communicate by messages hidden in these lyrics. For example, Hermes gets employees from outlets around the UK to attend his mother's concerts. He probably pays for their tickets or slips them a bonus. They won't ask why their boss wants to know. Instead, they send him the lyrics his mother uses that night in her third number-one hit. At first glance, she has minimal contact with her son, yet she can pass on news or instructions in secret at will."

"We need to break the code quickly," said Artemis. "What she told him or asked him to do for her a few weeks ago is irrelevant now. Future messages will give us a head start on countering whatever action she has planned."

Giles asked one of the agents to check transcripts of messages between Demeter and Hermes from her mobile. He warned him they might be cryptic or coded. Giles left the agent to it while he returned to work with Artemis on decoding the song lyrics.

As someone once said, it was going to be a hard day's night.

Friday, October 11th, 2013

Hermes and Nemesis had completed their first task. They sat in her sitting room, drinking tea. In the basement lay the body of Arthur Harman, seventy-two, former Worcestershire care home manager. The police had investigated allegations in 1996 that Harman was responsible for abuse at children's homes he had run in Worcester throughout the 1980s.

Victims came forward to give evidence against him. Harman consistently denied any wrongdoing. He insisted his accusers were unreliable witnesses. They had spent their whole lives in institutions. Fantasising about their lives was a standard method of escaping the harsh reality of their existence. But, over the years, the line between fantasy and fact blurred.

After a year-long investigation, the CPS decided not to

press charges. They saw no realistic chance of a successful prosecution. By 2010, Arthur Harman moved on from children's homes to care for the elderly. Rumours started circulating almost immediately. The police were slow to respond.

A newspaper reporter dug around and discovered that since 1997 when they dropped the original case, five former residents of the children's homes Harman managed had committed suicide. Naturally, this raised concerns at Olympus, and Arthur Harman was one of the first names on the list.

"He was a big man, wasn't he?" said Hermes. "A twelve-pinter, do you reckon?"

"It's unlikely," said Nemesis, stroking one of her cats, "my guess is ten and a half."

"You're the expert," said Hermes. "Do you have many ideas for your next batch of paintings? I'm looking for something to go on the walls of my office."

"I'm hoping to sell three or four at auction next week. Look through those first and choose whichever ones you prefer. I can tell you the sitter's name."

"We have several individuals to eliminate over the next few weeks. So you are going to be busy with that brush."

"Who's next?" asked Nemesis.

"The comedian Lenny James; his routines are rather crude. Too blue for TV these days. He's always telling the press he was conceived the night of the Queen's coronation as if that's a cause for celebration. He is fifty-nine. As old as most of his material. His best days were between 1979-1986. That was when his preference for teenage female fans was able to be given full rein. He got questioned and released on half a dozen occasions in the past three years. It's believed there could have been as many as forty victims, but only two have come forward. It was the same story as

The Price of Treachery

with Harman. Everyone knew he was guilty, but nobody dared run the risk of a jury siding with a face they had known and loved for years. The two women involved have been working girls since they met James. His lawyer said they were heroin addicts with nothing to look forward to but a slow, painful death. They hoped to earn a big payday by selling a sordid pack of lies to a red-top daily newspaper. Lenny James will eventually get a letter saying no further action will be taken, and another one will slip through the net."

"When do we do it?" asked Nemesis.

"Are you busy tonight?" asked Hermes, checking his diary.

"Not as far as I'm aware," said Nemesis. "I'll meet you outside the tunnel at ten o'clock."

Hermes finished his cup of tea.

"Until tonight, then," said Hermes, standing up from his chair.

"I'll come with you. But, first, I need to check on Arthur."

Nemesis watched Hermes disappear through the door leading to the courtyard next to his underground car park. How thoughtful of the early Victorians to install these below-stairs access tunnels for their workers.

Very few mews house owners knew of their existence. Those that discovered them had them sealed; or found they were too dangerous to use. Hers was in immaculate order. She made sure of that.

She turned her attention to her guest.

"Come now, Arthur, don't keep a lady waiting. I feel the urge to paint something this weekend."

At Larcombe Manor, Phoenix and Athena reviewed progress from the ice-house. The morning meeting had finished several hours ago.

Alastor and Minos were quiet. Ever since they discovered the extent of Thanatos's betrayal, they had questioned themselves.

"Why didn't we spot something, Athena," said Minos when she told them the morning after he escaped.

"He was always uncomfortable with how things were after Erebus left," said Alastor. "But he gave no clue he would do something so drastic."

"We worked here side by side for years, and yet, we never suspected he could turn out to be a traitor," said Minos, shaking his head.

"We've intercepted the message from the Plain reporting the loss of six M112 blocks of C-4. Along with various wires, a timer, and the paraphernalia a bomb-maker needs. What on earth does our ex-colleague have planned?" said Alastor.

Athena tried to reassure them. She stressed that the past was the past; it was the future that mattered. Over the coming weeks, she needed their help and support to combat the evils the Titans planned to unleash on an unsuspecting nation.

Although they had been quieter this morning than she wished, they grasped the importance of the work going on in the underground nerve centre. Giles had managed to decode the messages with the help of Artemis.

"It was to do with the substitutions, of course," Giles reported. "As soon as we isolated the words that differed from the original lyrics, we had a new phrase. So in each message, Honey B embedded a phrase of between five and nine words."

"Simple then," Phoenix said, "so what were the phrases?"

"Ah, but that was only the start, Phoenix," said Giles, with a grin, "the new phrase was a cryptic clue. Similar to the ones you receive from Zeus when he passes you a venue and an agenda, Athena. We then had to solve the clue before we could understand what she was telling Hermes; or what she wanted him to do."

"Does this mean we can intercept and interpret future messages from Demeter to Hermes?" asked Minos.

"It does, her UK tour is now over, but we have unscrambled the text messages she sent to Hermes from her mobile. These were straightforward cryptic messages. Provided that method of communication continues, then we will know what their plans are."

"Were any of the messages telling us anything we didn't already know," asked Alastor.

"Not really," said Giles. "An early one coincided with when Hermes arrived back in the UK from Ibiza. Others connected to intelligence that Thanatos passed to Hermes. She sent a kill message to Hermes the night you met him on the road home from Lymington."

"Has there been any communication between them since the meeting?" asked Athena.

"Nothing yet," said Giles. "She has talked with a security firm CEO on three occasions. We understand he was in charge of security on her recent tour. HSS is based here in Bath. They started operating recently, and their CEO is an ex-Detective Superintendent. His name is…."

"Hounsell," muttered Phoenix, "aka Orion, the hunter."

"That's him alright," said Giles, impressed, "how did you know?"

"I bumped into him at Glastonbury," said Phoenix, "we'd lost touch three years ago. I always knew he'd turn up in my life one day. He and Artemis used to work together."

"Is that going to be a problem?" asked Alastor.

"Not in the slightest," said Rusty. "She doesn't recognise Phoenix as the man she hunted for back then. From what she's told me, her ex-boss believes he is dead."

"We had better keep an eye on this Hounsell, or Orion as Demeter likes to call him," said Athena.

After the meeting ended and the others returned to work, Phoenix and Athena started planning how best to tackle the threats facing them. First, Athena read a report from Henry Case.

"We have surveillance outside of each of the four Titans' properties. Poseidon spent most of yesterday indoors before walking to a nearby Elmbridge restaurant for lunch. In the evening, he took a cab to the West End. He returned around midnight alone."

Phoenix looked at the report on Demeter.

"Since she returned from Nottingham, she has been staying at the Chelsea Harbour Hotel; it seems to be her regular pad when she's in London. The Honey B website says she's off to the Caribbean on a cruise ship in December for a tour lasting until the end of February. She hasn't contacted Poseidon, Hermes or Nemesis since Wednesday. Unless there's another method of communication that we haven't uncovered yet."

"What do we have on Nemesis?" asked Athena.

"Nothing," said Phoenix. "Agents have stood at the end of the lane by her mews house for a day and a half. There have been no visitors, and she hasn't left the place since returning to London from Nottingham. No wonder they say she's a recluse."

"We're missing something," said Athena. "Hermes was in his office yesterday. He had a late start today, which is not unusual. We both imagined there would be action straight after the meeting, yet they appear to have gone to ground."

"We haven't any further sightings of Thanatos either," said Phoenix. "If he's in London, then where would he be headed? We're watching the properties we reckon are involved, and he hasn't turned up there. You're right. We're missing something here."

"Poseidon was adamant we had to sanction the removal of names from the black book on Wednesday," said Athena. "Have any of the targets gone missing?"

"I'll get Giles to check for missing persons or suspicious deaths, although it could be a waste of time. We know they added other names after Curzon Street. We never got to see them. Demeter and the others didn't want us to know who they were going after among those key personnel who would galvanise opposition to their projected coup."

Phoenix called Giles Burke in the ice-house. A few minutes later, Giles rang back.

"A care home manager from the Midlands has been missing for twenty-four hours; Arthur Harman was suspected of abuse at children's homes in the past but never charged. He lived alone. The staff at the care home said he had been under a lot of stress lately. There are no reports of suspicious deaths with connections to cases of historical abuse or other criminal activity. Sorry."

"OK, Giles, thanks," said Phoenix, "keep us posted."

Everyone at Larcombe was waiting. It was the calm before the storm. Phoenix was uncomfortable with that scenario. He knew the storm would be upon them before they could prevent it unless they worked smarter rather than harder. So many innocent lives would be at risk if that happened.

Chris Rathbone arrived in London in the early hours of Friday. He made his way to a street near the mews house. Chris stood and watched; he spotted the surveillance operative in seconds. He was too experienced to miss him. Chris backed away and found a shop doorway to shelter in until dawn. His handler wouldn't appreciate his beauty sleep being interrupted.

A quick call at six o'clock resulted in him meeting his handler for the first time, but not face to face. Instead, they met on the tube station platform close to Harrods at nine. He stood by the platform edge as instructed; his handler arrived behind him two minutes later.

"Don't turn around. Just listen. Make yourself scarce today; find a hostel for tonight. Text me the address. We'll collect you before dawn. You'll be inside the house in minutes with no one being the wiser."

With that, Hermes left.

Chris Rathbone disappeared into the crowds, just another anonymous speck on the capital's streets. Time was on his side. His role in this coup was still two weeks away. The failed assassinations in the New Forest resulted in him being out in the open earlier than planned. His handler and the other people involved in this operation were more than capable of coping with any slight hiccup. Chris understood the game of risk and reward.

Why fret over another day of keeping out of sight of any Olympus agents hunting him? It was only a little added risk compared to a successful outcome's massive rewards.

The Price of Treachery

Artemis was hunting. She was aware of the lack of contact between the four people they were tracking. She knew Thanatos was still on the run. They had searched everywhere for him without a sighting.

When she mentioned how frustrating it was not to make progress earlier that evening, Rusty had explained to her: -

"He was trained at the same place as me. He knows how to avoid being seen. We were lucky to get a glimpse of him at Tidworth. That was probably due to tiredness. He wouldn't have slept until he got well away from here."

"You know Phil Hounsell is working for the singer Honey B?" she asked.

"We do," Rusty replied, "we don't believe he's directly involved in any of this. He's in security these days. How do you feel about it?"

Artemis sat at her computer now and wondered what she felt. She had told Rusty she was okay with things. Her commitment was to him and Olympus. Her former police colleague would only be a concern if he threatened that commitment by joining the Titans.

She was thinking of the relevance of his nickname, Orion, that Honey B used in the phone calls between them. He had been a mythical hunter, too, hadn't he? So who was he hunting for on the orders of Honey B?

She scolded herself for daydreaming. She had almost missed something. She looked into the history of the properties on the lane where Lady Primrose lived. The mews houses were tiny, low-level terraced cottages initially built for use as stables, built behind a much grander property to which the stables belonged.

They had a gardenless front. Many had no windows at the sides or rear. Wealthy Georgians and Victorians had built small service streets behind their grand villas and constructed stabling for their horses and carriages, with rooms above to house grooms and servants. Most had been converted for residential use, either incorporating the stable into the house or using it as a garage.

Artemis hurriedly searched for a detailed street map. She soon found the cobbled lane. What lay behind it? There was no indication of a garage. What happened to the stables on the lower level? If Lady Primrose was an artist, she needed daylight. The first floor would be where she would have her studio and a bedroom and bathroom. Her ground floor living accommodation was small but manageable, living alone. What lay beneath?

She studied the buildings and spaces behind the row of terraced houses. It all seemed so vague. There were several buildings between the houses and the next open area. Henry needed to send an agent to check them out. Were they lock-up garages, storage facilities, or units occupied by small businesses? Was it possible there was a rear entrance to any of the houses in Lady Primrose's lane?

Artemis alerted Giles Burke to her discovery. He rang Henry Case, and he made the call. The agent watching the front of the property, made his way along the main street to find the hidden courtyard shown on the map. Unfortunately, there were no street signs to help him.

A narrow street, just wide enough for the single horse and carriage it originally accommodated, threaded its way between two grand three-storey townhouses. He found himself in a haven of solitude yards from the hustle and bustle of Knightsbridge. To his right, there was indeed a row of lock-ups. To his left was the entrance to a more modern underground car park. Everything was quiet.

The agent wandered along the front of the lock-ups. They were primarily garages; others had business signs on the windows for shoe repairs and light engineering work. He walked past a doorway, set back from the fronts of the lock-ups. He turned back.

Why would there be a door here? Where did it lead? He returned to his post at the end of the lane and contacted Larcombe to report what he had found.

Chapter Thirteen

Saturday, October 12th, 2013

Phoenix and Athena were back in the meeting room for an emergency session. The news from London overnight had opened new lines of enquiry. Giles, Henry, and Rusty had joined them already; Minos and Alastor were on their way.

"I take it we're watching both the front and the rear of the mews house now, Henry?" asked Athena.

"That would prove tricky, Athena. The courtyard is too small and exposed to allow an agent to carry out covert surveillance. We have someone on the street opposite the narrow entrance. We can only watch any comings and goings. What happens inside will need something subtle to monitor."

"Do any of the surrounding properties afford a view of the courtyard?" asked Phoenix. "Can we get someone inside so we can observe from above?"

"We're looking at that possibility," replied Henry, "but many of these houses are residential and occupied. So if we can locate an empty business property among them, we could break in and keep watching for the rest of the weekend."

"When was your man in the courtyard, Henry?" asked Athena.

"Late evening," he replied, "he saw nothing except for this solitary unexplained doorway."

"Artemis tells me it was common for these properties to have a tunnel connecting the original access streets to the stables. Those streets have long disappeared under a century of urban sprawl. She wondered whether the door led to a lower floor or basement in the property belonging to Lady Primrose Charmbury."

"The lockups and so on that occupy the edges of the courtyard? Do they have any connection to the Titans?" Athena asked.

"There's nothing to suggest that, no," replied Giles. His phone vibrated.

"Sorry, may I take this? It's Artemis," he said. Athena nodded.

When he ended the call, he thumped the table.

"At last, a break," he said. "Artemis has looked into the operation of the car park. There are eight vehicles stored underground. They belong to people who live in luxury apartments on the nearby block. It's only a two-minute walk from there to the garage. Dominic Perkins has two spaces reserved in the car park. He keeps a high-performance sports car and a dark-coloured van there."

"Well, there we have it then," said Phoenix, "a definitive link between Hermes and Nemesis. Despite outward appearances, they are near neighbours, with a hidden method of entering and leaving her property. His van will be the one that rammed us in the New Forest.

Henry, your man needs to watch for that van and confirm whether Hermes has a passenger when he takes it out for a spin."

"Will do, Phoenix," said Henry.

Minos and Alastor had slipped quietly into the room.

"Good morning, gentlemen," said Athena. "I'll bring you up to speed later, but I need you to start looking into something for us. The Titans will start eliminating opponents in the next few days. Minos, I need a list of potential targets. People who the government would turn to for guidance in a period of national emergency. Alastor, your task is to identify public or private events they might hit in the next two to three weeks. Thanatos stole enough explosives from that MoD site to cause serious damage to both property and personnel. Where is the most likely target? Any questions, either of you?"

"No, Athena," said Minos. "We're glad to be doing something constructive to help."

The Two Stooges left the room. Henry went to the ice-house to brief his surveillance people; Giles and Rusty remained.

"Did anything odd happen since yesterday, Giles?" asked Phoenix.

"As I was leaving to come to the meeting, one of my lads shouted out that Lenny James hadn't turned up to open a budget supermarket this morning."

"Who is this, Lenny James?" asked Athena.

"He's an old comedian," said Phoenix, "opening supermarkets is all he gets offered these days. He's so out of the loop; he can't even get on Celebrity Big Brother. It could be something, though; Giles, did Arthur Harman ever reappear?"

"Not a whisper, Phoenix," replied Giles. "If they've

taken this James chap too, it could be linked to the original Yewtree black book."

"Is there any CCTV near this side street in Knightsbridge that would pick up the van if it was on the roads last night?"

"I'll start looking straight away, Phoenix," said Giles, and he left with a nod to Athena.

"We're moving quicker now," Athena said. "We've been running through treacle for a day or two. It seems as if we've got tabs on two of the Titans. We need to up our surveillance on Demeter and Poseidon to get a tighter grip. The first person I wish to find is Thanatos. Those explosives worry me. We have to neutralise the threat they pose. The consequences of allowing him to plant bombs in public places and murder, perhaps hundreds of innocent people, don't bear contemplating."

"Don't worry, Athena," said Rusty. "I'm sure Phoenix and I will do everything we can to see that nothing momentous happens on our watch."

While the emergency meeting was going on at Larcombe, two people were settling into the mews house. Chris Rathbone and Lenny James had arrived just before five this morning. Chris had received a text message from his handler. He had to get in the back of the dark van parked around the corner from the hostel. Chris had scrambled inside, slammed the door behind him, and the van pulled away.

"Sorry about the mess and the smell," his handler had said. They completed the rest of the journey in silence.

Nemesis had opened the rear doors when they arrived in the courtyard; she didn't speak. Hermes had reversed the van up to the doorway. Nemesis let herself in and beckoned to Chris to follow her. They walked through a long tunnel up a slight incline. A door at the end gave access to a basement. The fixtures and fittings were odd, but Chris Rathbone was just glad to be off the streets and in the warm.

Nemesis climbed the stairs to the top floor and showed Chris into her studio. A sleeping bag lay on the floor. She pointed to the bathroom next door and rejoined Hermes in the basement. They wheeled in Lenny James next. Unfortunately, he only went as far as the basement to a place once occupied by Arthur Harman. Arthur was still around, here and there.

Hermes and Nemesis climbed the stairs to the living quarters.

"A nice cup of tea would be welcome, don't you think?" said Hermes. He walked to the stairs and called up to Chris Rathbone.

"We're having tea. Would you care to join us? Then we can get properly acquainted."

On Saturday evening, Honey B relaxed in her Chelsea Harbour Hotel rooms.

They had already eliminated two of the original names on the list. On Monday, they would start on the real targets. The minor criminals they had chosen were a smokescreen to appease Zeus and the others.

Poseidon stayed out of sight, as they had agreed; his talents were better suited in other areas. Socialising and murder weren't really in his skill set. He was more of a schemer and financial guru. However, those talents would have their time.

Honey B checked her phone — nothing from Orion as yet.

She had kept him on a short leash since Wednesday. No question Phoenix and Athena were safe behind the barricades at Larcombe. A frontal assault was out of the question.

They had to persuade their enemies to come out into the open; for Hermes and Nemesis to kill them. She had devised a plan.

Orion had been sent home to Bath to begin the first stage. Each piece of information she had squeezed out of him during her tour now came into play. He was to reassume his role as a police Superintendent and visit Larcombe. It was a follow-up to his colleague's visit last September. His superiors were still concerned about the whereabouts of Garry Burns.

They weren't happy Olympus had told them the truth. Orion had a copy of the photograph taken of Phoenix and Athena in Curzon Street. He was going to use it to suggest Garry Burns was alive and well and living at Larcombe.

He was to invite them to Portishead HQ for questioning. Olympus had to maintain the façade that they were a genuine charity. How could they refuse a request from an officer of the law? He could suggest a date and time. Once they were through the gates and heading to Portishead, Hermes would strike. This time, he was going to be successful.

Honey B decided it was time for bed.

No sooner had she switched off her light and settled under the covers than her phone rang.

It was a message from Orion.

'All set; visiting the manor first thing Monday.'

"Good hunting, Orion," purred Demeter. She knew she would sleep well.

Sunday, October 13th, 2013

Giles Burke and his team had captured the film from the relevant CCTV cameras in Knightsbridge. Many hours of painstaking analysis had finally isolated the times when a dark van emerged from the narrow lane and returned.

He and Artemis were comparing the times with what they knew or suspected.

"They left a few minutes after ten o'clock," said Artemis. "The only event you logged as suspicious the following day was the apparent disappearance of the care home manager. He lived in Worcestershire, so if the Titans were involved, they could easily have driven there, killed him, and returned by the next time we see the van."

"They turned into the side street at four fifty-seven," said Gile,s "that's plenty of time. There's been no sign since of Harman. If there were any sign of foul play, the police would have found it. Did they kill him somewhere else and dump the body? Did they bring the body back to dispose of it, or was he still alive inside the van?"

"Whichever scenario we're dealing with, these two are cold-hearted, ruthless people. But, again, something opposite to their public persona," said Artemis.

"I agree," said Giles, "this next section shows the van leaving again. Once more, it's late at night. They are returning later this time, which might mean their victim lived further away."

"We haven't got a likely suspect except for that washed-up comedian, Lenny James, to fit that timeline. Where did he live?"

"Sheffield was where he lived, but the budget supermarket he was opening was in Chesterfield. So we found a Mr James booked in for one night at the nearby Premier Inn. That fits our timeline comfortably. I wonder what took them so long to get back?"

The two colleagues continued to nag away at their scraps of information.

"There are so many threads to follow," sighed Giles.

"Follow? That's the obvious answer," said Artemis. "Instead of reviewing the CCTV history, we need to use our new system to tap into the live feed. So we follow the van on its next journey and prevent more killings."

"I'm sure Athena considered that," said Giles. "We have to remember; Olympus has sanctioned direct action against people responsible for cases of historical abuse. She would be going against the Project's aims. The Titans could use that to remove her from control here at HQ. No, we have to tread carefully. We need to take what we know to Athena and Phoenix right away. They need to see this."

Giles rang the main house, and Athena invited them to join her. After they had seen the data, Phoenix wanted to act without delay.

"Why don't we go straight to Knightsbridge and visit Nemesis? These two missing persons could still be alive. God knows what they're doing to them. I can't sit on my hands any longer. I must be out there dealing with these people face to face."

"We have to be certain Hermes and Nemesis have taken the first steps in the battle for control of Olympus," said Athena calmly. Giles and Artemis shared a look.

"As unpalatable as it may be," she continued, "we must

wait until they travel to strike again. First, we need to identify their targets and then confirm they are significant players in the corridors of power. Then, if they are criminals from the Yewtree investigations, we stand back and let them get on with it. We can only act if we are one hundred per cent sure they have stepped over the line."

"I want to lead the crew we send to follow them," said Phoenix, "and I want Rusty with me. Two more operators will be enough. We will use two cars and switch positions regularly, so Hermes doesn't suss they've got a tail. We don't need to be too close. It will be easier to track them at night."

"I can arrange that," said Athena, "you travel to London today and wait. Then, Giles, you need to tap into the live feed on the nearby street cameras. Please take every precaution. As soon as they leave the underground car park, we must learn about their destination. Phoenix and his team will follow, and when they reach that destination, Phoenix will relay that information to Giles. But, unfortunately, we may not be quick enough to save their victim…."

"No," said Phoenix, "but if they've crossed the line, we take them out. Then, we return to London and pay a visit to a penthouse flat and a mews cottage. I can't wait to find out what secrets they hold."

"Right, that's as much as we can do today," said Athena.

"I'll fetch Rusty from the stable block. He'll know two agents who would be right for this mission. Do you want to walk with me, Artemis? You might not see him for a while."

Artemis blinked and pushed her glasses up her nose.

"Thanks," she said.

Athena watched as Giles left the room.

"Oh, by the way, Artemis, Minos informed me we have another follow-up visit from the police in the morning. It concerns the query you raised from the Charity Commissioners last year. It seems so long ago. I thought they'd forgotten it."

"Who are they sending?" asked Artemis. "I'll be underground tomorrow morning, so there's no chance of them seeing me. Nobody from my old life knows I'm here at Larcombe."

"I didn't get a name," said Athena. "I'll ask Minos later."

Athena gave Phoenix a quick hug.

"Take care," she said. Then, Phoenix and Artemis left for the stable block.

In London, the four Titans were plotting their next moves. Poseidon had travelled to London by cab from Surrey. The tail he had spotted as he reached Mayfair was soon lost. He rang Demeter on a throwaway pay-as-you-go mobile. There were perks to having a son in the business.

He and Demeter arranged to meet in Westminster. Fifteen minutes later, they were next to the London Eye, looking across the Thames towards the Houses of Parliament.

"Olympus has set the dogs on us," he said. "I had someone follow me into town. We must assume they are tapping our registered phones and hacking into our computers. From now on, we need to ask Dominic to supply us with burner phones. Our only contact must be through secure channels."

"I agree," said Demeter, "we are so close. The purge of the government's main advisers begins tomorrow tonight. They both stay in London during the week. As soon as this action begins, we have to act swiftly. We will only have hours before the disappearance of members of the emergency response committee causes panic. The public has read or heard about COBRA but doesn't fully appreciate its vital work. In essence, it's a get-together of ministers, civil servants, the police, intelligence officers and others that suit the matter at hand. When the government announces it has convened a meeting, it implies it's tackling an issue of immediate national significance. The loss of those non-ministerial members will effectively strangle them. They won't have anyone to tell them what to do."

"Our man from Larcombe is ready to go, I believe," said Poseidon.

"He is," replied Demeter. "He has a few hurdles to cross on Wednesday before he can deliver our next message, but he's confident of success. It will be the loudest Prime Minister's Question Time in history. Of course, it has a reputation for being rowdy, but this week it will be exceptional."

In Knightsbridge, Hermes and Nemesis were in the basement of her house. Lenny James was dead, and her equipment had been cleaned and stored away.

"I want to start on a fresh painting this afternoon," said Nemesis. "What shall I do with my guest upstairs in my studio?"

"Now everything is clear. Perhaps we could offer the basement as a workplace?" replied Hermes.

"As long as he realises he needs to finish before we return early Tuesday morning," said Nemesis.

Hermes left her tidying and climbed the two flights of stairs to her studio. Chris Rathbone was already hard at work.

"It seems odd you went to the trouble of stealing high explosives in easy-to-handle blocks and then dismantle everything," said Hermes.

Chris Rathbone stared at him.

"Do you honestly believe I could wander into Westminster with a few blocks of C-4 in my back pocket? Even with an authentic pass for the public gallery? No, security is as tight as at any international airport these days. I had to dream up a special method to transport the explosives inside the chamber."

"My colleague says you can construct whatever you plan to use on Wednesday in her basement. However, you must finish by the early hours of Tuesday. Will you complete things by then?"

"Have you collected the wheelchair?" asked Chris.

"It's in the van, but I can bring it inside now if you want to move your kit downstairs. I'd give you a hand, but I don't want to lose it. This stuff gives me the shivers."

"You fetch the chair; I'll move my gear."

"Good," said Hermes, "Nemesis wants access to the studio. She's feeling the urge to paint."

"Something else, aren't they?" said Chris, pointing to a stack leaning against the wall, "Do you want to try sleeping in here? It's as if the room's haunted."

Hermes looked at the canvases.

"They are pretty dark, I suppose, and not to everyone's taste."

"I tried to see what others might see in them, but I found the exercise draining," said Chris with a shudder.

"Exactly," said Hermes as he made for the stairs. "I'll get that chair from the van. See you below in a few minutes."

Chris collected his materials together and made his way carefully downstairs. He met Nemesis as she appeared from the basement.

"You will be finished by midnight tomorrow, won't you?" she asked.

"Don't worry," said Chris, "it won't take more than a few hours to finish the modifications I have in mind. So what are you painting this afternoon, a still life, maybe?"

Nemesis was halfway up the stairs to her studio. Her laughter echoed around her living room. Chris Rathbone hurried into the basement.

Hermes was waiting for him. He wheeled over the lightweight wheelchair.

"Tada," he said, "intriguing; how do you intend to use it?"

"While I was at Larcombe planning this operation, I applied for a pass for a Falklands veteran. It's usual for disabled ex-servicemen to receive help from a charity — Olympus and 'Help for Heroes' formed within months of one another. The authorities didn't question a request from a charity caring for people with PTSD, needing access for a disabled veteran. These lightweight versions are tubeless steel-framed, which allows me to create a bomb on wheels. I shall take my place in the public gallery, where they have step-free access and a space set aside, especially for wheelchair users. Then, when the action below is at its busiest and rowdiest, I'll get up, activate the bomb's timer, rest the chair against the bullet-proof glass screen and make my escape."

"How long will the delay be?" asked Hermes

"Fifteen seconds," said Chris, "at a quarter past twelve, there will be a huge bang."

Chapter Fourteen

Monday, October 14th, 2013

Athena had been up early today; she had spent a restless night. Phoenix was in London with Rusty and the others. She missed him being beside her when she awoke. Phoenix waited for any sign of movement in Knightsbridge.

Late last evening, Athena remembered to call Minos. Artemis must have been asleep when she rang the stable block to tell her the name of the policeman who was arriving soon. She had to leave things until Artemis got to the ice-house to start work.

It was time. Athena made the call at 8.00 am.

"Artemis, the name of that policeman is DS Hounsell,"

"Well, we both know he isn't a policeman any longer. He's been working for Honey B. If he's arriving at Larcombe with questions, we must assume they persuaded him to work for her alter ego, Demeter."

"I'll carry on and see him. I'll ask Henry Case to join me. We'll find out what he wants and go from there."

"Have you heard any news from London yet," asked Artemis.

"Nothing yet," said Athena, "they'll be okay. They're together. I wouldn't want to be fighting against them. I'd better get ready. I'll talk to you later."

Athena ended the call and contacted Henry. He was only too glad of the prospect of a visitor to the interrogation cells in the ice-house. Things had been so quiet of late.

Phil Hounsell drove over to Larcombe Manor from his home in Bath. It had been great to have a weekend at home with Erica and the kids. Okay, his boss was in his ear every few hours, but he was working and getting well paid for it.

As for Wayne and the lads, it looked as if they were off on another tour. Wayne was meeting up with the managers of an early Seventies group later to talk business. They tour around the UK from November until January. Wayne had emailed him a group photo. Phil vaguely remembered the name, but from the picture, it looked as if the original members had left over the intervening decades. He guessed the fans would be happy if they knew the songs and could still get into their trademark stage gear.

Phil had to stop at the cattle grid; there was a security barrier. He'd never driven along this road. Phil had heard of the charity, of course. At odd times, he'd seen the cars and vans with their logos featuring Mt. Olympus around the Roman city. It was a 'no through road', and Phil had never needed to visit the Manor or the farm further up the road. A guard raised the barrier after he had identified himself. The guard sent him to the front of the main building; it certainly seemed an imposing place. Phil saw a few military types working in the gardens. He parked his car and walked to the front door.

A burly individual, built like a rugby second-row, met

him. His grip was firm, and Phil was thankful for letting go of his hand.

"Good morning, I'm Henry Case, Head of Security. Please follow me. Ms Annabelle Fox, our CEO, is expecting you."

Henry Case showed Phil into a bright, well-appointed office. The clock on the wall ticked around to 8.30 am. The woman facing him was tall, attractive, and about five months pregnant, if memory served, when Erica had been expecting their children. It wasn't the only thing that struck him. She was the woman he had seen at Glastonbury in June, with the man he had mistakenly believed had been Colin Bailey.

"Good morning, Superintendent. I'm Annabelle Fox of the Olympus Project. You have questions, I understand. How may we help you?"

"My former colleague, Detective Sergeant Zara Wheeler, came here last September. She was following up on a query raised through the Charity Commissioners. At that time, she returned to Portishead with a photograph of one Garry Burns. Burns had been a patient here; I understand?"

"We don't refer to the men who come here as patients, Inspector," said Henry.

"My mistake. Ms Wheeler heard that Burns disappeared after leaving Larcombe. He might have gone backpacking."

"We haven't seen or heard from former Warrant Officer Second Class Burns," said Henry Case, "he discharged himself. He is no longer our concern."

"Perhaps you could explain this then," said Phil, producing the photo taken outside the Curzon Street venue in the summer.

Athena picked up the photograph.

"That is you and Burns, is it not?" asked Phil. "I might point out we three have met before. I believe I saw the two of you together at the Glastonbury Festival."

"What if this is that man Burns and myself?" asked Athena, "neither of us got accused of any wrongdoing. Maybe, Garry Burns has a legitimate reason for wanting people to believe he left the country. Maybe after his slow and taxing recovery from PTSD, he wanted to drop out of the rat race and live a simple life here, helping others."

Phil was struggling. This woman had all the answers. How could he insist they attend a meeting at Force HQ on the strength of what he had so far? He didn't know why that was important anyway. Honey B hadn't mentioned why she wanted these two out in the open. Until he sat here, up against it, he had only thought of the money she was paying him for his services. He realised what a mug he had been, but he ploughed on regardless.

"Where is Burns now? I should like to interview him alone. To see if his story matches yours."

"Well," said Athena, "if we're talking about storytelling, you're here under false pretences, are you not? You are no longer a policeman; you run a security firm called HSS from a small office in the city. You have been working for the singer Honey B for the past month. She sent you here, didn't she? What were you supposed to achieve? Most likely, she wants to flush us out into the open. Well, you've failed. I'm afraid you'll have to go with Mr Case now. He has questions for you. It would be best to answer them quickly and honestly. Goodbye, Orion."

Henry hovered over him. Phil wasn't stupid; he knew he stood no chance. However, he was confused; how did this woman know so much about him? How did she know

Honey B's nickname for him? Who the hell were these Olympus Project people?

"This way, Mr Hounsell," said Henry, "do you remember a band called The Eagles?"

"What? Yeah, vaguely. Why?"

"We're off to Hotel California."

At 9.00 am, Athena met with the few elite members still on site at Larcombe. Giles, Minos, and Alastor sat together when she arrived.

"I'll keep it brief this morning," she said. "Minos, do you have that list of potential targets? I need to forward them to Phoenix."

"I've reduced it to a potential sixteen names, Athena. If we lose those in a short time, it severely limits the response the government could give in a crisis. Moreover, almost all those names live in the capital full-time or stay in the city from Monday to Friday.

The most senior people are three men and a woman. They are advisers on security, economics, science, and terrorism. I have addresses for everyone; what car they drive; which stations they use if travelling across London by tube. If Phoenix needs more, I'll dig further."

"This is excellent, Minos," said Athena, taking the file he handed over, "I'll get this to Phoenix and Rusty later."

"If the Titans follow their normal pattern, they won't strike until tonight at the earliest," said Giles. "There was nothing on the CCTV footage overnight. Hermes had left for work in his sports car just before I left the ice-house. The others are still keeping out of sight. As for Thanatos, no sightings whatsoever."

"Thanks, Giles. Alastor, where are the likely targets for an attack using the explosives Thanatos stole?"

"I wasn't able to isolate any specific targets, I'm afraid.

We must consider the usual suspects. Airports, train and bus stations, busy public thoroughfares, government buildings, and sporting venues. There's only one significant Royal event scheduled. Prince George's christening takes place on Wednesday week in a private ceremony. Most of these possible targets have countermeasures to prevent attacks of this nature. Whatever Thanatos has planned, it will have to be audacious to make a devastating PR impact for the Titans. Minos has provided a list of significant people the government relies upon in a tough spot. The government might stumble along in the dark without advisers and avoid a catastrophe, relying on their wits. The Titans won't want that. So no, it makes sense that Thanatos will direct his attack towards the PM and his Cabinet."

"To attack the heart of democracy inside the Houses of Commons?" asked Minos.

"Alastor is right. Any attack on a prime location will need to be audacious," said Athena. "We'll send extra agents from the city to keep watch on Westminster. We'll continue to hunt for Thanatos and eliminate the threat when we find him. If he avoids detection until he breaks from cover to strike, we must do everything in our power to prevent him from reaching his target. What news from the ice-house, Giles?"

"Artemis and I have been working on what to do when Hermes and Nemesis carry out their next attack. If their target is on the list, Minos prepared, we have to hope Phoenix and Rusty prevent a murder. If this is indeed one of the advisers, we can confidently expect this to be their last killing. What will Demeter and Poseidon do next?"

"They'll go into hiding and take Thanatos with them," said Minos.

"What did you and Artemis come up with?" asked Athena.

"We convince his parents their son has returned to Knightsbridge safe and sound."

"Give me the full details of your plan, and I'll pass them on to Phoenix. They can take things on from there. Well done."

"Where's Henry this morning," asked Giles.

"In the ice-house with a prisoner. We detained Mr Hounsell for his good. It was clear he came here under orders to flush us out. As well as his other targets, no doubt Demeter wished Hermes to murder Phoenix and me in the next day or two. But, of course, she couldn't have known that Phoenix was already in the capital or that Artemis worked here. So the poor man walked right into a trap."

"I'd better add a couple of other items to my list," said Giles. "We want Demeter to continue to believe her Orion is in the game."

"I believe we've passed the tipping point, gentlemen," Athena said. "For the first time in a while, we're one step ahead of our opposition."

The meeting ended. Athena rang her partner and updated him on the meeting. She sent the files containing names and addresses, potential locations and proposed 'misinformation' to his laptop. It was now 10.00 am.

In the ice-house, Henry Case read his daily newspaper. There was no rush. His guest wasn't going anywhere.

In the first interrogation room on the third floor, Phil Hounsell sat alone. Despite his predicament, he had marvelled at the engineering that hid so much of this operation from view. He had seen how long the dark corridor had stretched beyond where he had stood while Henry Case unlocked the door.

If the floors above were as large, they must contain something vital to the Olympus Project. What could it be? A charity was off the cards after this. What had he stumbled upon; was he ever going to see his wife and children again?

One question kept nagging at him. Why was Honey B, a fading star, interested in what went on here at Larcombe Manor? Why had it been so important he persuade the two people in that blessed photo to drive to Portishead? Thirty years as a copper, and he didn't have a clue.

In London, Phoenix and Rusty were bored to tears. Surveillance can be mind-numbingly dull. After hours of sitting in the car waiting for something to happen, it wasn't just their minds that became numb. Even having the other agents spell them in two-hour shifts throughout the day wasn't a great help.

"Athena has just updated me on the morning meeting," said Phoenix with a yawn. "I've got details on our likely victims. Giles has had a few good ideas too. So we could be busy tonight."

Rusty turned on the radio. Unfortunately, it was tuned to that heavy metal channel again. Oh well, it stopped him from falling asleep.

Hermes finished work at six o'clock. He travelled back to the underground car park. The van was fuelled and ready to leave later. He thought he should check on Chris Rathbone's progress with his wheelchair conversion. He called Nemesis. She opened the outside door a few minutes later.

"Come in," she said, "I've got something to show you."

They walked through the tunnel to the basement. The wheelchair was resting against one of the chest freezers.

The Price of Treachery

"He finished everything," she said, "we're on for tonight."

"Good," said Hermes. "I'll get off home for a bite to eat."

"No, I've got something upstairs for you to see," Nemesis insisted.

Hermes saw her latest painting on the easel when they were in her studio.

"A Study in Scarlet?" he asked.

"That title's not new," she said, "but Arthur and Lenny contributed so much to it I may call it 'The Blood Donor' and risk the accusations of plagiarism."

"Where's your guest?" asked Hermes.

"In the bathroom. Chris needed to remove traces of his having handled the explosives. He's shaving his head too. Before Wednesday, he wants to alter his appearance as much as possible. Why don't you stay? We can eat together. I'd feel more comfortable with you here."

Hermes nodded.

"I'll go home, wash and change into the clothes I'll wear tonight, then pop back. So what are we having?"

"Don't worry, nothing from the freezers downstairs. I'll knock up a spaghetti carbonara while you're gone. Let's say we eat at eight o'clock?"

"That's fine with me. I'll see you later." With that, Hermes trotted along the tunnel and returned to his penthouse.

At ten o'clock, Chris Rathbone was alone in the mews cottage. He had enjoyed the meal, and the company was welcome, even if the atmosphere sometimes felt a little strained. They were an odd couple. He expected them back at two o'clock. They said they wouldn't disturb him.

In the ice-house, Giles and his team were on the alert.

"The van has pulled out of the side street. Check every street camera in the area to see which way they are going. Phoenix, did you get that?"

"I did, Giles. At last, we can do something positive. We're both moving into position now. Give me a heads-up as soon as you spot them."

Two minutes later.

"They're in Brompton Road, heading for Cromwell Road."

"Rusty, who do we have that's out this way on our list?" asked Phoenix.

"Several, depending on how far we're travelling."

"Giles, we have them in sight. They're turning onto Earl's Court Road. What's that, the A3220?"

"Yes, Phoenix, you're just around the corner from Stamford Bridge."

Phoenix kept an eye out for a bridge but saw nothing.

"They're turning off again," said Rusty, "we're in Fulham. This road takes us to where Sir Basil Atherton has a flat. He's a chief security adviser."

The van pulled up at the side of the road. Phoenix and Rusty parked one hundred yards behind them. Their colleagues in the other car drove past the van and parked in the next cul-de-sac.

"Stand by. There's no movement inside the van as yet. Does this property have a side or rear access? I don't imagine they will go in via the front door."

"There's a passageway between the properties I spotted as we drove past," said the driver from the other car.

"Sit tight and await further instructions," said Phoenix.

It was now 10.20 pm.

The Price of Treachery

Demeter and Hermes got out of the van. They disappeared into the dark passageway. They found the conservatory to the rear of Sir Basil's ground-floor bolt-hole at the far end.

Hermes slipped off his shoulder bag and got out the tools he required. Nemesis was poised, with her syringe ready to strike. The first of their victims would be paralysed and tucked up in the van by eleven. Then they could drive across the city to collect Margaret Hussein. Unless there were any delays, they could be back home before two. Every extra hour of sleep was vital over the next forty-eight hours.

The door to the conservatory was open. The pair slipped inside. Hermes started work on the back door. Inside the flat, Sir Basil was reading before bed. He thought he heard a noise. It was probably a cat. His neighbours seemed to have a dozen that called their place home. He tried to concentrate on his book again.

Hermes and Nemesis were inside the house.

"That's far enough," called Phoenix as he and Rusty crashed through the conservatory and into the flat.

Nemesis screamed and lunged at Phoenix. Her face was twisted with rage as she stabbed wildly at him with the syringe.

Rusty took aim and fired; he hit Lady Primrose in the throat and chest. She fell to the floor, mortally wounded. Hermes had pulled a gun and rushed towards Sir Basil, intending to use him as a hostage. Phoenix got off three shots; his trusty Sig Sauer didn't fail him. Hermes never reached his target.

Phoenix calmly stepped past the body of Nemesis and approached the adviser's bed.

"Sorry for the intrusion, Sir Basil," said Phoenix, as he

checked Hermes was dead, "we'll be out of your hair in no time. I'd advise stronger security in your conservatory. Proximity lights would help too. You never know who's creeping about these days."

"What the hell's going on?" Sir Basil blustered, "who are these people, and who are you?"

"We're the good guys," said Rusty.

The other two Larcombe agents now stood in the conservatory. Rusty beckoned for them to help remove the bodies.

"Goodnight, Sir Basil," said Phoenix as he pulled the conservatory door closed, "sweet dreams."

The nation's senior security adviser sat in bed and watched Phoenix leave. He caught himself thinking, 'Who was that masked man?' and realised he could never tell anyone what had happened tonight. They would think him quite mad.

On the far side of Ravenscourt Park, Margaret Hussein, a senior science adviser, slept undisturbed three miles away. She would have thanked Phoenix and Rusty for saving her life….if she had been aware of it.

"We'll get you home then, Hermes. Sorry if this isn't the night out you kept hankering after."

Rusty had pushed Hermes onto the back seat of their car. He relieved him of his mobile phone. Rusty wasn't surprised Hermes had more than one. He found the van's keys in Hermes's pocket and threw them to one of the other agents.

"Follow us back to Knightsbridge," he called. "We'll finish things off, then get back home."

The small convoy retraced their earlier steps. Finally, they pulled into the courtyard at ten forty-eight.

"I want to check inside and then go through the house

later," said Phoenix. Rusty shrugged; he opened the rear doors of the van. The agents stared at the interior.

"Out of interest, what did the syringe contain?" asked one of the agents.

"Something to incapacitate their victim," said Phoenix, "those floor restraints are to secure them while they travel back here. The killings must have taken place inside the house."

"Can you check if the lady was carrying her house keys, please?" asked Phoenix.

They retrieved the keys from the front of the van.

Phoenix opened the door to the tunnel. The agents entered. When they emerged in the basement, they stood in silence. A low whistle passed the lips of one of the agents.

Chris Rathbone had been unable to sleep. The new painting smelled more than a little. The subject matter disturbed him as usual. He couldn't relax, knowing the others would return at two o'clock. He was sitting in the living room when he heard a sound.

It was far too early for them to be back yet. Something must have gone wrong. Chris grabbed his backpack and escaped into the cobbled lane at the front. He had to forget the wheelchair for now. With luck, he could return to get it later.

In the basement, agents opened the freezers and examined the stainless-steel table. They uncovered and inspected the collecting trays and knives.

"A genuine house of horrors," said Rusty.

"I wonder what's upstairs?" asked Phoenix.

Leaving the two agents in the basement, he and Rusty climbed the stairs. The place was empty, as they had expected. The living area was tidy enough. There were smells of cooking, and the dishwasher was still full.

"Looks as if there were three for dinner," said Rusty, checking the cutlery, plates, and glasses inside. "Let's look upstairs."

The bed was undisturbed; the artist's studio was cluttered and smelt odd. Phoenix turned on a light. The painting in front of him made him gag.

"All those collection trays downstairs," he gasped, "the knives; Nemesis used her victim's blood in her paintings. No wonder those employees Hermes entertained in his penthouse were so disturbed. They're spooky."

"Come in here, Phoenix," called Rusty from the bathroom.

"I don't think Lady Primrose produced that much hair shaving her legs, do you? The colour doesn't match either. Does it remind you of anyone?"

"Thanatos? He was here in London; no wonder we couldn't trace him on the streets. So he's cut his hair very short or shaved off the lot. I wonder when he left and where he went?"

"What do we do now?" asked Rusty.

"Bring the bodies inside. Leave them on the table in the basement for now."

"We've over two hours before we need to send our messages to Demeter and Poseidon to notify them of a successful mission."

"So, we can get off home?" asked one of the agents.

"Check these phones," said Phoenix, "even the burner phone has GPS, I bet. Hermes will have supplied his parents with similar pieces of technology. We need to send the message from here in the basement, not from the M4 near Chippenham."

Rusty shook his head. Phoenix never missed a trick. He half wished the Titans weren't so technically 'savvy' because another two hours with these body parts wasn't something he fancied.

There were so many horrific items in plain sight that none of the Olympus agents gave the lightweight wheelchair folded up against the end wall a second look.

Chapter Fifteen

Chris Rathbone checked his watch. It was midnight.

It must have been Phoenix downstairs, perhaps with other Olympus agents. They must have caught Hermes and Nemesis. He had no way to contact the people with whom Hermes worked. Until Chris had arrived in London and moved into the mews house, the only person he knew was his handler, Hermes.

He knew it might be hours before the agents left. He had to stick to the plan. If he could retrieve the wheelchair from the basement before Wednesday, he could still carry out his part of the deal. He had to disappear. It was time for another two nights in doorways on the city streets.

Inside the basement, the four men chatted about what lay ahead.

"Do the Titans have other assassins besides these two we neutralised tonight?" asked one of the Larcombe agents.

"Good question," said Rusty. "There's been no sign of anyone else, but we cannot discount Thanatos. Whatever he has planned is imminent, so the removal of the advisers must have been scheduled for this week. Tonight was the first attack. The others were to follow quickly if we've got this right. I think we'd better search both places for any hint as to who came next on the list. Then we can continue to spread misinformation until we catch up with Thanatos and the others."

"Well, that gives us something to do while we're waiting," said Phoenix. "If we find a list, those whose names are on it, including Sir Basil, will have to be taken to a safe house. Twenty-four to forty-eight hours should be enough. After that, we must make the Titans believe Hermes and Nemesis have taken their targets. Then, one of you two check upstairs; Rusty and I will check the penthouse."

The following two hours were productive. Rusty found a file on a laptop in the penthouse that listed the names and addresses of the targets. He spotted Margaret Hussein's name. She was one of the targets for tonight.

Hermes and Nemesis had been getting more brazen, believing themselves unstoppable. The cheeky monkeys had targeted two victims per night for tonight and tomorrow. Only four advisers, but Rusty could tell they were key personnel.

The Titans had chosen well.

Phoenix checked the phones. He looked for the style of the message that passed between Hermes and Demeter. He knew they were brief and cryptic. He wanted to see whether there was anything specific relating to the deaths of people such as Harman and James. Something that gave him a clue on how to phrase the one he needed to send.

Rusty returned from the penthouse.

"They had two planned for tonight, then two more tomorrow night."

"Just as well we found that out," said Phoenix, "who were they picking up after Atherton?"

"Margaret Hussein, the senior science adviser. She lives three or four miles further on from Fulham."

"These messages that Hermes sent look simple enough to manufacture. Can you see anything in them to trick us?"

Rusty took the phone and had a look.

"Jokers to the left of me," he read, "that's Lenny James for sure."

"Yes, but he's deliberately used the right lyric from that annoying song. Unlike his mother did for him when she passed messages," said Phoenix. "He left out the apostrophe that should be there to identify Lenny properly. Hermes was knowledgeable; he'd never make a grammatical error such as that. It's another level of security so that Demeter knows it's him sending it."

"What do you propose to send then? Do the same messages go to both Demeter and Poseidon?"

"According to his phone log, Hermes only told Mummy. We'll need to get Giles to check if, when, and how she told Poseidon. Let's get this first one sorted; if that goes pear-shaped, they'll be onto us anyway."

Phoenix wrote down the names – Sir Basil Atherton; Margaret Hussein.

"Not a clue," he said, puzzled, "for Harman, with his history of abuse in children's homes, Hermes sent The Kids Are All Right. So what's he done there? Should it be Alright?"

"Yeah, that was The Who song, I think," said Rusty. "The clue is in the surnames."

"Sorry?" said Phoenix.

"I'm not surprised," said Rusty, "considering your dislike of sport, mate. Atherton and Hussein are former

English cricket captains, So the song title or lyric needs to be cricket related."

"Any ideas?" asked Phoenix, out of his comfort zone.

"Try something from Cricket Lovely Cricket, the calypso," said Rusty.

He Googled the lyrics to check his memory.

"Here we are with those two little pals of mine, Ramadin and Valentine. So why not send With those two little pals of mine?"

"That could work, Rusty. Brilliant. Hold on; I'd better stick the apostrophe in 'pals' to complete the deception. What do you think?"

"I reckon it's subtle enough and has the content. Let's give it a try."

Phoenix checked his watch. It was 1.56 am. He pressed send.

"It's obvious from the list you found in the penthouse that we need to remain in London. Then, we can search for Thanatos, move the four advisers to a safe house, and send the appropriate message to fit the timeline. If tonight's message works, then we'll be composing one more. We know the targets now. We've got the rest of the day to get it right. If no more killings were planned after Tuesday night, it looks as if Wednesday is when Thanatos will strike. It's imperative we identify his target."

"Where do we stay," asked one of their colleagues, looking around the basement.

"No point sleeping in the cars," said Phoenix, "and this place gives me the creeps. So we'll use the penthouse. I'm sure Hermes won't object."

They locked the door from the tunnel behind them and walked across the courtyard towards the apartment block.

"Just one thing still puzzling me, Rusty," said Phoenix, "who the heck was Ramadin and Valentine?"

Tuesday, October 15th, 2013

Demeter read the text message from Hermes when she awoke at nine am. Everything was still going to plan. By tomorrow afternoon, she and Poseidon could come out of hiding. They would have a great view of the future, their future.

She relayed the message to Poseidon. Then she got up and took a shower. As the water cascaded over her surgically enhanced breasts, she thought of Orion. He hadn't called her yesterday after his meeting. Perhaps everything wasn't going to plan after all. She stepped from the shower, dried herself and dressed.

She rang Orion. It went straight to voicemail.

"Family emergency; off to Scotland for a few days. Leave a message, and I'll get back to you."

"Bloody inconvenient," she yelled and started planning what to do with Phoenix and Athena. They had to be eliminated before Wednesday, if possible. Hermes and Nemesis were busy. Could this Thanatos that Hermes recruited be her saviour? How could she contact him? Might it be too risky to send him back to Larcombe? He might not get back by Wednesday afternoon. No, it was no good. They would have to tackle Larcombe later.

When hotel staff visited Honey B in her apartment that day, they remembered what a bitch she could be when the mood took her.

The Price of Treachery

In the ice-house, Henry Case was with Giles and Artemis. They discussed the news they had received from London.

"An excellent night's work," said Henry, "two of the Titans killed, both of their targets saved from a dreadful death. By lunchtime today, the four senior advisers will be tucked away in our maisonette in Park Steps, St. George's Fields. We don't want them roughing it in Chiswick, I suppose."

"Demeter contacted Poseidon and passed on the false message from Phoenix," said Giles. "That seems to have done the trick for now. So how have you been getting on with your guest?"

"I'm convinced he was just a pawn. He doesn't know what Honey B is up to on her darker days. He told me everything I needed to know. I got him to record a new voicemail message to delay any concerns for forty-eight hours. I can't imagine Honey B will come west to check her hunter is where he says he is."

"Poor Phil," said Artemis, feeling sorry for her former boss and lover, "what will you do with him now?"

"He's not a candidate for the pet cemetery. I can put your mind to rest on that score. We'll hang on to him, then release him into the wild when it's over. First, I need to persuade him to keep his mouth shut."

"It's probably best if you stay clear of him, Artemis," said Giles. "There's no reason for him to know where you live and work now."

"Come on," said Henry, "Athena will be waiting. We've just got enough time to make the morning meeting. It's already five to nine."

The atmosphere in the meeting was both electric and optimistic. Olympus had gained a definite advantage overnight. Athena had talked with Phoenix and was up to speed with developments. This morning, the main topic had to be how to find Thanatos and prevent him from carrying out a bombing.

"If he was in Knightsbridge, as Phoenix and Rusty believe, where would he go after they disturbed him?"

"He would hide in plain sight, on the streets," said Alastor, "or at least, that's what I would do with his training."

"What is his target?" asked Athena.

"It has to be somewhere significant. We've been down this road before," said Minos. "If the removal of the advisers was a significant step in their campaign, then logic suggests members of the government are his target. So, it could be Downing Street, Westminster, possibly even Whitehall, somewhere like that; places with existing security measures designed to prevent an attack. The situation requires a strike that delivers a huge blow to the centre of power. The more audacious, the better, as far as the Titans are concerned. We must apply our resources in and around these buildings to prevent Thanatos from getting through our cordon. Do we have sufficient numbers of agents on the ground in London to achieve that?"

"It's a fine balance, Minos," said Athena. "We can't commit too many agents and give the impression Olympus is a private army. On the other hand, I'll defer to Phoenix and Rusty's experience. If they need extra crews drafted in, we'll get them."

Athena ended the meeting, and her people returned to their posts. The clock ticked on. She checked with Phoenix on the progress with the advisers. They were on their way to the safe house. She asked if they had any sightings of Thanatos. Rusty and the others were scouring the nearby streets. Nothing as yet. Giles had told Phoenix they were monitoring live CCTV feeds to help him.

Athena asked if he needed more operatives.

"I wouldn't mind Brad and his crew from Milton Keynes if they're available. But, other than that, we're fine. We don't want to be tripping over one another."

"Take care, darling," she said, "by the way, I felt the baby move for the first time this morning."

"Put your feet up this afternoon; nothing will happen until tomorrow. Of course, we'll keep searching for Thanatos, but other than that, I've just got to compose a message before two o'clock tomorrow morning."

"How are you getting on with that?" she asked.

"The two advisers on the list for tonight were Neville Kennedy-Smith and Thomas Courage; they cover economics and terrorism. So how do I find a cryptic clue for a song title or a lyric from those two?"

"Ask Henry Case. He's the expert on beers and lagers. Smith's and Courage are well-known brewers. There has to be a drinking song out there somewhere. So get your heads together and use your initiative; good hunting today. Call me if there's any news. I'll text you if Brad can come to London for a day or two."

Athena ended the call and did as Phoenix suggested. She rested.

Phil Hounsell sat in splendid isolation in the ice-house, wondering what would happen to him.

Chris Rathbone sat on a bench in Hyde Park. He had decided being outside in the open was better than skulking around side streets trying to avoid CCTV cameras. These wide-open spaces gave him a clear view of anyone hunting for him.

Later he would drop his backpack off at Paddington left luggage; he must stash the gun and knife before tomorrow. He was returning to the mews house in the early hours to try to retrieve the wheelchair.

Demeter was at Chelsea Harbour, annoying the staff. Poseidon was lunching at his favourite restaurant in Elmbridge; he would walk home in a while. No insurmountable problems were facing them before tomorrow.

Phoenix and Rusty sat in a café with a bacon roll and a mug of coffee; it was their turn for a break. The others searched for any signs of Thanatos. Brad had rung ten minutes ago to say they were on their way. Olympus would have another team of four agents in Knightsbridge tonight. Where they might need to be tomorrow remained a mystery.

The watching and waiting continued.

At midnight, Phoenix, Rusty, and the others rested in the penthouse. Brad's crew took the first watch from ten o'clock until two. As soon as the text message was delivered to Demeter safely, the Larcombe boys would resume their search.

The hunt for Thanatos would continue through the Borough of Kensington and Chelsea.

"This place looks better since we took the paintings off the walls and stacked them in the one-bedroom," said Rusty.

"As long as I don't have to sleep in there, I'm fine," said Phoenix. "Let's use the information Henry has passed us to compose our next text. He's suggested 99 Bottles of Beer.

I reckon we need something that links the supposed

victims' surnames with the fact they're no longer with us. That's been the essence of the earlier messages."

Rusty thought for a while but couldn't come up with anything.

It was one of the others that had a brainwave.

"This was due to be the last of the killings. They both have surnames of brewing families. So why not use last orders at the bar?"

"Genius," shouted Phoenix, "that will do nicely, mate."

There was a knock at the door just before two o'clock; it was Brad and his team. Phoenix sent the text, adding the apostrophe in the word 'orders'. The four Larcombe men descended in the lift. They set out for another corner of the Borough from where Brad's team had just completed a fruitless search.

Chris Rathbone stood in the shadows in the cobbled lane outside the mews house. It looked deserted. He let himself in and crept across the living room without turning on any lights.

The place was empty.

He went downstairs to the basement. It smelled worse than it had when he stayed here. He flicked the light switch and flooded the room with bright light.

The bodies of Hermes and Nemesis lay on the table, their vacant eyes staring at the ceiling.

Chris shivered; he was right. Their mission had failed. He gave the table as wide a berth as possible and sought out the wheelchair. There it was, leaning against the wall near the door to the tunnel. Chris grabbed it and hurried upstairs. He turned off the lights and didn't look back.

Chris paused by the front door and steadied his breathing. The lane was quiet. He slipped outside, closing the door quietly behind him. As soon as he could find a level surface, he would unfold the wheelchair and take his seat.

For the next ten hours, he was going to be the disabled ex-serviceman who had requested a pass to the public gallery in the House of Commons.

A former soldier wounded in the Falklands who had always wanted to attend PMQs to feel the atmosphere in the bear pit of British politics.

Wednesday, October 16th. 2013 – 11.00 am

The Olympus crews were on standby in the Borough, waiting for a call that told them they had identified the target or that Giles Burke had finally spotted Thanatos.

Demeter received the final text message from Hermes earlier this morning. She had told Poseidon the news and arranged to meet him on the South Bank. They were to take a trip on the London Eye. A panoramic view of the city, but a front-row seat of the Palace of Westminster. What a view it would be today.

Athena was restless. She didn't want to wait around in her room. Athena strode across the lawns to the ice-house. She wanted to be at the sharp end of the surveillance alongside Giles, Henry, and Artemis. She joined them in the control centre.

"Please tell me we've got good news?" she asked.

"The activity around both Houses has been busy, Athena. There's nothing to report so far. Downing Street and Whitehall are quiet."

"Can we access any cameras closer to the action?" asked Athena.

"This shows one of the access points," said Artemis. "When visitors arrive, they are funnelled through check-in, like at an airport. There's a queue forming. That's for the public gallery. There's no sign of our man or the Titans yet."

It was eleven-forty-five pm. Prime Minister's Questions time was due to begin in fifteen minutes. A crowded Chamber awaited him.

Chris Rathbone had reached the access point for disabled visitors. He had a visually impaired woman in front of him. Chris had deliberately cut it fine. He wanted to use the sympathy card if he needed it. He ensured his progress was laboured, suggesting he was tired and weary. The security staff started to check the woman's documents. He checked his watch.

"Don't panic, mate. We'll get you inside before the fun starts," said one of the guards.

"Is that him?" cried Giles.

He spotted a shaved head he had sat across the table from for so many meetings.

"That's him," said Athena, "why is he in the wheelchair?"

"He's not carrying the bomb on his person," said Henry, "he's bloody sitting in it."

Giles alerted Phoenix. Both crews sped towards the House of Commons.

They were eight minutes away.

Demeter and Poseidon had arrived on the South Bank. She had booked their tickets online. As noon approached, they would take their places in the pod. They would be at the top when the explosion came, perfectly placed to see the beginning of the end of democracy.

The cars containing the Larcombe and Milton Keynes'

crews threaded their way through the midday traffic. Six men exited the two vehicles on Abingdon Street. The drivers left the area and circled Whitehall and The Mall. They were in radio contact with the men on the ground and Giles in the ice-house.

"Where is he now, Giles?" asked Phoenix, leading Rusty, Brad, and the other agents towards the visitor's entrance.

"He's being vetted now. The process has only just started. You need to hurry. The time is eleven fifty-six. He's chatting and smiling. These guys will have received training on how to approach and handle disabled visitors. His behaviour will put them at ease and distract them. The security staff has checked his pass and ID; they're patting him down. They're not paying any attention to the chair. He'll be through in thirty seconds. Can you see him yet?"

"Yes," shouted Rusty.

"Stop that, man," yelled Phoenix.

The security staff turned around; five armed men in army combat uniforms were facing them. Moving up slowly behind them came Brad. He was wearing a bomb suit.

Chris Rathbone heard the shout; he recognised the voice. The timer was in his underpants. The guards were polite enough not to rummage around down there.

Thirty seconds and he would have been in the building. Phoenix had bettered him yet again. He spun the wheelchair around and rolled towards the Olympus agents. He thrust his hand inside his trousers to activate the timer.

He was going to die, but at least he would take out the cream of the Olympus agents. Phoenix realised what Thanatos was planning and opened fire. The traffic noise drowned out the sound of the six shots from his silenced P226. The wheelchair rolled aimlessly towards Phoenix and Rusty. Its occupant was dead.

Brad ordered his two crew members to remove the body, and he collapsed the wheelchair and carried it back towards the street. The first car moved into position. Brad and Chris Rathbone were soon in the rear seats. Phoenix and the other agents stood on the pavement, looking relaxed. The second car slowed up to collect them.

"Thank you for your cooperation," Rusty said to the guards, "this exercise was to test your security systems. No doubt your superiors received the e-mail. Don't worry about the man in the chair. My colleague was firing blanks. You'll be receiving our full report in the coming weeks."

He left the guards looking dumbfounded. On Abingdon Street, there was now no sign of any army personnel. After a little more than three minutes, everything was back to normal.

It was noon inside the House of Commons, and the Prime Minister prepared to answer the day's first question.

Demeter and Poseidon stood in the pod, looking towards the House of Commons. They slowly rose into the overcast sky. The clouds threatened rain later. They were one hundred and thirty-five metres above the South Bank at twelve-fifteen. Demeter held her breath. Poseidon showed little emotion as ever; there was a brief twitch below his left eye, nothing more.

"It's time," whispered Demeter. "Failure was not an option."

The pod had passed the zenith and was beginning the twelve-minute descent.

"The Larcombe mole has failed us. We must meet with our son and his companion straight away. Then, we need to regroup, plan our next move, and continue the fight," said Poseidon.

Below them on the South Bank, there was activity.

Artemis continued monitoring CCTV in and around Kensington, Chelsea, and the City of Westminster. In addition, she was to inform the car drivers of any potential traffic hold-ups which would delay their arrival to pick up their passengers.

After the cars had moved away into traffic, her attention was drawn to the film of foot traffic on the South Bank fifteen minutes earlier. It had been captured as part of the operation but left unreviewed as events developed across the river.

She saw two people fall into step beside one another one hundred yards from the Eye. There was something in the manner it was done that unsettled Artemis. Her policewoman's brain told her it was 'wrong'. They knew one another, for sure, yet they showed no acknowledgement. There was no greeting, no embrace.

Artemis closed in on the faces of the couple. It was Demeter and Poseidon.

Artemis called Giles across to help them.

"Can you get us into the CCTV on the Eye itself?"

"It might take too long; we'll use the webcam that covers the Eye; let me see how close in I can get," said Giles, tapping keys furiously. "What did you catch?"

"Demeter and Poseidon. I think they might be travelling on the Eye,"

"Front-row seats for the expected bombing, I wouldn't wonder,"

"Can we get Phoenix and Rusty there in time?"

"We can try," said Giles.

He left Artemis, watching the Eye descending. She switched cameras and waited for the batches of sightseers to emerge from the pods and spill out onto the concourse.

The Price of Treachery

Giles called Phoenix and diverted them to the South Bank.

"They have just stepped back onto the South Bank," said Artemis.

Phoenix and Rusty were running. Demeter and Poseidon were heading away from them; the other agents were waiting nearby.

The Queen of the Titans and her former lover didn't sense any danger.

"This way," said Phoenix, grabbing Demeter's arm. Rusty persuaded Poseidon to join them as they guided them towards Belvedere Road. Once inside the cars, they set off back to Bath.

"You'll never get away with this," hissed Demeter, struggling against the ties that secured her hands.

"I'm afraid we have bad news for you," said Phoenix, turning towards the woman next to him. "Your dreams of a coup will have to be shelved. Your son Dominic and Lady Primrose were killed late on Monday evening. As for the traitor from Larcombe, who you imagined would blow up part of the Commons chamber today, I'm afraid he's dead too."

"Dominic can't be dead; I've heard from him daily."

"Last orders at the bar? Erebus left a huge legacy behind him. He even passed on his skills as a cruciverbalist to those of us who admired him so much."

"Damn you," spat Demeter.

"I always vowed I would take revenge on those responsible for his death," said Phoenix. "My colleague is putting Poseidon in the picture in the other car. So the game's up, Demeter. We are returning you to Larcombe Manor. I'm sure you always wanted to take a tour around the facilities."

Everyone at Larcombe awaited their arrival. Finally, the

Titans had been defeated; the threat to democracy had been removed.

Athena was still in the ice-house. At three o'clock this afternoon her partner would be home, and Artemis and Rusty would be reunited. They could look forward to a brighter future.

Demeter and Poseidon would arrive here too. Their future was secure. Henry Case was going to take them deeper into the ice-house.

There they would discover the price of treachery.

Epilogue

On the eighteenth of October, a small detail of men from Larcombe left the ice-house just after sunrise. They buried five bodies in the pet cemetery: three men and two women who had plotted to change the face of Britain for their own ends.

The following day, Henry Case had a final session with Phil Hounsell. If he could forget ever having set foot on the estate, then Olympus were prepared to let him return to his family. However, one hint of any loose talk would mean a price to pay.

Phil drove back to the city and hugged Erica and the kids. HSS might struggle to survive without their generous benefactor, but sometimes the simple life has its attractions.

Giles and Artemis were extra-busy in the intelligence section.

They contacted the safe house in St. George's Field and had the four government advisers released. Their masked captors treated them well. They learned that the brief break in their routine had been in the national interest.

Several clean-up crews went to the mews house. Under cover of darkness, they removed a succession of 'white goods' and their contents. They scrapped the rest of Lady Primrose's belongings. Painters and decorators were employed to refurbish the living accommodation.

Olympus had acquired a new safe house. Lady Prim was a recluse; after all, it wasn't unusual for her neighbours to go for weeks without seeing her. In time, they would learn she had sold up and moved to Newlyn. The light was better there for her painting.

They had to cancel the Caribbean cruise for Honey B because the singer's whereabouts were unknown; staff at Chelsea Harbour Hotel celebrated in the West End.

The Elmbridge restaurant missed Leo Andrews's visits for a few days, but then he was soon a forgotten man.

As for the mobile phone company, it soldiered on, but without its mercurial leader and his TV ads, it was losing ground to the competition.

The cruise ship Honey B should have been entertaining sailed with another fading star. Instead, three days out, it passed the wreckage of a small private jet. The captain notified the authorities on shore.

No bodies surfaced, but items found floating on the surface indicated the three passengers on board were family members. The media had a field day. Headlines such as a heartrending end to reconciliation, and Caribbean catastrophe, heralded the news that after decades of unhappy relationships, the singer Honey B was planning to return with her son's father.

The paintings in Hermes's penthouse bedroom were taken into the auction house to raise money for charity. It takes all sorts, doesn't it? Prices still ranged between six hundred and a thousand pounds, and every one of them sold.

When each death had been recorded and ratified, Athena would produce similar wills for the Titans and Thanatos as for Erebus. Every penny of their estates went to the Olympus Project.

Athena had contacted Zeus and the other loyal Olympians to break the news. Everyone was shocked at the degree of betrayal and supported the action taken by Athena and Phoenix without exception. Furthermore, they welcomed the injection of funds due in the coming months.

Zeus said he hoped they could make the meeting in Curzon Street on Wednesday, January 8th. They would discuss the appointment of four replacements then.

In the months that followed, Olympus agents faced other trials. But the fight against crime never stops. Phoenix, Rusty and the others continued to dispense their particular brand of justice.

At Christmas, when Athena and Phoenix entertained Rusty and Artemis in the manor house, Artemis was invited to join the Larcombe elite. From the first of January, she would replace Thanatos at the morning meetings.

On New Year's Eve in the late afternoon, Athena went into labour, and Phoenix called the ice-house. Athena moved to the medical centre; the baby had decided to arrive two weeks early.

In the distance, Phoenix could hear a television, the unmistakable sound of Big Ben striking midnight, followed by the firework display. A new year had dawned.

"Come and see your daughter, Phoenix," said the Doctor.

Phoenix walked into the room. Memories came flooding back from when Sharron was born. Was Athena alright?

Athena was tired but happy. She was holding their baby.

"Darling," she said, "meet your daughter."

"We never did get around to choosing a name, did we?" asked Phoenix.

"Oh, the past few months' events decided it for us, Phoenix."

Athena handed the little mite to him to hold.

Phoenix cradled his daughter in his arms.

"What shall we call her?" he asked.

"Hope."

Next in The Phoenix series

vinci-books.com/new-dawn

A new dawn brings fresh horrors as an enigmatic puppeteer pulls the strings of evil.

In the sixth instalment of Ted Tayler's Phoenix series, the Olympus Project battles a rogue surgeon and a shadowy puppeteer controlling a criminal empire. Reeling from a coup, Olympus must rebuild and confront this sinister force. Can they stop the corruption threatening the nation, or will they fall to the darkness?

Turn the page for a free preview…

A New Dawn: Chapter One

Monday, 3rd March 2014

"It's your turn to fetch her," said Athena.

Phoenix was swinging his feet out from under the duvet and heading for the next-door nursery. Half-asleep was the default mode so far this year. He had heard Hope's preliminary sniffles and whimpers as he lay beside his partner. Experience told that those whimpers would have increased in volume tenfold by the time he padded along the corridor and into her bedroom.

Hope screams eternal was a phrase adapted for use soon after their daughter arrived on New Year's Eve.

Sure enough, as he opened the nursery door, the first high-pitched yell greeted him. Hope's little red-cheeked face pressed up against the side of the cot. Phoenix scooped his daughter up into his arms and held her close.

"Hello, princess," he said, "I can tell why your mother didn't name you, Patience. You don't enjoy hanging around, do you?"

The Price of Treachery

A few gurgles were all he got in reply. Hope squirmed left and right, trying to see into each corner of the room at once. Phoenix was thankful the winter had turned out to be the mildest he'd known. Just a few precious moments alone with his little girl and Phoenix would deliver Hope to her mother. He could afford to let that warm bed wait a while longer.

Phoenix recalled the early days spent in 36C Meadow Road on the Westbourne estate with his first wife Karen and their daughter Sharron. Then, the central heating was forever on the blink. He worked nights at Shaw Park Mines and hadn't been as involved with the night feeds as on this occasion.

Karen had been breastfeeding, at least for a while. But, because he slept during part of the day, Karen's Mum, Kath, dropped in to help. Both women lavished attention on Sharron, but it had been her father she idolised from the outset.

He did his growing when he was in the flat before going to work and at weekends. He and Karen had both been far too young to marry. His plan was more about taking people out of this world, not bringing them into it. Nevertheless, their daughter provided someone he could truly love for the first time, a natural response to an infant who loved him unreservedly.

Back in the present day, Hope was becoming restless. Phoenix walked back to the main bedroom. Athena sat up in bed, wide awake and prepared for battle. A clean, dry Baby-grow, a fresh nappy, a milk bottle, and an impressive array of ointments, powders, and wipes were laid out in readiness. Things had progressed in thirty years.

Phoenix laid Hope on the changing tray and removed her damp clothing. The room felt comfortably warm, and

Hope kicked out her legs, enjoying the freedom nakedness offered. She grabbed at her toes, missed and rolled over onto her side. Athena moved into action, wiping, dusting, and making unintelligible noises that Hope found amusing.

Phoenix then dressed the little mite and handed her to Athena, who had Hope's night feed poised and ready to go. As mother and daughter settled into their now familiar positions, Phoenix sat on the edge of the bed and watched.

"It took a while, but we have got her into a routine," said Phoenix, stifling a yawn.

Athena nodded. Hope was fast demolishing the bottle of milk. Athena set the feed to one side and cradled her daughter against her shoulder; she gently rubbed and patted Hope's back.

"I wonder what it was like caring for a newborn infant in this old barn of a place for Erebus and Elizabeth?"

"Helen, their only child, arrived the year after me," said Phoenix, "the Hunt family money would have protected them. They wouldn't have faced the problems many other young parents did then."

"It was forty-five years ago, though; it must have been primitive," said Athena, with a grin.

"Cheeky beggar," said Phoenix.

Hope gave a long burp. She was ready to return to the bottle.

"Someone else thinks that was below the belt, too, by the sound of it. Do you want me to carry on, darling?" he asked.

Athena handed Hope over to him and watched as he encouraged their daughter to finish the bottle. Athena checked the clock on the bedside table. If she settled to sleep straight away, she might get three hours' sleep before they were due to rise — the nine o'clock meeting was the first thing on the agenda, as usual. But, no matter how pleasurable, domestic duties took second place in Olympus' activities.

A few minutes later, Hope was snoozing in Phoenix's arms. He wiped a few milk bubbles from her lips.

"Say goodnight to your mother, Hope," he said. Athena kissed their daughter's forehead, and father and daughter headed for the door.

Athena watched them leave, her heart full of love. How lucky they were. There might be plenty of clouds on the horizon for the Olympus Project, but here at Larcombe, only one matter genuinely troubled her. Since the turn of the year, Phoenix had been the perfect father and partner. How could he return to the fray when the time came?

He arrived four years ago, a loner, prepared to risk life and limb to bring criminals to justice. Their relationship surprised her and yet fulfilled her in equal measure. Now, she couldn't imagine life without him.

Phoenix had expressed concern several times over the dangers faced when tackling missions the Project handled. Only a few short months ago, they both escaped death in the New Forest at the hands of Hermes. The menace of the Titans had since receded, but evil still lurked around every corner.

Hope's arrival was fantastic news for them both, but the Project's activities meant its agents were always at risk. A loner might accept the odds; a family man might understandably have second thoughts about the wisdom of putting himself in the firing line time and time again.

Athena knew she needed to tread carefully. No matter how much she wanted to protect Phoenix, in the end, any decision to step back into a non-combative role must be his alone. Yet, deep inside, she doubted whether he'd ever be content in that capacity.

As much as he enjoyed the planning and preparation of missions he, Rusty and other agents carried out, she knew he relished being in at the kill. How did the old saying go? It's not enough for justice to be done; it has to be *seen* to be done.

When Phoenix returned after checking that Hope settled herself for a brief respite, he found Athena asleep. He marvelled at her ability to focus one hundred per cent on the minutiae of the many tasks she tackled each day. Then switch off and snatch a few precious moments of rest.

His trusted friend Rusty Scott was just the same. When they first went on missions, he recognised it must be second nature for members of the armed services. They snatched forty-winks whenever an opportunity arose. In the field, they never knew when the next chance would come to relax. Although Phoenix never served in the forces, his skill set made him ideal for the Olympus objectives. He often wished to 'switch off' as quickly as his mate and Athena, his partner.

Phoenix never lost sleep over the people he killed. His conscience was clear in that regard. Only people who deserved to die suffered by his hand. Where was the problem?

Yet, he had faced death at Cropredy and Eton Wick in the past year while on Olympus operations. He and Athena took a day trip to the coast to visit Erebus's yacht, 'Elizabeth'. One of the Titans attacked them as they returned to Larcombe via the New Forest. Those had each been a close call. If he were a cat, he would be adding the number of used lives.

He had Athena and Hope to care for now, which was

why since the New Year, he often lay awake staring at the ceiling, wondering what the future held. Then, when sleep enveloped him in her arms, there were the dreams with which to contend. Not nightmares yet, but disturbing dreams, nonetheless.

A new dawn had broken over Larcombe Manor. A new day; a new week lay ahead. Phoenix stood at a crossroads. He was uncertain which way to turn for the first time in his forty-six years.

On the other side of the Georgian house, Rusty Scott and his partner were awake and preparing for the day ahead. Artemis had showered and dressed. Rusty was still thinking about it.

"Come on," Artemis urged her lover with a friendly poke at his back.

Rusty stayed under the covers for a few more seconds.

"I'm only just coming to terms with this, you know," he said as he swung his legs out of bed.

"What, being naked in front of a younger woman?" asked Artemis.

Rusty strolled unselfconsciously around the bed to where Artemis sat, brushing her hair.

"I've been comfortable with us from the first day we met, sweetheart," he said, taking the brush from her hand. He brushed her hair, and they looked at one another in the dressing-table mirror.

"No, it's this apartment. Since I arrived here, I've lived in the stable block quarters. They were male-orientated, but we rubbed along there, didn't we? When Athena elevated you to the hierarchy here, she naturally wanted us to distance ourselves from the other ranks. We needed to be close at hand if Olympus matters took an urgent turn for the worse. That had to be a plus for the Project, but I feel uncomfortable here, in Thanatos's old rooms."

Artemis touched his hand to indicate he could stop. She took the brush from him, laid it on the table and stood. She put her arms around his neck and looked up into the rugged face of the man she loved.

"He was a traitor, Rusty," she whispered, "and he paid the price. Athena had the place redecorated and fitted out with new furniture. Nothing of your former colleague remains. Just what's lying in the unmarked grave in the pet cemetery. We're together and among friends. Our work is interesting and rewarding. I've never been happier."

Rusty shrugged.

"You think you know someone," he said. "All those years I worked with him, day in, day out. Even though he could be a pain sometimes, I never suspected a thing. Phoenix dubbed the originals Erebus recruited at the project's outset as 'The Three Stooges.' It suited them. Erebus led the way, and they followed like sheep. Although Phoenix poked fun at them now and then, he never doubted their loyalty."

"Thanatos felt slighted when Erebus favoured Athena to assume responsibility here when he retired," said Artemis. "I wish I'd met the old man; he sounds like a special person. Nevertheless, Thanatos felt power was his right and sold out to a faction that offered him the possibility. But, unfortunately, he backed the wrong horse."

With that, Artemis gave Rusty a shove.

"Now, get in that shower. I'll get us something to eat before we go to the meeting."

Rusty did just that. As the hot water cascaded over his head and broad shoulders, he tried to push the dark thoughts out of his mind. He knew Thanatos wasn't the real cause of his unease; it was Phoenix.

A life of domestic bliss wasn't an attribute Rusty associated with the vigilante killer he'd known for four years. Instead, he had enjoyed training the new agent, refining the skills he already possessed and adding more. They formed an easy friendship that had grown so strong; they were like brothers.

Since little Hope had arrived, although they had attended meetings together and discussed, planned and put into operation Olympus direct actions; neither he nor Phoenix had left Larcombe Manor on active service. Rusty was itching to get back in the field. He wasn't sure if his brother-in-arms welcomed that prospect.

As nine o'clock ticked around and the first meeting of the new week was upon them, Artemis and Rusty left their apartment and crossed the landing. The sweeping staircase took them to the ground floor. As they passed the oil paintings of famous ships and portraits of the Hunt family ancestors, it was impossible not to remember Erebus. How would the old gentleman tackle this situation?

"A penny for them?" asked Artemis.

"I was thinking of the old man. You were right. Erebus *was* special. I don't think he would have sat on his hands for three months, waiting for Phoenix and Athena to sort things out. He would have anticipated the problem and more than likely met up with Phoenix in the orangery after a fortnight. That's where they always went — just the two of them. It was always interesting and productive if I was lucky enough to join them. He had a knack for cutting to the chase. If a decision was needed, he took it. There was no argument."

"Why not ask Phoenix to meet *you* there then?" Artemis suggested. "Get him away from the main building, tell him your concerns and sound him out on his future. I'm not daft. You've got itchy feet. Fighting is what you are trained to do and keeps you alive. Sat around the main table with Athena and the others isn't where you flourish."

They had reached the meeting room door. Rusty could hear voices; Phoenix and Athena had arrived ahead of them. The nanny, Maria Elena Urbano from Estepona on the Costa del Sol, was now looking after Hope.

The first arrival at Larcombe Manor at the dawn of 2014 had caused a stir; when the twenty-five-year-old beauty with long jet-black hair breezed onto the estate several days later to start work, the effect was even more noteworthy.

"Minos and Alastor are just behind us," whispered Artemis.

Rusty opened the door and ushered her through in front of him. He glanced back towards the staircase. The two senior Olympus servants appeared to stick closer together than ever; they followed him inside in perfect step.

"Good morning, everyone," said Athena. "I see we're waiting for Giles and Henry, as usual."

"It takes longer to get ready in the mornings than it used to, Athena," Rusty grinned.

"Yes, apart from the aftershave," added Artemis, wafting her hand in front of her nose in an exaggerated fashion. "They must decide what to wear and then check the mirror half a dozen times before they leave their quarters...."

"Then they drag their feet walking across from the ice-house so they can bump into Hope and her nanny, by accident, on their morning constitutional," said Rusty.

"She's attractive, that's for sure," said Athena. "I'll speak with Maria Elena; get her to change her routine. We need those two to be giving one hundred per cent concentration on Olympus matters. I shouldn't need to say that goes for everyone around the table. So far, the year has been quiet. The wet and windy weather was the major feature. We successfully completed the direct actions we sanctioned for our teams in London and Midlands. We took two 'crash for cash' entrepreneurs out of the game, making our roads safer and insurance costs cheaper. As for our schools, we uncovered attempts by Islamic extremists plotting to take over several schools. We passed the information to the Home Office; provided they act on that information, they can thwart those attempts."

The door opened and in rushed Giles Burke and Henry Case.

"Sorry, we're late," blustered Henry, "an unavoidable delay."

"Of course you were," muttered Phoenix, looking across to where Rusty sat.

Rusty grinned at his friend, but there was no reaction. Phoenix had 'zoned out' and was staring into space. Rusty wondered where his mind had wandered. Meanwhile, Athena was calmly getting the meeting back on the agenda and prefacing the first item.

"Our intervention is required to stop the menace of drugs sold to our children. Minos, this subject is close to your heart. Can you run through the background material, please?"

Almost nine years ago, Sir Julian Langford, QC, had lost his only son, Harry, to a cocktail of drugs. On the surface, nineteen-year-old Harry appeared to be a happy-go-lucky teenager with the world at his feet. However, in his darker moments, he suffered a crisis of confidence. Harry felt the weight of expectation on his young shoulders. While in a depressed state, he chose to take his own life.

While this was a tragedy for Sir Julian and his wife Claudia, it was even tougher to understand it happening in the relatively low crime area around Maidstone, in Kent, where the Langford family lived. That incident alone might have triggered a desire to join an organisation such as the Olympus Project. His time as a prosecutor and on the bench as a judge persuaded Sir Julian to join Erebus at Larcombe Manor.

He had noted a steady increase in the number of criminals before him, despite the establishment's constant preaching of the opposite message. They were kidding the public into believing we were winning the battle. He had seen first-hand the watering-down of justice that saw courts handing out shorter, softer sentences even for horrific crimes. Defence lawyers seemed to have the odds stacked in their favour in this modern age. Criminals often walked free from his court over a small slip by the police or the CPS, guilty or not.

After he had arrived at Larcombe Manor, he became known as Minos - the judge of the dead of the Underworld. Over the past eight years, he had been a vital cog in the wheel that drove the Project forward. His main wish was to tackle those responsible for manufacturing and peddling drugs and to ensure they received the appropriate level of justice.

For Minos, the suspended sentences so often handed out, partly due to overcrowded prisons but mainly due to a weak-willed establishment, held memories of different times. As a result, he was a strong advocate for the return of capital punishment.

"I'm afraid we face a long and difficult battle with this problem, Athena," Minos began. "The tentacles of this evil reach into all corners of the nation; into every level of society. Nowhere is safe anymore. I have details of a mother whose daughter became addicted to drugs while at an expensive public school in Surrey. She has started an online blog warning other parents that their loved ones could get groomed by dealers targeting independent schools. They select naïve pupils from wealthy homes because they know they have access to funds to feed their habit. Also, in the past, these same privileged children have been led to believe they are immune. They don't believe drugs can touch them. They spend many months away at school, far from the warmth of a loving family home. Their only compensation being they have too much money. This lady's daughter is recovering from her cocaine addiction; she told her mother her dealer charged her well over the normal price for her fix. He told her, 'You can afford it, darling. Why worry? Daddy will always cough up more if you run short.' What shocks me is that the education system pays little or no heed to the potential dangers. Pupils at this public school were ignorant of the sophisticated grooming techniques used by dealers. They choreograph every step carefully. From a bit of harmless fun when they take that first 'hit' to chronic dependence on recreational drugs. After that, a gradual decline into despair and death, as we are all too aware. Meanwhile, another case from the Midlands highlights how young these children can be. Two thirteen-year-old lads took their first drag on a cigarette on the way to school. Two years later, the boys' parents were alerted by school staff, informing them they caught the boys smoking cannabis on school premises. Aged sixteen, they left school with few qualifications and no ambition other than to get wasted as often as possible. Ecstasy, crack cocaine, and heroin were the next steps on their downward spiral. Their parents now had no clue as to their whereabouts. They had resigned themselves to waiting for the knock on the door that told them their son had taken his final fix."

Minos paused. He looked up to gauge the reaction. Not one pair of eyes met his. Everyone was staring at the shiny surface of the elegant Georgian table directly in front of them.

"It hits home hard, doesn't it?" he said, "it could affect any of you, as it did me. I thought things were bad in '05 when Harry died, but things have worsened, as these figures demonstrate."

Minos slid a pile of reports to his left, where Alastor sat. His colleague removed a copy and then passed the collection around the table so the others could study the figures. The room fell silent for a while.

Alastor spoke first. "The government's latest survey shows twenty per cent of secondary pupils have taken an illegal drug," he said. "Cocaine use has doubled in the past year. Thirty-five thousand eleven-year-olds around the country have tried Class A drugs. Up to half a million fifteen-year-olds have at least tried hard drugs, if not become addicted to them. Whatever policy this country is following. It isn't working. These numbers are scandalous."

"What the heck is 'Frank' doing these days?" said Phoenix, sitting up straighter in his chair. "That bloody multi-million-pound campaign was designed to reduce drug and alcohol misuse. A decade on, and it's dead in the water. Deaths from cocaine were in the low hundreds for teenagers a decade ago. This report suggests they've risen six-fold."

"At least there's one thing we're excelling at," muttered Rusty. "We might be well down the rankings in education and health care standards, but we hold the dubious distinction of having the highest level of cocaine use in Europe."

"You certainly don't overstate the problems of the task

facing us, Minos," said Athena. "However, we mustn't let that weaken our resolve. Where do we lay the blame for this escalation in the past decade?"

"The failure to control our borders has allowed hard drugs to flow into our leafy suburbs and schoolyards," said Henry Case. "By softening our stance on cannabis classification and dithering over whether we should go further or not, we led many to believe it's okay to use the drug. We can see the results of this in the pages of this survey. Young lives destroyed, a whole generation of children betrayed."

"What has been the government's response to these figures?" asked Giles Burke.

"This survey covered the use of drugs and alcohol among secondary school pupils," replied Minos. "Despite the alarming picture that the drug statistics paint, the government welcomed the report. The figures show a small fall in the numbers found drinking and using types of less addictive drugs."

"Unbelievable," said Phoenix.

"If I were a parent of a child attending school, I would be horrified," said Artemis. "We entrust our children to schools for large amounts of their lives until they're at least sixteen. Surely, we should expect the schools to safeguard them from the dangers of drugs? Not through education alone, but watching the school perimeters and checking who and what enters the premises?"

Minos flipped open another file on the table in front of him.

"In times of austerity, it becomes challenging to cover all the bases, Artemis. I have examples of brazen dealers preying on kids after they left school and walked home. Police increased their patrols around bus stations in North

Wales after reports of dealers targeting school transports. Dealers have no morals, no scruples, no conscience."

"Can we concentrate on two or three worst offenders?" asked Rusty.

"There are dealers who are more prolific than others," said Minos, "my dossier is here for analysis. Take your pick. You will find plenty from which to choose."

"We must start somewhere," said Phoenix, "to do nothing isn't an option. On the other hand, removing the problem from a few schools across the country might get the government's head out of the sand."

"Based on their reaction to this survey, it might take a lot of shifting," said Rusty.

"Phoenix and Rusty will assume responsibility for the direct action we take," said Athena. "I'm sure I can rely on the two of you to achieve the results we expect. Can you produce an action plan for next Monday's meeting?"

"No problem, Athena," said Phoenix, "it will be good to have something positive to contribute again."

"The drug menace won't disappear overnight," said Athena. "We will need to revisit it time and time again, even if the government wake up and make meaningful inroads. One thing is certain. I want the landscape to look very different from the one portrayed in this survey before our daughter starts school."

Henry Case and Giles Burke were next up as they delivered their security report updates. Artemis sat quietly, watching and listening, as her superiors ran through the list of threats facing the country from home and abroad. If the public ever became fully aware of the scale of problems the security services tackled daily, widespread panic would inevitably follow.

It was clear the official security organisations were strug-

The Price of Treachery

gling to cope. There was constant pressure from terrorist organisations and organised crime, increasingly from cyber-criminals, yet the highest pressure came from their government. Year after year, they were required to achieve more and more with fewer resources.

Artemis had experienced several years of this impossible task within the police force. But, in her short time with Olympus, she appreciated how valuable the secret organisation's input was, behind the scenes, in smoothing out the hot spots.

The meeting was ending. Athena closed by informing everyone that the next Olympus hierarchy meeting was in four weeks at Curzon Street, London. Zeus had postponed the initial meeting in early January following Hope's birth. Flowers, cards, and little gifts had arrived at Larcombe from the remaining Olympians. Zeus was keen to promote the new Olympus's image as one big happy family after last year's troubles.

One item on the agenda for the meeting was evident. There were new faces to introduce. Following the demise of Demeter, Poseidon, Hermes and Nemesis, there was an urgent need for fresh blood. So Zeus had searched high and low for people with the financial capacity to help bankroll Olympus' missions and ideology aligned with that epitomised by their founder, Erebus.

It appeared from the confirmed date of the meeting that quest had been successful.

Giles and Henry waited for Artemis to join them and headed towards the ice-house. They would soon disappear below ground to carry on the highly sophisticated surveillance and intelligence gathering in which the Olympus operations room excelled.

Minos and Alastor hovered. Athena could tell they

needed a quiet word with her. She knew it was unlikely necessary; they needed to be reassured that their perceived status in the organisation was still intact. Athena saw these few minutes massaging their frail egos as a small price. After all, they were more than happy to graft away on the analysis and interpretation of the data generated by Giles and his staff.

Rusty saw his opportunity. As Artemis scuttled over to join Giles and Henry, he collared Phoenix.

"So, when do we start on this drug problem?" he asked.

"Meet me in the orangery in fifteen minutes," replied Phoenix.

With that, Phoenix left the meeting room and headed for the stairs.

Rusty glanced over to Athena. She had just finished chatting with the Two Stooges.

"What did he say?" she asked Rusty.

"We're meeting in fifteen minutes in the orangery," he said.

"That's good," sighed Athena. "A few hours in his old surroundings might snap him out of this melancholy."

"Don't worry," said Rusty. "I'll keep him there until he breaks."

Athena smiled. She knew Rusty had the Project's best interests at heart. It was good to learn that at least one other person in the organisation had noticed her partner's darker mood since the New Year.

"Handle him with care, Rusty," she said as she swept through the doorway and practically ran up the stairs to find Phoenix. With luck, they could spend a few minutes together with Hope before Phoenix left for the orangery.

"I don't think kid gloves are what he responds to," whispered Rusty. "I reckon a sharp dig in the ribs is what he needs right now. Then we can both get back to doing what we do best."

Rusty closed the door behind him and headed out of the house. The late morning sun was bright but weak as he walked briskly towards the building Erebus had held so dear.

Everything at Larcombe Manor was coming alive after the winter. Despite the chill in the air, he could sense the changes occurring. Spring was just around the corner. It was time for the estate's grounds to come alive again. The time for Phoenix to rise again was long overdue.

A New Dawn: Chapter Two

Little had altered in the magnificent orangery since Erebus had left Larcombe for his brief retirement on Ibiza. Although the sparse furniture was twentieth-century functional, rather than its original luxurious fittings, Phoenix imagined little had changed in general since the early nineteenth century.

Wealthy landowners had used orangeries to house orange and other citrus trees to protect them from Britain's harsh winters. By the time the Hunt family had this edifice built, glazed roofs were the order of the day to allow as much sunlight into the building as possible. The ability to afford such an adornment made their wealthy family appear even more noble and aristocratic.

The impressive structure featured external stone and brickwork, while the interior was decorative and plastered. South-facing windows encouraged the maximum light to flood through, and the walls facing north were thick to protect against the cold. Phoenix had counted the fifteen tall windows as he strolled past his first day at Larcombe when the old gentleman took him on the grand tour. As the months and years passed, the one hundred and eighty feet long orangery had found its way into his heart, just as it had his mentor's.

Phoenix understood how protective Sir William Hunt felt towards this place of sanctuary. It hadn't been somewhere to use for their meetings, a convenient spot perhaps halfway between the main house and the stable block where Phoenix had had his quarters. But it offered so much more.

As he sat waiting for Rusty to arrive, he sipped from a cup of coffee. The sun was streaming through the plate glass, warming him. It felt good to be alive.

Phoenix recalled a conversation when Erebus had described the fine dining that had gone on here back in his ancestor's time. The 'great and the good' were invited to the manor house for the Hunt family to flaunt their wealth.

Times change; his father had used the orangery for afternoon tea, particularly in the height of summer, although these occasions were exclusive to his family, not for visitors. Erebus had continued this tradition with Elizabeth and Helen.

After the tragic death of his only child, and Elizabeth's gradual mental decline, he returned here alone to reflect on carefree summer afternoons with loved ones. Those solitary periods of grieving had been the breeding ground for Olympus. A thirst for revenge, a desire to seek a reversal in the decline of justice. Above all, to ensure the punishment fits the crime.

Four years on, the legacy of the older man remained. Phoenix understood his place now in the grand scheme of things. His life with Athena and Hope was precious. He would protect them to the death, but it was he who must take up the fight against the evils Erebus had created Olympus to defeat.

Zeus, Athena, and the other Olympians managed the finance and the ethos and identified the organisation's most appropriate targets. He was the bringer of fire to cleanse the world of those who committed the most despicable crimes.

The door opened, and in walked Rusty Scott. A steward followed him, carrying a tray.

"Sorry, I was so long getting here," said Rusty. "I thought we might be here for a while, Phoenix. I got us this grub. Is that coffee in the jug hot?"

"It is," replied Phoenix, lifting the domed lid from the silver tray. His friend had to wait for the food to cook. The stack of food looked incredibly appetising. He licked his lips. Erebus was right; times change. The humble bacon roll had supplemented fine dining and afternoon tea.

The steward left them alone and returned to the main building. Rusty fetched himself a cup of coffee, then sat opposite his pal.

"Right," he began, "what's going on, Phoenix? You've been out of sorts for ages. You'll both be dog-tired with the new baby, that's only understandable, but it might go deeper than that. Are you thinking of withdrawing from active service?"

"It's been at the back of my mind, that's for sure," admitted Phoenix. "I keep asking myself whether I should place myself in danger with Athena and Hope to look after. I was sitting here, waiting for you to turn up, thinking what Erebus would want me to do. It didn't take long to conclude. I'm like the actor who lands a role and realises it was the one he was born to play. All his other performances are worthless compared to that role. Erebus identified me as the person he sought to wield his sword of vengeance. Who am I to go against his wishes, whether he's no longer with us or not?

"Hallelujah," cried Rusty. "Artemis and I were worried you might be ready for your pipe and slippers. Carrying out direct action missions is what we're best at, mate. Horses for courses, as they say. But I don't want to take it easy yet, either. We make a good team; I'd be hopeless on my own."

"When we were in the meeting this morning, I was thinking of those early days when you were getting me fit and training me," said Phoenix. He finished his coffee, got up, and walked across to get a fresh brew.

"You're almost the last of the handful of SAS trainers still stationed at Larcombe since the Project began, Rusty. It's been a while, too, since we've recruited new agents. So when Athena informed us of fresh blood at the top, I thought we needed fresh blood here, too. We've got agents who served in Kuwait, Kosovo, and Iraq, but we've held our agent numbers steady around the world in the past two years. I don't want you tied up with training any new intake; you're too valuable out in the field."

"Well, I haven't missed training the newbies, I'll admit," said Rusty, taken aback by the direction the meeting was taking. He'd assumed they would discuss possible changes for Phoenix, not for him. "But I'd like to keep a handle on it," he added.

"Naturally," said Phoenix, "my vote is for you to update the training manual and oversee your new master trainers. They do the work, and your role would be advisory."

"Where do we source these 'master' trainers?" asked Rusty.

"Athena heard a whisper a month ago that someone wanted to reconsider their role within Olympus. Kelly Dexter wants to start a family, and Hayden Vincent still has nightmares over Eton Wick. His leg wound wasn't that serious, but as we both know, it was a hairy mission, and we lost good men that day. I think he wants to take a step away from the front line."

"They could prove to be a good fit here," said Rusty, "we know them well already, and they're excellent agents. So, OK, they've got my vote. So, Kelly wants to start a family, then? It will be good for Athena and Artemis to have another female around the place."

"Maria Elena will be busy too; she'll be running a crèche before she knows it. So you'd better prepare for big changes in your life, Rusty. Artemis will become broody."

"Heck," said Rusty. "I'm older than you, don't forget. I'm not sure I'm right for fatherhood. Let's not think about that for now. Why don't we concentrate on the job that Athena sent us here for first? Shouldn't we be getting on with planning our response to this drug problem?"

Phoenix moved the files he had on the table to one side. He took the lid off the silver tray and picked up a bacon roll.

"Let's have lunch," he said, "there will be plenty of time for planning that later."

"This reminds me of the odd lunch we had together with the old man," said Rusty, munching on a roll. "God, that's good. Artemis is trying to wean me off fast food and fried stuff, but it's what I've always known."

"Me too," said Phoenix, "my first wife wasn't much of a cook. Her mother, Kath, was brilliant. Especially at Christmas, although there were only seven or eight for dinner, she cooked enough for twenty and hated seeing it go to waste."

When the rolls were gone and the jug of coffee emptied, the two friends sat quietly for a few minutes, wondering what they were doing to their waistlines. Phoenix stood up, stretched, and Rusty realised it was time to get back to work.

"Athena wanted to add another item to the agenda this morning," said Phoenix. "But we agreed to leave it until after the next Olympus meeting. There's a new threat emerging in the Middle East. It is an area that will continue to be ravaged by war, no doubt, just as it has been for twenty years. However, I believe this latest outfit, ISIS, poses a bigger threat than Al Qaeda ever did to our shores. This terrorist organisation emerged ten years ago from the remnants of Al Qaeda in Iraq. It laid low after U.S. troops went into Iraq in 2007 and began to re-emerge in 2011, taking advantage of the growing instability in Iraq and Syria to carry out attacks and bolster their ranks. Fallujah and Raqqa fell to them in January. They are poised to launch an offensive on Mosul this summer."

"What's their main objective?" asked Rusty. "Why do you believe they pose a credible threat to the UK?"

"They aim to form a caliphate stretching from Aleppo in Syria to Diyala in Iraq to create a so-called Islamic State. Evidence suggests young Muslims in mainland Europe and the UK are being radicalised and persuaded to join the fight. The freedom of movement the pro-Europeans are so keen on means ISIS members may already be in every major Western city, recruiting both men and women. The incidence of terror attacks as a part of their overall campaign is guaranteed; those attacks will target civilians and weaken European governments' resolve to get involved on Middle Eastern soil. The Americans withdrew from Iraq, as did the UK, and public opinion in the States is against going back in large numbers. I guess US special forces may be there in the low hundreds, but significant numbers of boots on the ground are something else."

"If they come here causing trouble, we'll help the authorities take them out, as we always do, Phoenix," said Rusty.

"That's why we need to recruit more agents," said Phoenix. "We have adequate numbers to tackle the threats that face us at present, but not an all-out terror campaign. When I say 'we', I mean both ourselves and the UK authorities. Since 2010 this government has imposed year-on-year budget cuts on the armed services. There have been reductions in the workforce across the board. Police and border control numbers slashed. As a result, we are less able to defend ourselves than in the darkest days of the early 1940s. It will take a massacre of unbelievable proportions to get the government to abandon this mania for austerity and wake up to a few harsh facts."

"There may not be so many of us these days, but quality counts," said Rusty.

"We might not get the chance to test ourselves, Rusty. In the old days, wars were started by politicians, who argued until they were blue in the face. Then when they failed to get their way, they declared war on one another. While they stood back and watched, the likes of you and I went to fight a few bloody battles to see who picked up the spoils. Today's conflicts wage on Twitter and Facebook; if someone sailed their fleet up the Thames and landed troops in Central London, it would be all over social media in minutes. The public would demand to know what the government would do. The armed forces would fill out forms; check budgets to see whether they could afford to put bullets in the too few guns available. If I were them, I'd invest in a few thousand white flags and hang the expense."

"Are you sure you're okay, mate?" asked Rusty. "Only you're more negative than usual, and that's saying something."

"It's the lack of sleep. If I could sleep for eight hours, that would be fantastic. To make Athena's parents are coming to stay at Larcombe this weekend. They came to Bath to see their only grandchild early in the New Year. Giles needed me in the ice-house, and Athena took Hope to meet them at the Royal Crescent Hotel. Naturally, they wanted to know where I was. Athena had to cover for me."

"I thought her father knew the basics of what you were up to here?" asked Rusty.

"Geoffrey's no fool. Athena and I discussed the problem, and, well, you know how it goes, mate, discretion is the better part of valour. So Athena decided it would be possible to collect them from Bath Spa station and bring them to Larcombe this time. She plans to put them in rooms at the front of the house, overlooking the fields and the driveway. We'll keep them away from the business end of the operation as far as possible. The thing that's got me wound up is they mentioned the 'M' word on their last visit."

"Tricky," said Rusty with a smile. "Have you made any progress in deciding who you'll be when this marriage takes place? If it's such a hassle, why not proceed with the baptism, anyway? Nobody worries too much if couples marry these days, do they?"

"That's another thing contributing to my sleepless nights, Rusty. Athena's parents are old school and keen on seeing their daughter walk up the aisle so that Geoffrey can give her away. Grace Fox wants to invite loads of their friends to the wedding and reception. Athena and I would be happier, either staying as we are or just having a simple ceremony in front of witnesses such as yourself and Artemis. I might get away with using my real name if it was low-key. However, Athena is against me using any assumed identity Henry Case might produce. Can you imagine trying to persuade Grace Fox not to splash news of their daughter's wedding across the pages of The Tatler?"

"Hmm, I said it was tricky, mate," said Rusty. "Glossy, half-page photographs of a man who died four years ago, with his beautiful wife might bring unwanted attention to Olympus."

"Not to mention on me," said Phoenix. "This weekend could be a nightmare."

"Let's lighten the mood," said Rusty. "Why not take me through your files and bring me up to speed? Then we can plan where to target our direct action. Even the murky world of drug dealing has to be better than what you're facing."

Phoenix laughed and turned over the file cover at the top of the pile on the table.

"These figures prepared for the Mayor of London's office earlier this year showed over eighty London gangs operating outside the capital. Gangs from more than half the thirty-two boroughs are involved, with those from Hackney, Brent, Greenwich, and Newham known to be the most prolific. In addition, Metropolitan Police data monitored the rise of fourteen 'super gangs' now active in more than one police area outside the capital."

Phoenix turned over surveillance photos from the icehouse one by one. They showed transactions happening in dozens of locations across the east and south-eastern side of the country — Oxford and Cambridge; Guildford and Epsom in Surrey; Crawley and Harlow in Middlesex.

"Giles and his team found this evidence after only a few hours trawling through CCTV footage. It's blatant, Rusty. They don't give a toss whether anyone sees them or not. God knows how many deals they make inside pubs and clubs, in the local parks and open spaces. It's an epidemic. These dealers are now so prolific that they operate in every police area across Britain. They're active in towns and cities within easy reach of London. Gangs deal in many parts of Essex and as far afield as Wiltshire and Hertfordshire. They're everywhere. Three-quarters of drug-related arrests made by police in towns in Kent are for crimes perpetrated by London-based gangs."

Rusty pored over the photographs, scanned the figures and blew out his cheeks.

"Where the heck do we start?"

"What these reports continue to emphasise is the gangs have expanded their supply methods. Artemis told Giles they termed it 'cuckooing' in the police forces she worked with at Durham and Portishead. The phrase has been in use for five or six years. It describes where dealers arrive in a new town and identify a vulnerable local addict. Then they move in, taking over that person's home and sometimes, like a cuckoo, force them out. The house or flat becomes their regional base, often staffed by teenage gang members."

"This isn't random, is it," said Rusty. "It's based on a well-established technique to establish a fresh sales territory like those adopted by dozens of major businesses. That must take loads of organising; street kids can't handle this level of sophistication. The guys at the head of these gangs are intelligent. They're genuine entrepreneurs. It's a pity they don't use their skills in legitimate businesses; they would wipe out the national debt in the UK in short order."

"True, but I can't see them settling for a zero-hours contract and getting paid peanuts when they can rake in the profits this game offers. So their next step after finding their new nest is establishing a customer base. They pass out business cards to prospective clients. Buy or extract phone numbers of known drug users from local dealers," said Phoenix. "They can send text messages offering introductory deals to draw in new punters. More gang members move in from London if a town or city district promises real potential. Some stay in the crack house they've recruited. Others find a bed-and-breakfast place to stay in for a few weeks."

Rusty continued leafing through surveillance photos and facts and figures in the files on the table. The afternoon sun had disappeared behind the main building, but the underfloor heating had started working. He knew it would be possible for him and Phoenix to continue working in comfort for several hours. He glanced at his watch, trying to gauge when the next call to the kitchens might be necessary. He could send for more coffee and something to take the edge off their hunger.

"We'll give it another thirty minutes," said Phoenix, spotting what Rusty had done. "I'll work out a plan of action this evening. Perhaps we could get together again after tomorrow's meeting? Maybe even take a trip to the Home Counties to see this innovative sales programme in action?"

"No guns, just a recce?" asked Rusty.

"Yeah," Phoenix replied, "the people we want won't be anywhere near the point-of-sale. We need to play this as we have in the past. Strike at the head of the snake. Leave the body to wither and die. As you said, the street-level gang members don't have the nous to run the organisation. If we can identify the brains behind a few of the busiest gangs and eliminate them, then these campaigns by the sales forces will falter. We can give subtle hints to the local coppers, pointing out where the cuckoos are based. With luck, they'll tidy up the loose ends. No doubt, they'll apologise for not having done it sooner. They've done the spadework for us in these reports. A lack of officers on the ground explains why they only seem to pick the lowest fruit on the branch. They can see the juicy prizes at the top of the gang structure, but they're out of reach."

"Out of touch, more like," grunted Rusty. "They spend thousands of hours trying to dig up dirt on politicians and personalities who've been dead for a decade. Meanwhile, our kids get poisoned under their noses, and they appear to do little to tackle the problem. Except for gathering data and writing reports."

Rusty started reading from a report by the National Crime Agency. It revealed the seven police forces closest to London had identified over eight hundred London-based criminals selling drugs in their areas. The gangs had been drawn to the middle-class, more affluent regions by what they saw as lucrative and easy pickings.

"Think about what we know from that first report," he said. "If eighty separate gangs are involved, maybe with more than one main guy at the helm, you're talking one hundred bodies the police will still need to catch and imprison. We can cast adrift foot soldiers by taking out the leaders. Make it easier to sweep up your loose ends. This NCA report also found criminal rivals in these satellite towns are easily subdued by the London gangs, who routinely use much greater levels of violence. However, some gangs have access to machine guns, and experts worry clashes between such groups will soon break out in provincial towns."

"I didn't say it was going to be easy," said Phoenix, "but remember what I said in the meeting. We must do something. The threat of increased violence is always there, but the gangs' best weapon is the mobile phone. These days they can buy pay-as-you-go phones virtually anonymously. That allows them to run a criminal business and cause enormous human misery. Minos underlined the result of their actions in the facts he presented this morning. We have seen an increase in the misery of drug addiction and the exploitation of vulnerable kids forced into helping these gangs."

Phoenix collected the photos and files together. He had had enough for the day. He wanted to get back to Athena and Hope. A shower might help him to feel clean again. Rusty accompanied him as they walked back towards the main building.

"Our first targets should come from those gangs that concentrate on school-age children," said Phoenix.

"I agree," said Rusty. "Then we can look at the colleges and universities later when we have the opportunity to revisit the problem."

"See you in the morning," said Phoenix.

Rusty bounded up the stairs towards his apartments, then slowed as he remembered that Artemis was below ground in the ice-house. His partner had another three hours until her shift finished.

Phoenix strolled more leisurely to the rooms once occupied by Sir William Hunt and eased open the door as noiselessly as he could. Athena was asleep on the settee. Hope nestled in the crook of her mother's left arm, wide-awake but totally at peace with the world.

Hope spotted movement and gazed towards the door. When she recognised a familiar face, she gave Phoenix one of her million-watt beams and gurgled a welcome.

"Ah, the innocence of youth," said Phoenix. "How soon it dies."

**Grab your copy...
vinci-books.com/new-dawn**

About the Author

Ted Tayler is the international best-selling indie author of the Freeman Files and Phoenix series. Ted lives in the English West country, where his stories are based. He was born in 1945 and has been married to Lynne since 1971. They have three children and four grandchildren.

His thought-provoking mysteries appeal to readers of Sally Rigby, Joy Ellis, Pauline Rowson, and Faith Martin. His action-packed thrillers are a must for fans of Mark Dawson and J C Ryan.

Gus Freeman's cold case investigations are carried out with reasoned deduction rather than bursts of frantic action. In each of the 24 books, unsolved murders are accompanied by romance, humour, and country life. The core message in the 12 Phoenix novels is that criminals should pay for their crimes. Unfortunately, the current system fails to deliver the correct punishment, so Phoenix helps redress the balance.

Acknowledgments

The love and support of my family; without them, this would have been impossible.

www.ingramcontent.com/pod-product-compliance
Ingram Content Group UK Ltd.
Pitfield, Milton Keynes, MK11 3LW, UK
UKHW040120190326
469155UK00004B/1255